Tony Cornberg i~ ~~~~ ~ue
upon Tyne where ~~~ ~ self-
employed criminal a~ ~ce. He is
also Director of the In~ ~ Tutors which
undertakes enhanced Crin~ ~d vetting for those
involved in one-on-one ~ ~n with children and
vulnerable adults.

TONY CORNBERG

THE WHITE
POWDER
BUSINESS

Matador
9 De Montfort Mews
Leicester LE1 7FW, UK
Tel: (+44) 116 255 9311 / 9312
Email: books@troubador.co.uk
Web: www.troubador.co.uk / matador

ISBN 10: 1 905237 96 0
ISBN 13: 978-1-905237-96-8

Cover illustration: © Getty Images

Typeset in 11pt Plantin Light by Troubador Publishing Ltd, Leicester, UK
Printed in the UK by The Cromwell Press Ltd, Trowbridge, Wilts, UK

Matador is an imprint of Troubador Publishing Ltd

"In its purest form, heroin is a white powder"

http://www.addaction.org.uk/Druginfoheroin.htm

"Whilst it is recognised that the possession of large quantities is likely to be more consistent with supply than personal use, it is important to consider other factors…"

http://www.drugscope.org.uk/wip/23/pdfs/dstpsecond.pdf

"Looks, throws, catches, hustles –
part o' one big team."
Al Capone in *The Untouchables,* 1987
(dir. Brian de Palma © Paramount Pictures Corporation)

It is a business, after all. A Firm. Danny Walsh was at the top of this one. And the board of directors consisted of him and five others. They were the people he trusted. Perhaps trusted is going a bit far. No-one really trusts anyone except themselves, and some people don't even do that. But these five men were the people that Walsh was closest to trusting out of all the people with whom he had worked.

Billy Cameron was what could be described as a right-hand man. A strange name for someone, perhaps even more so since Walsh was left-handed. He was enormous. He dealt with, as Walsh called it, 'customer service' and debt collection. Maybe debt *creation* would be a more accurate description in the circumstances. He had known Walsh since they were kids. They had grown up together on the same estate and spent their childhood effectively practising for the lives that they now led. They had started out in the classic way – as tearaways. After a while, they got a bit more sophisticated and people started to employ them. And before they were twenty years old, they were pretty much on their own. A product of circumstance more than their own skills in truth – there was a period of two years or so when all the members of the local Firm, as was, were in prison at the same time and so Walsh and Cameron had seized the opportunity to keep it going. And once everyone came out of prison, they ended up working for their previous employees. Quite a come-down – and it had been more than a little hairy to begin with; the former big-shots weren't altogether thrilled to relinquish their empire. But that was a fair while ago. They are all washed-up has-beens now. They spend their days sitting outside upmarket bars and cafés, getting the odd wave from members of the Nouvelle Vague. Walsh's Firm.

Then there was David Nozé, or "Black Davey" as they called him. He wasn't even black, he was North African. And then only because his father was – his mother was as English as Cornish pasties and rain. But since the rest of the Firm was white, they called him Black Davey. He had moved into Walsh and Cameron's estate when they were all around fourteen. He was the odd-one out on the estate. Seen as an impurity. His parents were talked about. He was singled out, had few friends. That's why his teens were angry years and that's why he had come to Walsh and Cameron's attention. They showed him no prejudice. He was exactly the same as they were in one sense. To them it really was a matter of what's inside that counts, though this was not as romantic and flowery as it might appear. Angry people make better robbers, simple as that.

The rest of the inner circle was made up of people who didn't grow up on the same estate as Walsh and Cameron. Dean Stobbs was someone who Walsh had met during a brief period in youth custody. And they had shared a cell. He had no nickname as such – there was nothing about him that stood out particularly. So, as is perhaps unsurprising, Dean Stobbs was merely referred to as "Stobbsy". He had become involved with Walsh once he was released from custody. At the time, Walsh had needed someone to listen to the Police scanner while he and the others carried out commercial burglaries. Stobbs was approached by Walsh once he got out of prison and he turned out to be pretty good at the job. From there, he just became part of the fixtures and fittings of what eventually became a powerful enterprise.

The four men picked up two others over the following year or so. Jimmy Turner was another inmate turned co-worker. He was given the name "Houdini" after several failed escape attempts. Not the most accurate nickname in the world, but it seemed to annoy him and so it stuck. He had shared a cell with Terry Connolly who had only been in custody once in his life. He had absolutely hated it. It wasn't supposed to be fun in prison but it had affected him really badly and he was so determined never to go back that he became almost paranoid. Houdini had introduced him to Walsh and the others and it became obvious that he was useful to have around if only for his paranoia. Any plan they formulated together came under his intense scrutiny – he was always looking out for potential flaws, ways they might be caught. And so their work became organised in the extreme and they were never caught, due to the input of the man they called "Cautious Terry".

Six men. Walsh, Billy, Black Davey, Stobbsy, Houdini and Cautious Terry. It worked. And for a long time. Perhaps if they had kept it to six then it would have always worked. But it's no good standing still is it? Businesses have to grow or be swallowed up by larger organisations. And in this game its all about control. Lose that and it's all over.

* * *

Simon Silver was of the opinion that most crimes were drug-related in some way. And not just the possessions, supplies, cultivations and so on. But wider than that. Domestic burglaries, it seemed, tended to be committed by heroin or crack-cocaine addicts. Street robberies were often the same – people needing to raise some cash to satisfy the day's cravings. Assaults and murders committed by people on ketamine. And if you want to be technical about it, alcohol is a drug, and goes hand in hand with drunken fights and public order offences. He couldn't think of a crime that wasn't drug-related. Fraud, maybe. But most frauds go undetected. For the most part, the average fraudster is too clever to get caught. Either way, Simon had noticed that you don't get many fraud cases in comparison to drug-related crime and drugs crime itself.

Most days in Simon's criminal practice involved some sort of drugs issue. A convicted burglar up for sentence, armed with a drug-dependency for mitigation purposes. A violent offender wanting to plead to a lesser offence on the basis that they were drunk at the time of the assault. But today was different. And it was the first of its kind as far as Simon was concerned. Possession with intent to supply heroin to the value of over a quarter of a million pounds. A gangland case. A major gangland figure. Been asked for personally apparently. Quite flattering. Scope for some big-headedness. Truth be told, Simon was as nervous as the first day on his feet seven years ago.

It was a plea and directions hearing. There was nothing to it really. Especially with this case. There was no defence for this man. And that meant a guilty plea. Get him to sign the brief to show that he understood what he was pleading to and why. Go upstairs. Wait to get called on. Guilty plea, adjournment for pre-sentence reports by the Probation Service and then come back for sentence. Easy.

Not quite. People like this never plead guilty. They run trials. For several reasons. They want to see if they can get off. That's the main reason. They are always facing jail even on a guilty plea, so it's worth having a go. Getting a five year sentence on a guilty plea is far worse than getting ten years after a trial. At least you know you had a good fight. You would spend the five years wondering whether or not you might have been acquitted. So when Simon went down to the cells to meet Danny Walsh for the first time, hoping to confirm the guilty plea that was coming, he was slightly surprised.

"Not guilty all the way, Mr Silver, honestly. I'm not pleading to nowt," said Walsh.

Simon sighed and almost looked like he was pleading with Walsh to listen to reason.

"Look – it's your case," he said, "but you've got no defence!"

"They weren't my drugs. That's my defence."

"Well whose were they?"

"I don't know, could have been anybody's."

"You know what the Prosecutor is going to say don't you? He's going to ask you how all that heroin came to be in your car. What are you going to say to that?"

"I'm going to say that I don't know. Someone must have planted it there. My fingerprints aren't on the stuff anyway – they can't say it's mine can they?"

"Well, they can to be honest, because it was found in your car."

"So? Someone could have put it there."

"How?"

"Here – do you not believe me? I'm telling you the truth, it's not my fucking stuff!"

Walsh was getting irate now. And perhaps with that, more believable.

"It's not that I don't believe you, I'm just thinking ahead. How am I going to convince a Jury that it wasn't your heroin?"

"Well, there's no fingerprints for one thing."

"OK, fair enough, but then the Prosecutor will just say you must have been wearing gloves."

"Aye but that's a doubt, that means not guilty."

"Ideally, you're right. But there's more than just the fingerprint issue here isn't there?"

"Like what?"

"Well, you know, people who have made statements against you, about you being a heroin importer, you've read the case papers haven't you?"

"Aye I've read them, but it's just bollocks, that."

"You'll need a better explanation than that."

"Whey, the Police'll have just been round and made deals with them."

"I know, they probably have, but in fairness, Danny, if they say it in Court then the Jury get to hear some pretty damaging stuff about you."

"Aye but they'll maybe not stick to what they put in their statements"

"That's a big risk"

Walsh sighed this time, and his hands covered his face.

"I know."

He looked up at Simon.

"It's just…I'm not guilty of this, you know?"

Simon didn't know. He didn't care. But he was starting to believe him. And maybe soon he would start to care more.

* * *

Walsh was brought up to Court with four security staff. He was deemed to be an escape risk and so he sat in the dock wearing handcuffs. Defendants are usually relieved of this imposition, innocent until proved otherwise as they supposedly are, but once in a while they have to be cuffed. Simon was reminded of the only other handcuffed defendant he had represented. And he ticked himself off for having sat alone in the cells with Walsh without someone there to take notes for him. He should have learned that lesson from Hopper. You need a witness with you when you make decisions about pleas. OK, next time I go down to see Walsh I'll make sure Caroline comes with me. Where is she anyway?

"Are you Mr Silver?" asked a nervous young girl sat in the Solicitors' row behind Simon. He turned round to face her.

"Yeah – hi," he said with a look of confusion on his face.

"Hi I'm Shelley, from Openshaw and Co."

"Oh right – are you here for the Walsh case?"

Please don't be.

"Yeah – I've just started working here though, and I haven't done a PhD before."

Simon was the sort of person who remembered what it felt like to be starting out. And he was sympathetic. Anyway, he wasn't bothered about Shelley's inexperience, he had something else on his mind.

"Oh don't worry, it's dead easy. He's just going to plead not guilty and then they'll just set a trial date. Er…I thought Caroline was coming down for this anyway."

"Oh, well I'm just covering for her while she's away."

"Has she gone on holiday? Alright for some eh?" Simon laughed.

"No she's on maternity leave."

Come on, keep personal and professional life separate.

You can do it. You can.

Can you?

No, you can't can you?

"She's pregnant?"

"Yeah, so she's off for a few months. Her dad wants her to get married before it's born, but she says she won't!" laughed Shelley.

Glad you're laughing. I'm about to start crying. How am I supposed to concentrate now? I just want to go home. Pregnant?!

"I think her boyfriend's lush!" Shelley went on. Simon just turned away. Shelley cursed herself. You don't say stuff like that in Court! But then why not? Who's Simon Silver anyway? He's just some bloke. Who does he think he is? I bet he thinks

7

I'm just some daft little girl who's come down here to take notes and look pretty.

In truth, Simon was thinking about Caroline. And nothing else. He hadn't even noticed that Shelley was attractive. He would, though. Just not yet.

A knock on the Judge's door.

"Court stand!" shouted the Usher

The Court stood.

"Are you Daniel Walsh?" asked the Clerk of the Court.

"Yes," replied Walsh.

"Sit down."

Kate Holloway stood up.

"May it please Your Honour, I appear to prosecute this matter, my learned friend Mr Silver appears for the Defendant Daniel Walsh. Your Honour, the Defendant is charged with possessing heroin with intent to supply. I anticipate a Not Guilty plea to the indictment, though I should perhaps leave this for my learned friend to deal with."

That didn't really need saying, Simon thought. Oh well, there's no real recipe in this job. He stood up.

"Your Honour, perhaps the indictment can be put."

"Yes," said Her Honour Judge Kristensen

"Daniel Walsh, stand please," said the Clerk, standing up himself.

Walsh stood up in a relaxed, perhaps arrogant manner. The last time he'd been in the dock he was only eighteen. That was nearly twenty years ago.

"Daniel Walsh, you are charged on this indictment with one count of possession with intent to supply a drug of class A. The particulars of the offence are that on 21st March 2002, you had in your possession a quantity of heroin to the value of two hundred and sixty thousand pounds, with intent to supply such to persons unknown. Are you Guilty or Not Guilty?"

"Not Guilty," said Walsh.

"Not Guilty," the Clerk confirmed, and wrote to that effect on the indictment.

"Sit down please."

Simon stood up now.

"Your Honour, I have filled in a PDH form," he said, handing it to the Usher. "I estimate a 5-day trial given the amount of witnesses required, Your Honour."

He only said "Your Honour" twice in the same sentence because he knew she was going to disagree with the 5-day estimate.

"Five days Mr Silver? Really?"

Thought so.

"Your Honour, the nature of the defence is such that no witness is agreed and so the defence requires all of them to attend."

"No, surely you don't need everyone, Mr Silver."

Oh come on, don't make me have to work!

"I'm afraid so, Your Honour."

"Well what is the defence?"

"Simple denial, Your Honour."

"Simple denial? What does that mean?"

"Your Honour, simply that the charge is wholly denied."

"Miss Holloway?"

"I have to say I agree with Your Honour. In fact, those instructing me have sent letters to the defence asking for more details of the defendant's case. It is rather vague."

"Where is the defence statement Miss Holloway – do I have a copy?"

"You should have, Your Honour, though it was sent in later than it should have been."

Simon looked at Kate. Come on! What did I ever do to you?! Stop getting me into trouble! Shelley's heart would have started to beat faster too, but she didn't realise that her father's firm was being criticised.

Her Honour Judge Kristensen found the defence statement in her own bundle of papers. It didn't take long to read. And once she had read it she looked up at Simon. He knew he was about to get it. But get what? This is the bit where you have to be ready to think on your feet.

"Mr Silver, this is probably the worst defence statement that I have ever seen."

You can't stay quiet. But you can't really disagree. So what do you say?

"Your Honour?"

That's no good. But it's said now.

"Well, Mr Silver, Miss Holloway is quite right, this is far too vague."

Simon turned to Shelley and whispered to her, though quite audibly.

"Have you got the defence statement?"

Shelley didn't know what a defence statement was. She pretended that she did. But Simon saw right through it. And since all eyes were on him, since it was him that was holding the Court up, he could be forgiven for being a bit stroppy. But then, it was probably Shelley's first day. Kate Holloway rescued them both. And she made it known that she was doing so for her own benefit as well as theirs.

"Your Honour, I have a spare which my learned friend can use," she said, passing a copy over to Simon and giving Shelley a dirty look in the process.

"Thank you Miss Holloway," said the Judge.

Simon read through the defence statement, all the while feeling the eyes of the Judge on him, willing him to finish quickly. It *was* vague in fairness. But he was going to have to argue that it was perfectly clear. And without preparation. How do you do that? With Judges like this, you let them speak first. And try to counter what they say. So you stay quiet for a while and look like you are stuck for what to say. They like to pick on you when they can see you floundering.

The pause got on HHJ Kristensen's nerves.

"I take it you have heard of the Criminal Procedure and Investigations Act Mr Silver?"

You know I have. And you know there's no need to talk to me like that.

"I have, Your Honour, yes," replied Simon.

"And what does it say Mr Silver?"

So far so good – you know this bit.

"Your Honour, it asks that the defence serve a defence statement which sets out the nature of the defence."

"No, Mr Silver, there's more to it than that, as I suspect you well know."

"Your Honour?"

"It should specify the defence in general terms, as you say, but further than that it should specify the allegations with which the defence takes issue and also state why."

Shit.

"Mr Silver?"

The problem with this sort of situation is that you have too many people to impress. You have to show your opponent that you don't take things lying down. They have to know that you aren't a pushover, otherwise the next time you come up against them, they'll try to negotiate their way out of anything. If you're prosecuting them, they'll ask you to accept a plea to a ridiculously lesser offence. Or they'll refuse to accept your offer of a lesser plea if you're defending. That's no good, because you've got your client to impress too. They need to know that you're going to fight for them. Dress the job of Barrister up as much as you want. Status, decision-making, responsibility. And so on. But in truth you're just a voice. You represent someone's interests and you put their case as they instruct you to. If they want to call the Police liars, then that's what you have to do. You can tell them what will happen, but you can't tell them what to do. And if you look weak, like you won't fight, then they'll instruct someone who will. And the Judge will see that. You have to impress them too or they bully you into giving the job up. They need to know that you'll politely argue that chalk is in fact cheese. And when you see them socially, they'll come and talk to you. If you look like an idiot, then they'll just talk *about* you. It's all about reputation, this game.

The other problem is that when you are standing up in Court, being asked a question, and your mind wanders in the way that Simon's does, you annoy people. It's no good standing there open-mouthed without a thing to say. Yes, you are just a voice, but you are a voice all the same. And you get paid to talk. Simon was being paid to talk about the defence statement. That's the Solicitor's job. Shelley's job. But she didn't prepare this defence statement. It wasn't her fault. But whoever did had done a real half-hearted job of it. You are, in truth, supposed to specify, in your defence statement, the allegations in the case that you disagree with. And you are, the Judge was right, supposed to say why you disagree with them. But then isn't it obvious why you don't agree with an allegation? Why would you agree if you were innocent? There's a good start. Try that.

"Your Honour, I understand the point. This defence statement may, at first glance, seem far too vague." Simon paused for effect, and then went on. "Then again, Your Honour, while I am certainly not one to challenge the validity of English Law, I do have certain reservations about the relevant sections of this particular Act, in fact, I always have."

Not *strictly* true, considering that you have just thought about this, Simon thought.

"Oh?"

"Your Honour, I agree that the defence statement appears vague. After all, it merely states that the Defendant denies the allegations against him. It doesn't say which allegations specifically, nor does it say why he takes issue with them."

"No, it doesn't does it?"

"Your Honour, if a Defendant is entirely innocent of a charge, then what more can he say other than just that?"

This seemed to puzzle the Judge. Unconventional ideas tend to do that.

"How do you mean, Mr Silver?"

"I mean, Your Honour, that to be asked to specify exactly what you take issue with would be, in this Defendant's case, to ask him to identify each and every allegation against him. Now if a defendant were guilty, let's say, then he might wish to disagree with parts of the Crown case – that the Police have got the wrong car for example, or that he didn't *quite* say what is written on the interview transcript."

He paused again, waiting for it to sink in. And then went on.

"But when someone is guilty of none of the charges against him, it is quite an imposition to ask him to identify everything with which he takes issue. The point being, Your Honour, that this would mean a guilty man has less work to do than an innocent one."

She seemed to latch on to that. Kate was still sitting down too. That was a good sign. And with them seemingly on the ropes, Simon went on raining punches.

"This Act, Your Honour, seems to be very helpful in terms of defendants who are *quite* guilty, but does no service whatsoever to those who are innocent. This defendant refutes the Crown's case in its entirety. It is therefore far simpler for him to say just that, rather than go through the case and refute each point individually."

"Well, yes I can see the logic in that, Mr Silver, but the defendant has still failed to specify why he takes issue with the Crown's case."

One sentence should do it.

"Well, Your Honour, he takes issue with it for the simple fact that he is not guilty of it."

The Judge seemed to ponder this. And after a while, she spoke, with a smile for the first time so far today.

"Yes, Mr Silver, looking at it from that angle I agree it does seem rather odd. It is an imposition, to use your word, to ask Mr Walsh to particularise that with which he takes issue. Yes, taken as it is, I think you're right, the defence statement is acceptable."

"Grateful, Your Honour. This takes us to the original point about the trial estimate of five days."

"Say no more, Mr Silver, I can see that you will need to test all of the evidence if you disagree with it all. Any observations Miss Holloway?"

"No, Your Honour."

They discussed witness availability. They discussed Counsel's availability. Walsh didn't really listen to any of it. He was just pleased to have Simon represent him. It was clear that he was up for a fight.

* * *

Career criminals are just that. They don't have jobs. Crime is their employment. And so when a career criminal comes to Court, they don't tend to come alone because their colleagues don't need to ask for time off work. And so you end up being watched by more than just your client. And these people aren't impressed by your job. To them it has no real status because they are far more wealthy than you are. To these people, status is judged by money, not by breeding.

Five people had sat and watched the hearing. They approached Simon as he left the courtroom. The larger of the five men spoke to him.

"Do you reckon we'll get a visit? Can we go down and see him?"

"Er, give me five minutes – I need a quick word with him. Then I daresay they'll let you see him," replied Simon.

Who were these people? They hadn't been introduced. But they needed no real introduction as such. Simon had seen them around the Court building before. And they had probably seen him too. They were obviously friends of Walsh. And that meant that they worked with him. They had an interest in this particular Court case because their livelihoods would probably depend on it, and if not, they would certainly be affected by it. Being one man down, to these people, was something to be avoided at all costs. Especially when the man concerned was the main player, as Walsh was.

Simon felt really in the thick of it now. Fair enough, it was only the plea hearing. But the trial date would come around soon enough. And this would be an important trial for Walsh and his cohorts. There was a lot riding on it for them. That meant extra pressure on Simon. He wondered if they knew that this was his first real gangland case. But why should that be a problem? He was a criminal lawyer, and this was a crime. It should be no different to any other trial. But it felt different. It *was* different. They made you fight more. They made you feel the need to fight harder than you perhaps usually would. That's quite a thing to say. Why should your effort be any different from case to case? Maybe it was just the fact that Simon was more frightened of this kind of work. You hear stories about these people, you know.

Simon left the Court building and headed back to Chambers, for no real reason other than to pick up papers for the next day. He preferred to work on papers at home rather than in Chambers, there were less people to distract him. In fact there were no people to distract him at home.

He drove past the Court on the way home. He even looked to see if the five men were standing outside. They weren't. They were probably still in the cells visiting Walsh. He wondered whether they were talking about him at all. Were they impressed? Would they recommend him? In truth they hadn't seen enough of him in action to form a proper view and he told himself that in all fairness, he had done a good job today. He wanted to impress them though. It was about time he got some big work. He needed the reputation as a big hitter. He was ready for it now, and the work that came with it. But why impress these people in particular? Because they were gangsters?

Simon started thinking about the word 'gangster'. He even said it out loud a couple of times. It sounded a strange word. What did it mean? Someone who was in a gang? Someone who led a gang? It was one of those words that has a feeling attached to it. A feeling of seriousness. A social position gained through violence. People to whom the rules do not apply. People who are welcomed by others by the fear that they instill in them. You know not to argue with them. To question them. You don't get to do that. Because you know that they aren't like normal people. They kill people don't they? Or mutilate them in imaginative and original ways. That's what the films would have you believe. And we all watch them.

Simon was a big fan of gangster films. He started thinking about which film would best describe today. "Reservoir Dogs" perhaps? Simon remembered the famous scene after the group left the restaurant and walked down the street together. They were better dressed than the men from today, in all fairness. But it reminded him of the scene nonetheless. And the feelings attributed to it. The fact that they were an unbreakable group. The fact that we would all like to be part of such a group. The thrill of the lifestyle. The feeling of belonging. The feeling of being needed, relied upon. Being popular perhaps. Rising above other members of society, even if just in your own mind. It's exciting.

This was the first of several parallels that Simon drew during his involvement with the Walsh case. He couldn't help thinking about some of the films he had seen, looking for similarities. Because the truth was, he had spent his university days immersed in gangster films. He wasn't unusual. They appeal for a reason. Maybe he yearned for involvement in such a life. Maybe we all do. Based on films that we see. About fictional people. Gangsters. But here he was, talking to real gangsters. It sounds juvenile. It probably is. But he couldn't help thinking about it. He had never felt so awake.

"Is this you and me talkin', you know, like, lawyer-client thing, and you can't tell nothing I say to you?"
Ordell Robbie to Max Cherry in *"Jackie Brown"*, 1997
(dir. Quentin Tarantino © Mighty Mighty Afrodite Productions Inc)

Seven years ago, Simon had given his life up for a job he had dreamed of doing since he was a child. He would tell himself that this *was* his life and he had in fact given up nothing at all. But in truth there had been several changes. No more late lie-ins during the week. Up with the larks to beat the traffic so that you get to Court in good spirits. Every day, except the weekend. But then again, such is the routine that you end up waking up at the same time even on days off. And perhaps that's no bad thing. When you work during the week, you appreciate the weekend and you don't like to waste a minute of it.

He had also had to give up going out during the week. It messed with his routine. It made him too tired. He had always been the world's worst person for getting up in the morning and a late night, particularly a late drunken night, was more a risk than an inconvenience when it came to waking up in good time for work. However, there was more to it than that. When you work in Criminal Law you tend to avoid going out too regularly anyway; you end up seeing people you would rather only see at Court. And you don't need the Police to think you're in the company of people you have represented. It doesn't look too clever.

So what Simon ended up doing was going out at the

weekend only. And to the more quiet places, the places that didn't tend to attract trouble. He had always told himself never to go to bars and clubs that had been the subject of criminal cases. And the more cases he worked on, the fewer options he had in terms of nightlife. It's quite an imposition really. And he felt almost offended by it. Why should work affect private life? No-one else has to make such a sacrifice. He would be out at night, just like any other reveller. But to be truthful, he couldn't have fun if he was looking over his shoulder all night for members of either of the two factions of criminal activity. A Defendant might talk to him. Police might see him and wonder. Or perhaps a Police Officer would talk to him. And a Defendant might see him and wonder. You can't win.

Over the weekend that followed Walsh pleading Not Guilty, Simon saw no Police Officers. And fortunately, no Police Officer saw him. Because while he was standing at the bar, watching his drink being poured, someone approached him and tapped him on the shoulder.

"Are you Mr Silver?"

Simon turned round slowly. Who was this? Either way, he wanted to pretend to be someone else. People that he knew socially called him Simon. People at work called him Mr Silver. He was not at work right now.

He immediately recognised the man. And there was no doubt that the man knew exactly who Simon was. There was no use in pretending to be someone else, for the sake of one quiet night. Because Simon was very aware that he would be seeing this man in Court very soon.

"Yes, hello, I remember seeing you earlier this week," he replied.

The man thrust his hand out for Simon to shake, which he did.

"Billy Cameron," said the man. But Simon already knew that.

"Mr Cameron," replied Simon in acknowledgment.

"Here, man, call us Billy," he said, almost taking offence.

"OK, hello Billy," Simon laughed.

"Are you on your own?"

I can't lie. Can I? No, I can't.

"Yeah."

"What are you doing in here?" asked Billy, with a look of genuine curiosity on his face.

"Just a quick drink – why?" asked Simon, feeling the curiosity.

"Nowt, I just didn't think you would come in here, with it being one of Danny's places, like."

"Is it?!" asked Simon. So much for being careful!

"Aye man! Did you not know?!"

"No. Shit, I probably shouldn't be here."

In fact, Simon definitely shouldn't have been there.

For his part, Billy just laughed.

"Fuck off man, there's nowt wrong with going out for a drink!

"There is if you're on your own in your client's bar," replied Simon, immediately wondering whether to finish his drink or just leave it.

"Here, there's a few of us over there at that table," Billy said, pointing to a corner of the bar, empty but for a group of five men. The surrounding tables were empty. There were people standing up all around the bar. But the tables remained empty. Perhaps that part of the bar was strictly invitation-only. And Simon was being invited. It occurred to him that the other tables were empty for a very good reason. Who would dare sit near these men? But come on, they're just men. Maybe it was nothing, maybe people just prefer to stand.

But what to do about the invitation? Be rude? Or be stupid? Either choice would have consequences. Be rude and it would get back to Walsh – he might take offence and instruct someone else. Be stupid, go over and sit with these people and Simon might well be kissing goodbye to Prosecution work in the future. Because the Police would find out about it. They always do. And they would wonder what he was doing in their company.

But perhaps it was time to stop prosecuting anyway. Maybe if he got in with these people he would get enough defence work so that he wouldn't miss prosecuting people. These men might recommend him. But then, Simon had always promised himself that whatever he achieved, he would do it on his own. If work came as a result of being sociable with these people then he would feel that he hadn't earned it for the right reason. Or is that being too strict with yourself? Word-of-mouth is a perfectly acceptable method of advertising. And as a Barrister he couldn't advertise himself on the television or in the newspaper because you're simply not allowed to. So maybe he should join them.

Simon was intelligent enough, and perhaps realistically paranoid enough, to think through the consequences of the choice he faced. And he justified every single consequence that came to him. Whichever negative effect he thought of, he rationalised it. This was not like him, he was usually more sensible than this. But the truth is, he wanted to sit with them. To be seen with them. To be associated with them. He knew what they were, as did everyone else. Gangsters. Feared, but accepted. Malevolent but without attracting revulsion. A strange cocktail of feelings is reserved for such people because simply put, we would all sit at their table with them, just to see what it was like.

Simon picked up his drink and walked over with Billy Cameron to be introduced to the Firm. He remained there for one drink, was offered another, which he accepted. And then another. And soon it was his turn to buy a round, which he did without further questioning himself and without the need to put his hand in his pocket. They talked and laughed. People looked at them. Simon started to feel comfortable. And they felt comfortable enough with him, for some reason, to tell him about Fivers.

Cautious Terry looked at Simon.

"I'll tell you about Fivers, Mr Silver. But, look, don't say anything to anybody right? Not many people know about him."

"Hey, don't worry about that."

"Well, I do worry Mr Silver. It's kind of my job."

Simon smiled.

"First of all, call me Simon – and second, don't think I'll go around gossiping ok? I get told all sorts of confidential stuff at work."

"Well, this is confidential right – seriously."

"OK, go on, Terry."

"Right – Fivers, this lad who used to work for us…"

* * *

"Whoa! Here man, slow the fuck down! I'm too young to die!" shouted Danny.

"Ahh come on, you love it, man!"

"I fucking don't. Seriously, Houdini, if you crash this car I'll fucking shoot you."

"Alright, alright."

It had snowed heavily overnight and the roads around Newcastle were an absolute nightmare, more so than usual. Houdini was driving Danny Walsh's car, Danny himself was in the passenger seat. Billy, Davey, Stobbsy and Terry were crammed in the rear seats. Danny rarely drove the car himself, he got someone else to do it. And today it was Houdini's turn.

They were on their way to look at a club that Danny was thinking of buying. A great way to tidy up some money, owning a club. And also a great way to control the supply of things that you shouldn't really be dealing in. Danny was heavily into drugs back then.

They were all going to be late to the meeting. But none of them cared particularly. Everyone knew Danny by reputation and he never faced criticism, at least not from sensible, self-respecting people. The snow was slowing everything down that day.

Billy had the bright idea of suggesting a short-cut. The whole of the north-east seemed to be on the same road and while the traffic was moving, they never went over ten miles per hour. Not fast by any means. But fast enough in this kind of weather to crash the car, hence Danny getting wound up. So Billy suggested getting off the main road and going through some back roads and housing estates. Danny agreed and Houdini was instructed to follow the order.

They took the next exit and, Billy was right, the traffic pretty much disappeared. Maybe everyone was heading for the main roads since they were the least dangerous in the snow. Gritters tend to ignore the minor roads. So they drove along a few small roads for a while. Until someone a few cars in front got a little carried away and turned a slight corner too fast.

"Ahh, man, fuck this!" said Houdini as he looked into the distance and saw the car hit the pavement and spin back into the road, met by the force of the car behind it. Houdini slowed down and turned into a housing estate. He knew the roads round here. He had been chased along them a number of times, fleeing the houses he had tried to burgle in the past. He knew that there was a way to get into the city centre this way.

The roads on the housing estate were covered in snow and Houdini had to slow right down to avoid careering off the road and into someone's garden. The journey was irritating enough with everyone squeezed into the car. And now they were crawling along an estate. Danny took to breathing in deeply and looking out of the window. Even someone like Danny Walsh appreciated the sight of the fallen snow on the trees and in the gardens. Cars parked outside houses had perfect, untouched snow on their roofs. It was a few inches thick everywhere that it had lain. Even on the road. Few people had driven along this road today. Then again, it was early and there was, in all likelihood, only a handful of people in this area who had any reason to go out in the morning. The whole estate was almost a holding-area for the unemployable. Only Houdini could have picked a place like this to target during the time he burgled houses. There was, in truth, little to be stolen round here.

Danny had a smile on his face as he thought of this. He felt at ease, certainly more comfortable than the four sardines in the back seats. And the view from the car window was soothing. It was so quiet. There was no sign of life in any of the houses. The snow on the roofs made it look like the whole estate had engaged in mass redecoration. Every one of them was covered in a fresh, thick layer of snow. All, that is, except one.

In the middle of a terrace of white-topped houses was one that had no snow on it at all. And Danny immediately knew why. His heart jumped.

"Stop the car a minute Houdini," he said.

"What's the matter like? Do you feel sick? Is ten miles an hour too fast?!" Houdini laughed.

"Shut up, man. Look up there," he said in a soft voice, pointing up towards the house.

"Hey look at that – there's no snow on that house. How's that?" asked Houdini.

"Yeah, how's that," echoed Danny, "I'll tell you how that is Houdini, someone's got a little business going on up there."

Houdini still didn't quite get it.

"A cannabis farm you thick twat!" said Billy.

"Oh aye, 'cos the roof must have got hot and melted the snow."

"Well done, mate! Took you a while but you worked it out in the end! All by yourself as well! Nee fucking safety net either!"

"Fuck off man, I'm just the driver!"

Danny laughed.

They all watched the house a little longer.

"I wonder who the fuck lives there," Danny mused. Even when he thought out loud, he swore. That was just his way. You got used to it after a while.

No-one said anything. This was Danny's to call. He made the decisions. They just followed them, once Terry had given his usual paranoid view of course.

"Well," said Danny, louder than before, "let's go and buy a nightclub, lads. We'll come back here later on. See if we can find out who's making money in my town."

When he said things like that, it reminded the group who was in charge. For all the banter and camaraderie, this was Danny's party, and Danny's alone. Moments like these served to tell the Firm not to forget it. And they remained silent as though deep in contemplation. Truth be told, they were in contemplation. Asking themselves why he didn't refer to Newcastle as "their" town. After all they had done together he still felt it to be *his*. And they didn't argue with him. To do so would be to challenge his authority. No-one had ever succeeded in doing so and many had tried.

*   *   *

It was dark now. The club was bought, for a fraction of the asking price by the way. And the Firm had celebrated by sampling a few of the drinks that the club still had in stock. They would have stayed for longer than they did were it not for some other business that they had to attend to. And so they left the club, locked up and piled into Danny's car as before. Everyone was slightly drunk except for Terry who insisted on driving in case the car was pulled over by the Police for a so-called "random check".

The snow had pretty much melted by now and the roads were clear, although Terry was eager to drive within the speed limit so as not to attract attention. They arrived back at the house they had seen earlier that day. There was still a hint of snow on most of the houses but Danny had made a note of the house number anyway. Terry pulled the car up on the opposite side of the street and Danny sat silently thinking about how to play this one.

"D'you reckon I should just go and knock on the door?" he asked the group.

It sounded risky. On his own, Danny might be in some trouble if there were a few people inside. You would expect a reputation like Danny's to immunise him from trouble but then his reputation wouldn't deflect a bullet if the occupant of this particular house got a bit carried away.

"I'll come with you just in case they don't recognise you," said Billy.

"Terry?" asked Danny.

"Just don't go shouting the place up Danny, we don't want curtains to start twitching. Some nosy neighbour might reach for the phone if they think there's some trouble."

"Aye, no bother."

Billy and Danny got out of the car and headed across the road. They walked up to the door without hesitation and Danny knocked loudly on it while Billy walked back a few paces to see if he could see anything inside. The door was answered swiftly. Such was the keenness of the resident to make money. He was a young lad, about 19 or so. He came to the door and glanced quickly up the street before looking into the eyes of the man stood at his door.

"Alright?" he said.

"Aye, just wanted to score some tac, mate," said Danny.

"Not from the house, man. Meet us down the road."

"OK. But I am at the right place though aren't I?"

"Well aye. How much do you want?"

Danny said nothing. He just stepped aside to allow Billy to barge forwards and make a grab for the youth.

He tried to shake himself free, all the while shouting 'I've done nowt! I've done nowt!'. Danny put a hand on Billy's shoulder to tell him to ease off.

"Hey, we're not the fucking Police. We just want to talk to you."

"Get the fuck off!"

Easing Billy off him did not mean the same as letting go of him completely. He wasn't going to calm down. And that meant attracting attention. So Danny and Billy invited themselves in.

Danny closed the door behind Billy who still had hold of the boy.

"You can let go of him now, mate," said Danny, careful not to mention names, at least not at this stage. The kid had clearly not recognised Danny as yet, and he was happy enough for things to stay that way for the moment.

A woman in her forties, though in truth she looked far older than that, came through to the hallway to see just what the hell was going on.

"Mam, go back into the kitchen," said the boy.

"Who are these? What's going on?" she asked.

"Mam, just go back in will you?"

"You better not be in trouble mind, Adam. Are you the Police?"

"Like the lad says, go back into the fucking kitchen," said Danny.

This time, she did.

"Right then, *Adam*," said Danny, "let's have a look upstairs eh?"

"What for?"

"You know what for," said Billy.

Access to the loft was gained through a hatch in the ceiling and a ladder that had to be unfolded. Danny climbed up, followed by Billy. The boy followed them up too. The heat was noticeable immediately. The whole of the loft was kitted out with all sorts of equipment for cultivating cannabis plants. The only drug-related thing that Danny couldn't see was evidence of how much the kid had been making. There was no sports car parked outside. The house was in a state of near-disrepair. This meant that either the kid was daft enough to pay money into a bank account or he had it stashed in the house somewhere.

They climbed back down the ladder. Danny poked his head around a couple of the second-floor rooms before finding the kid's bedroom and he immediately went inside and started opening cupboards and drawers. He found nothing for a few moments. The kid said nothing either. Then Danny had a look under the bed. There were a few boxes. That's when the kid's heart sank.

"Is this the money?" said Danny, pulling one of the boxes out from under the bed.

The kid stayed quiet. Danny was about to find out anyway.

"Fucking hell! How much is in here?"

"I don't know," said the kid.

Danny waved his hands around inside the box, disturbing the tidy order in which the notes had been placed.

"How come they're all five-pound notes?"

How life can change with one simple answer, well-thought out and at speed. Sometimes fate has a hand in such things. Sometimes it's down to a high IQ. In this case, it was due to an interestingly high level of criminal imagination. A curious ability to see a multitude of paths that lie before you, intertwined into the distance, and select the one that takes you the furthest.

"'Cos that's how much I sell at a time," he replied.

"Just fiver deals? You're not very ambitious are you?!"

"There's less of a chance of getting caught if you keep things on a small-scale," he replied with a sigh, continuing a lie that seemed to be working.

He appeared to be lecturing Danny about the workings of the drug world. Danny was the expert here, not the kid. But he wasn't particularly offended.

"But you *have* been caught haven't you?!" Danny laughed.

"Fair point," said the kid, smiling.

"How long have you been doing this then?"

"About six years."

"Six years?! Fucking hell, son, and you've never been caught?"

"Not until today."

Danny looked at Billy.

"That's impressive, that is."

The kid was not convinced about how sincere Danny was being. Danny could see that. He stood up to face him.

"Hey, seriously, that's good going, son."

"So how come you found me anyway?"

Danny laughed.

"Pure chance, mate, yours was the only house with no snow on it this morning. So I thought something must be going on in the loft – and I didn't think it was a campfire!"

"Caught out by the fucking weather…" mused the kid.

Danny smiled.

"Aye, bad luck, lad."

Danny picked up the box.

"So, all the boxes the same are they?"

"Yeah, all full of fivers."

"Well, 'Mr Fiver deals', I'll tell you what we're going to do. I'm going to take this box with me. Kind of like compensation for, you know, taking my customers. And you can get rid of all the shite upstairs."

The kid listened intently.

"The rest of the money is yours right? But you stop dealing as of now. How's that?"

"Well, to be honest right, you've just come into my house, I don't know who the fuck you are, and you've sworn at me mam, stolen loads of cash from me and now you're saying I have to stop dealing. So, I mean, you can probably, like, imagine how, you know, confusing that might be."

Danny placed the box under his left arm and threw out his right hand.

"That's true, you don't know me do you? My name's Danny. Danny Walsh. You might have heard of me."

The kid's face changed.

"Yeah, I've heard of you."

"Then you'll probably have heard stories. Stories that don't really fit with what's happened here, with you being stood up instead of lying on the floor covered in your own blood."

"Aye, you hear the odd story from time to time. Gossip, like."

"It's only gossip because people gossip about it. Doesn't mean it's not all true."

The kid sighed now.

"So, like, where do I stand? Are you going to come back for the rest of the money or, like, grass us up?"

"I've told you, it's yours to keep. Just don't deal any more."

"What, and that's it?"

"That's it. You don't believe me do you?"

"Well, my head's up my arse at the minute, I don't know if I believe you or not. No offence, like, but imagine you were me."

Danny did his famous good-cop-bad-cop bit and stood back, apparently considering the kid's point of view.

"Aye, it must be a bit weird for you. Standing in your bedroom, talking to people you've heard of but never met before. I would be a bit confused I suppose."

"Like I say, my head's up my arse. Like, you know, if you advised somebody not to take your advice, would you be happy or sad if they ignored you? Know what I mean?"

"What?!"

"Doesn't matter. I just mean, it's a bit hard to work out what's really going on."

Danny liked the kid. He was either completely mental or profitably clever. Either way...

"Tell you what, do you know a club in town called Vapour?"

"Aye."

"Well I bought that club today. Come there tomorrow morning and we can talk about your career. You've obviously got a decent head on your shoulders. You talk shite, but you seem bright enough."

"So hang on, you're going to take one of my boxes of fivers and then offer me a job?" asked Adam in disbelief.

"Maybe, if you've got what it takes."

The kid thought about it.

"Alright, on one condition."

"Oh aye?" Danny's face tightened.

"Go and say sorry to me mam for swearing at her."

Danny laughed, as did Billy.

"OK son, I will."

He did. There is, after all, a certain code of honour to be upheld. You don't upset women or the elderly. Perhaps because they tend to be the only ones who aren't particularly impressed by you.

*   *   *

"Count that," said Danny climbing back into the car and handing the box to Stobbsy and Terry in the back seats.

"What's this about like?" asked Terry.

"The kid's been dealing, and that's some of the money he's made."

"Just some?"

"Aye, I felt sorry for the little bastard. He was unlucky. We only found him by chance. So I let him keep the rest. Anyway, I had to really, I stopped him dealing. If I'd taken the lot he'd have been straight to the bizzies. Nowt to lose, you know?"

"Well how do you know he won't go to the Police anyway?" asked Terry.

" 'Cos he won't. I offered him a job."

Terry had a look on his face that Danny knew all too well.

"Terry, don't start, I know what I'm doing."

"You're the boss," he replied, without looking at Danny.

"Alright, go on then – if you've got something to say."

"Danny, I'm not saying anything, man. But if he goes to the Police then we're all fucked. And to be honest, I don't like the fact you've made that decision for everyone."

One thing Terry failed to be cautious about was the way in which he spoke to Danny in front of other people. And he realised what he had said and regretted it immediately.

"Danny, I don't mean to be rude, it's just sometimes you get a bit carried away and it's not good for your business you know?"

"Tell you what then Terry, once Houdini's dropped us all off back at the club, get your car and come back here. You can stay and watch the house all night and make sure there's no Police. How about that eh?"

"Are you serious?"

"Terry, you worry too much."

★   ★   ★

Inside the house, Adam took the remaining three boxes out from underneath his bed. His box of fivers was gone now. And so it was perhaps time to find a new place to stash his three remaining boxes, neatly separated as they were into tenners, twenties and fifties. He walked downstairs. He felt terrible for having brought this to his mother's door. She was clearly upset.

"Mam, do you want a cuppa?"

"Aye, go on, son, I will."

★ ★ ★

"Ah, the ambitious Mr Fivers!" shouted Danny, "come and sit over here, mate!"

He was being far too friendly for the kid's liking. But he was sitting down drinking a cup of coffee and didn't look too intimidating. Anyway, the kid had come to the club without being forced to do so. He hadn't really felt the need to fear this man. He was curious about the gang perhaps, even though he knew who he was dealing with here. And that meant that a lot of the people from his area would know too. They would see him involved with the big boys. His respect would maybe grow into notoriety. Truth be told, that's what he was starting to dream of. Becoming the big man. The trouble was, Danny Walsh was the big man. That was not going to change, in the near future at least. His hunger for involvement had clouded his fear. But now that he was here in the company of this almost fabled man, his mind was cast to the stories he had heard. People who crossed Danny Walsh never talked about what he had done to them in return. There was a reason for that. But to Danny, this kid was an unambitious street dealer unwilling to take the risk of selling large quantities, unwilling to do time in prison.

"Alright Fivers," said Billy.

"Fivers?" asked Houdini.

"Aye, he only sells fiver deals," said Danny, updating his less than razor-sharp colleague.

33

"Only fivers? Fucking hell, kid, you'll never make any money doing that!"

"Well, he's not ambitious," said Danny, "are you Fivers?"

"Well," announced the kid, sitting down, "better to be a prince in a kingdom of many than a king in a kingdom of one."

Danny laughed.

"He talks some bollocks this one!"

"Aye, what are you – a fucking poet?!"

The insults came thick and fast. Fivers didn't mind them. These were men to be respected. Like it or not, they could say whatever they wanted to. He was hardly going to argue with them.

"So, Fivers, what do you think of the place?" asked Danny

"Not bad, not bad. I've been here before a few times, actually," Fivers replied.

"Have you? I don't think I ever came here before I bought it."

"Does it still get busy?"

"I think so, I don't know to be honest."

"Oh."

"Oh what?"

"Well, you know, what if it doesn't pull customers in?"

"I'm not looking to make a profit, Fivers. A bit like you with your fucking fiver deal empire!" Danny laughed.

"I'm not trying to criticise, it's just, well...it doesn't matter."

"No, go on."

"Well, no offence, right? it's just that, to be honest, do you not worry about being seen to spend all this money on a club that stays dead quiet? The Police might think it was just a way to hide money."

"Fucking hell, Fivers, you're worse than Terry!"

Fivers bowed his head a little.

"Anyway, mate, I didn't spend all that much on it. Got it as payment of a debt. I only spent about 10 grand on the place."

"Fair enough. None of my business anyway."

"That's the attitude. See, Terry? Fivers knows when to shut up!"

"There is another thing, though, Mr Walsh."

"Fuck's sake. What?"

"Well, you know how I used to deal?"

"Aye, that's right, Fivers, you *used to deal.*"

"Well, I kind of got to know the score, you know, about the dealers on my, like, level. Anyway, I never sold anything in this club 'cos, you know, the place was already taken by someone else."

Danny sat up. As did the others.

"Really?"

"Yeah, I tried it once and I got kind of, like, discouraged from doing it again."

Danny looked at the others. If drugs were being sold in Vapour, then it wasn't by this Firm.

"And so I was thinking that, well, that dealer is going to be a bit pissed off that he can't deal here any more. He'll know about your reputation, just like I do. And if he gets pissed off he might try to set you up. The last thing you want is to get shut down in the first week. 'Cos you know, Mr Walsh, the pigs'll be dying to find some reason to get you out of here."

"Too fucking right," agreed Danny. There was a pause. An expectant one.

"So Fivers – am I going to get a name? Or wait all day?"

"Well, I only know his nickname. But I do know where he deals. And where he lives."

Danny smiled.

"Good lad."

Danny always worked on the basis that there was no time like the present. And so he wanted to find this lad that same day. Besides, he was on a roll, two dealers in two days would find themselves without incomes. Fivers was in the good books as far as Danny was concerned. Probably because he felt sorry for him in a way. He only found him by chance. And he seemed like a good kid. Respectful. Humble. He knew his place and Danny liked that. He wasn't ambitious. Apparently.

"Let's go for a drive in my car, Fivers," said Danny, handing the keys over to him and beckoning for him to follow him out of the club.

Fivers followed behind, but not before having said goodbye to the lads.

Danny's car looked brand new. He obviously took care of it. Fivers was not sure why he was being allowed to drive it, but then he didn't pass up the opportunity. He had never driven a Jaguar XK8 before. Thankfully, at least the snow had melted so the chances of an accident were normal instead of high. A small but welcome mercy when driving the beloved car of Newcastle's premier villain.

He climbed in and immediately noticed how comfortable the seat was.

"Alright this, eh?" asked Danny.

"Aye, it's comfortable, like."

"Took me fucking ages to buy this. Police fucking hate me driving it!"

"I suppose they want to know how you could afford it."

"Exactly. The way I get the money to buy stuff like this tends to be a bit unpopular with that lot."

Fivers laughed, for the first time today.

"How did you manage to get the money then?"

"Well, nobody knows this, right, but I'm still paying it off. I just got a mate to arrange the finance for me."

"Oh right."

"Anyway, be careful when you pull out," said Danny, "some fucker's bust the wing mirror, look."

Danny pointed to the passenger side wing mirror. Or, at least, the place where it should have been.

"Did you see who did it?" asked Fivers.

"Na. Someone just clipped it I reckon. Then fucked off."

"Bastards."

"Aye. Fucking fortune to fix, these things!"

"Have you ordered one from the dealership?" asked Fivers, surprised that someone like him would want to pay full price for something.

Fortunately, Danny Walsh knew a scrap dealer, as he quickly pointed out, in his own style.

"Fuck that! My mate's got a scrap yard, he's keeping an eye out for me. Soon as he gets a blue XK8 in, he's going to let me know and then I can have a wing mirror."

"That's nice of him."

"Aye well, he's one of the lads, you know? Deals in scrap metal, but not *just* scrap metal, if you know what I mean. They call the lad Barnesy – he's got a place up near the coast – calls it 'Absolute Scrap', the daft twat!" Danny laughed, though he did like the name.

Fivers laughed too, but knew what 'one of the lads' probably meant. Barnesy, the scrap dealer, was obviously part of the Firm. Running a front, dealing in all sorts, protected by Danny, probably helped him dispose of things from time to time.

He wondered how many people Danny knew. People who just look like they are running a normal business but are, in fact, involved in the odd sideline here and there.

"So where are we going?" asked Fivers, pulling away surprisingly smoothly.

"To this kid's house. The one you said deals at my club."

"Hang on, Mr Walsh, we're not going to do anything daft are we? In daylight?"

"No, I just want to have a look at him. And where he lives. Then we can come up with a plan of action."

"Oh right."

There was silence for a while. Then Danny spoke.

"You can go faster than this you know, it's not a fucking 2CV."

"OK."

★　★　★

Fivers pulled the car up at some shops.

"What are we doing here?" asked Danny.

"Well, this is the area where the lad lives."

"Some shops?"

"No, but I thought we should park here instead of outside his house."

"Oh right. Fair enough. Is it far?"

"No, it's just up that road," said Fivers, pointing to the right with his arm outstretched, very aware that he almost hit Danny in the face in doing so.

"So, what are we going to do? Wait here in case he goes to the shop some time today?"

"Well, no. But this is the area."

"Aye, but where's the kid?"

"I don't know."

"For fuck's sake, Fivers, you've brought me up here for nowt!"

"Well, sorry like, but you said you wanted to see the area where he deals."

"Aye, OK. Tell you what, let's draw him out, like in the fucking OK Corral!"

Fivers laughed again. Danny Walsh was clearly insane. He shouted, then he made jokes. His unpredictability was to be treated with caution. This guy could change his mood in an instant.

"How are we going to do that?" asked Fivers.

"I don't know, call at his house – tell him you want to score some gear."

"I'm the last person he wants to see. He'll get paranoid."

"Oh aye, you fell out didn't you…"

"I've got an idea," said Fivers, taking his phone out of his pocket.

"Whoa, hang on, what are you doing?"

"I'm going to ring one of his mates."

"Who?"

"Well, the reason he found out about me dealing in Vapour was because of a so-called mate of mine. He thinks I don't know about it, but I do."

"Oh aye? You still speak to someone who set you up?"

"People always have their uses, Mr Walsh."

Danny seemed curiously torn between being impressed and being dubious.

"Alright Mick?"

Danny could hear words on the other end but couldn't make them out. He only had Fivers' words to go on.

"Look, I need your help," he said.

"I'm going to Vapour tonight. I want to start dealing there again. I'm sick of just selling tac on the streets."

Danny could hear 'Mick', whoever he was, saying something but couldn't make it out.

"I know he does, but that's why I need you. I need you outside to keep a look out for him, let me know if he's coming in."

"I don't care if he does! I'm still pissed off about last time. I'll split the money with you, mate."

"You will? Champion. Meet me by the Monument at 9."

"Aye, see you then, cheers."

"What was that about?" asked Danny.

"Playing the twat for a mug. Three guesses who he's ringing up right now."

"Oh right – so he's going to come down to the club and expect to find you there?"

"Exactly."

"Nice one."

"You could have made that call from the club though, couldn't you? Instead of wasting my petrol."

"Oh, well, I suppose so...sorry."

Danny laughed.

"Don't worry about it Fivers I'm only taking the piss! It was my idea to come up here anyway."

"So should we go back to the club then? Tell the others?"

"Aye, go on."

★ ★ ★

Danny looked at the group, which already seemed to have a new member.

"So that's the plan right? Fivers is going to go and meet this kid at the Monument and walk down here. Fivers reckons the lad is going to set him up and so it probably won't be long before this dealer kid comes in. Then we can all meet him."

"Aye, sounds alright," said Terry, without being asked. It seemed as though Fivers had thought of everything in advance anyway.

"Right, Fivers, get yourself away home," said Danny, handing him a twenty-pound note, "get you and your mam a takeaway for your dinner."

"Oh, cheers, Mr Walsh."

"Who's Mr Walsh?!" laughed Houdini.

"Leave him alone, he's being polite!" said Danny. "Seriously though, Fivers, call me Danny – the Police are the only people who call me Mr Walsh!"

"OK – see you all later, lads."

Fivers left the club. Predictably, Terry was the one to speak first.

"Well, this is all very new isn't it?"

"What do you mean?" asked Danny.

"Well, I mean, who's this kid, like? One minute you get Billy to smack him about, the next minute he's hanging about the place coming up with fucking plans for us all to obey."

"Now you listen here, he's a good kid. Anyway, it's my plan not his."

"That's fair enough then. I'm just being careful."

"Aye well there's no need," said Danny with a look that made no-one want to speak for a while.

"So, what does everyone want to do for scran? Fish and chips?" Danny suggested.

"Aye, sounds canny," said Davey.

"Right, Houdini, wander up to the Chippy and get five fish and chips."

"Fuck's sake."

★ ★ ★

Although he operated on a far lower scale than Danny, Fivers was of the opinion that it wouldn't do to be seen driving around in a car. He was unemployed and lived in an area far from salubrious. It annoyed him. He felt it a great example of the conformist nature of English society. Judging people by the car they drive. Judging people by the fact that they don't have a car. It doesn't happen anywhere else in Europe, just here. If the Police saw him driving a car then simply put, they would

41

wonder where he got the money to buy it. It might seem to border on paranoia but in truth that is how this country works. Things like that are noticed. Danny could justify his car. He was paying it off. No-one would bother investigating that. If he had shelled out cash for it then perhaps he would expect a call from Officers who work for a living and can't afford such a car. But Fivers had no such luxury. He could not justify driving any kind of car. It meant risking exposure. And he had been making too much money to take that sort of risk.

He sat at the back of the bus on the way back to his mother's house thinking about how strange it was that he lived in a house that he could afford to buy outright three times over yet he was travelling by bus. He knew, of course, that he couldn't be seen to spend very much at all. He was perhaps worryingly self-disciplined. And while it annoyed him for a short time, he imagined the consequences of being seen to throw money around. Suspicion. Investigation. A jail sentence. Having the money confiscated. And, perhaps worst of all, losing his customers to someone like Danny fucking Walsh. God, it makes you shudder.

He thought through the events of the last twenty-four hours now. Yesterday, he was happily watching the television with his mother. Then someone had come to the door and scared him to death. They had stolen a box full of five-pound notes. But then he had been offered a job. And now he even had a nickname. He was, after such a short time, well on his way to being well in with the most notorious people in the North-East.

Then his mind turned to something far more important than that. The fact that he was getting a takeaway for his mother and him, something that she would really appreciate. They hardly ever had takeaway food, she couldn't afford it. He could, but it would be no good for her to find out what he was up to at night when he claimed to just be going round to his mate's house. It would destroy her. Like it destroyed her when her husband was killed over a drugs debt while she was in hospital giving birth to her only son.

He felt guilty every time he thought about that. She really had no idea. He felt like he was betraying her every night he went out selling. But it was all for her. All he needed was enough money to set them up in a nice house. Maybe employ someone to make the garden look nice for her. She could have someone cook for her, make her cups of tea while she sat in the sitting-room with her feet up. She deserved it. He wouldn't need to sell drugs any more.

OK, maybe they wouldn't have staff. But they would be living in what most people call a normal house. No need to worry about the choice between eating well or paying bills on time. It would be takeaways every night! Or not, whatever. At least they would have the choice. And that's how Fivers mitigated his guilt.

⋆   ⋆   ⋆

Fivers caught the bus back into town that night. He wasn't nervous – he wasn't carrying anything on him that he shouldn't have been. After all, Danny had stopped him from dealing. That reminded him, he still hadn't cleared the loft out yet. Best get that done in case Danny found out.

He arrived in the city centre. It was just a few minutes to 9 now. Mick should be coming soon. He saw him coming from a distance and set off to approach him. He always thought it weird to do that. Perhaps everyone does it. Walks towards someone with whom they are meeting, even though when they do meet, they will be walking back in the opposite direction again. His mind always wandered like that.

"Alright mate?" Fivers asked.

"Alright Adam?" replied Mick, though it was neither a question nor a statement.

Fivers smiled to himself. People don't call me Adam any more, he thought.

They walked down to the Quayside to Vapour. Billy Cameron, the token doorman outside the as-yet unopened club had seen him coming and signalled for Houdini to set the sound system going. He stuck a door supervisor licence badge to his jacket pocket and stood outside.

"Evenin'" said Fivers, as he walked inside.

Billy Cameron gave him a vacant nod for the benefit of Mick, who was instructed to remain outside and be on the lookout for 'Millsy', the dealer who Fivers was about to set up.

Mick had, as Fivers had predicted, been in touch with Millsy within minutes of hearing of Fivers' plan to re-establish himself as a Quayside dealer. He stood outside of Vapour, the music thumping and the lights flashing as they always did. Waiting for Millsy to arrive. He was excited at the thought of what Millsy was going to do. And since he had become officially involved with Millsy, rather then being simply a friend, he took the same offence at Adam's audacity. Such audacity had caused Millsy to give himself a night off from dealing and come down to Vapour. He wondered how much money Adam was going to make inside Vapour before Millsy arrived. The more the better – it was all to be taken from him. And split between Mick and Millsy.

When Millsy arrived, Mick was even more excited. Something of a parasite really. Unwilling to mete out his own violence but happy enough to get a kick out of watching someone else do it. He found himself wondering what he should do next though. Call Adam on the phone to tell him Millsy was here, as arranged? Or just watch as Millsy went inside and emerged with Adam pleading to be left unharmed. He decided that there was no need to worry about Adam finding out that he had been stitched up. After tonight, according to Millsy, Adam's life in Newcastle was going to change forever anyway. Mick's friendship with Adam was to be confirmed as a thing of the past.

"Is he inside?" asked Millsy.

"Yeah he's been in about five minutes," replied Mick.

"Have you rung him?"

"No, I wanted to wait for you."

"Well, it's fairly kicking in there, we can't just wander in and pick him up. You'll have to get him outside."

"OK, I'll call him."

Mick pulled out his phone and dialled his friend Adam's number.

"Adam, he's here. Get the fuck out!"

Billy was still on the door. He had to stay there to make it look to Mick and Millsy that the place was open for business. But the longer this was taking, the more risk that other revellers would turn up expecting to be let into the club which was, as yet, not ready to serve customers. It was all taking too long. He had to do something. If he didn't, the two lads may well have smelled a rat. He looked to Mick and Millsy.

"Not coming in, lads?"

"No, we're meeting someone," replied Millsy.

"Well, you'll have to move along from there, you're making the place look untidy."

Millsy was the sort of person who would usually take a doorman on. And probably not do too badly either. But tonight, his energies were saved for something else and fighting with a doorman would make him lose his focus. Perhaps he should do as requested. But when he thought about it, he couldn't leave the door area – he might lose sight of Adam. That was unacceptable. The only other option was to go inside. Either that or end up in a brawl with a doorman, giving Adam the chance to slip past without facing what Millsy intended for him.

Millsy walked past Billy and into the club. Mick didn't follow.

"You as well – come in or fuck off," said Billy.

Well, why not? Fivers was going to find out about Mick's dealings with Millsy soon enough. And it didn't matter. He was finished anyway.

He too walked past Billy, who gave him a nod. And when he was fully past, Billy removed the door supervisor badge from his jacket pocket and entered the club too, closing the door firmly behind him.

Houdini saw them both walk inside and immediately turned the music off. Mick could see what was coming. He turned around, intending to escape through the door, but Billy was there to greet him. He didn't touch him. He didn't need to. The look that he gave him was a powerful one. A slight shaking of the head as though to suggest that Mick would leave when *he* said so and not a moment before. He reinforced his message with a blow to Mick's face which, due perhaps to the fact that it was expected, hurt all the more.

Millsy was only a few paces in front of Mick at the time. He too could see what was going on here. Davey walked up towards him and he didn't move while Davey patted him down, checking him for concealed weapons. He found none. This guy was clearly arrogant enough not to feel the need to back himself up with a firearm. But what Davey did find, as he rifled through Millsy' pockets, were several small bags filled with Ecstasy tablets. He looked Millsy in the eye, tutted to him and held one of the bags in the air. A sign to beckon over a man who was most offended by the fact that there were drugs, other than his own, in the club.

Danny walked slowly over to Millsy, sipping occasionally from a bottle of lager.

"Sit down," he said.

"What?"

"On the floor, now. Sit down."

Millsy knew he had no choice.

Fivers appeared from somewhere, Millsy didn't notice where. He joined Danny in front of Millsy. Danny put a hand on Fivers' shoulder, looked at him and winked. Then his eyes went back to the man sitting cross-legged on the floor.

"I've been hearing stories about you," he said.

"Oh?"

"Yeah. Not good ones either."

Millsy started to get nervous.

"Two things really, mate. First of all, this is my club and I don't like people coming in with pockets full of drugs to sell. It messes with my sales you see."

"Well, he's a dealer as well," replied Millsy in a shaky voice and pointing up at Fivers.

"No he isn't. Are you Fivers?"

"No, I know better than to get mixed up in that sort of thing," replied Fivers.

"Exactly. You hear that? He knows better than to sell drugs, especially in my club."

There was a silence. Perhaps predictably. After all, what could Millsy say to that.

"Second thing. I heard a rumour that you had a bit of a go at my pal here. That's not true is it?"

"It was between me and him, nothing to do with anyone else," replied Millsy.

"That's where you're wrong, mate. It's my business now. Go on, Fivers, get your own back," said Danny, removing his hand from Fivers' shoulder and standing back.

Fivers reminded himself how badly he was beaten up by Millsy. And the first few kicks to his face were pleasurable. Those that followed were just to make a point.

Mick found himself standing on the dance floor area, between his friend and Billy, who remained by the door.

Billy looked at him.

"Don't worry, son, you're next."

* * *

"So where's Fivers now?" asked Simon, realising that he had hardly drunk a sip from his bottle since the story began.

"Fuck knows," said Terry.

"I think he disappeared after that thing with his mother," said Houdini.

The others looked at Houdini disapprovingly. Simon noticed. Clearly, he was not going to hear about that story tonight. Maybe another time. It was a good few weeks before the trial. Maybe he would find out then.

"Once in the racket, you're never out of it"
Al Capone in *The Untouchables,* 1987
(dir. Brian de Palma © Paramount Pictures Corporation)

When you are late to Court but the prison bus hasn't arrived by the time you get there, nobody knows you are late. And you say a quiet thank you to whoever you believe in for relieving you of a problem. But even in the light of that, Mondays are still Mondays. Add to that the fact that you haven't slept much, having stayed up to prepare the case and you get a Simon Silver Monday.

Once the prison bus arrived, Simon went straight to the cells. On his own. He should really have known better than to do that, from past experience, but he was only going to pop his head in. The case was prepared. Walsh was happy enough with what Simon had done so far, in fact he was professional enough to recognise the fact that he had no chance of getting a not guilty verdict. So this was just a bit of PR.

Walsh had the usual deloused look that inmates tend to have in the mornings – more sanitised than merely clean. And he was in decent enough spirits, looking forward to having his fight in Court. He was in no way guilty of the charge he faced but he was almost resigned to being convicted anyway. Such was the beauty of the way in which he was set up. But who had set him up? Well, the question was really more like 'which copper'?

Walsh knew what he would do if he ever found him. But he also knew that he would never find him. And as a professional he did not allow this to cloud his mind. Focus was required. It's no good getting bogged down by emotion. There's no room for that. All of his energy was to be poured into getting acquitted.

He walked into a conference room.

"Hello Mr Silver," he said as he joined him.

"Have a seat, Danny," replied Simon.

He sat down.

"I've just come down to say hello really, before we go up to Court. There's nothing to be done to be honest – we've done everything we can now so I just wanted to pop my head round the door."

"No bother, I appreciate the courtesy. How are you feeling anyway? Confident?"

"As confident as I can be. You know the score Danny, we're up against it here. But I'm ready for a fight, if that's what you mean."

Walsh smiled.

"That's all I need to know," he replied, standing up, "now I suppose I'd better let you go and get dressed. There'll be a cup of tea waiting for me round the back so if you don't mind I'll go and have that."

"OK then," said Simon, joining Walsh in standing up, "I'll see you upstairs."

It's always nice to work with professionals. They are always polite. But they like to win. And if they don't, you can feel the concrete setting around your body. This was going to be a struggle and Simon had made sure that Walsh knew just how much of a struggle it was going to be. That way, when the inevitable happened, he would feel like less of a target. It was probably his own imagination getting the better of him. Maybe it was a bit unrealistic. But then again, you don't apply for the job of gangster, you earn it.

★　★　★

The trial was listed to kick off at 10.30, but it was a fair bit later than that by the time it did. It was quite a big trial and Kate Holloway had asked for some time just to make sure that all of the prosecution witnesses had turned up. There is always a glimmer of hope that key witnesses don't turn up and the Crown is forced to offer no evidence. But Walsh wouldn't walk today. If witnesses were happy to make statements against someone like Walsh then coming to Court would make no marginal difference to their fear. They clearly weren't frightened to make statements so they wouldn't be scared of telling their story in Court. Then again, if that was true, and they didn't turn up then that would suggest that they had been frightened off, spoken to by Billy and the others perhaps. Simon's new friends. He didn't want to know. And, by eleven o'clock, they had all arrived anyway so he thought no more of it.

Kate was full of the joys of spring as usual. She was being more cocky than she needed to be today. She knew she was going to get a conviction. And so did Simon. But he told himself that it was only because the evidence was so damning. Any idiot could get a conviction on this one. Not that Kate was an idiot. In fact, she was one of the few people that Simon was actually wary of. She was well known to spring the odd surprise from time to time. She had a First from Cambridge to back herself up too. But this case didn't require someone like her. A pupil could do it for God's sake.

In fact, why have they used her? Maybe the Police are worried that they might not get Walsh, that he would emerge the innocent victim of a set-up. That must be it. But then why would they worry? They've done a cracking job with the evidence. The Officer in charge clearly knows what he's doing. And he's only a Sergeant. What's his name again? David Whelan or something. Probably just being careful, all in all. They seem to really want Walsh off the streets.

In fact, the Prosecution had briefed Kate for the very fact

that they knew Simon Silver was getting the defence brief. And they needed someone of her calibre to make sure they didn't end up with an acquittal. Simon didn't know this of course. If he did, he would probably have become so big-headed that his wig wouldn't fit.

Her Honour Judge Kristensen had reserved the case to herself. It wasn't clear why. Maybe she just fancied an easy few days. This was not going to be a particularly taxing case. She would not need to direct the Jury on very much law. The truth was, though few people knew it, that she was a pupil when Walsh was first convicted. And he had stuck in her mind. Sometimes they do. Young defendants who don't get upset. Who are in fact very polite. Professional, even. Ones to watch. She sat behind her pupil-master and watched Walsh get convicted almost twenty years ago. She remembered having been attracted to him. To his way of life. To her, he took danger with him in everything he did. He was exciting, something that pupillage is not. Sometimes she had thought about him before she went to sleep.

There was little to say before bringing in a Jury pool. From that pool, twelve people would be selected to hear Simon Silver's pathetic attempts to convince them that they couldn't be sure enough to return a guilty verdict. It would be an easy few days for them too.

The public gallery was full. But five men in particular stood out. Simon hadn't seen them for a few weeks. Not since that night in the bar. He had been too busy to go back there and see them again. It would have been a great excuse for avoiding them. But he didn't want to avoid them. He wanted to go back there and talk to them again. Be seen with them again.

He could pick them out through the tinted Perspex that separated them from the main body of the Court. He saw Billy Cameron nod his head towards him to say hello. He found himself doing the same back. And then his heart jumped as he wondered whether anyone had noticed. It seemed that they hadn't. He saw Black Davey fiddling around in his jacket. Walsh was asked to stand.

"Daniel Walsh, the names you are about to hear are the names of the Jurors who will try you. If you object to them, or to any of them, you must state your objection as they come to be sworn, and before they are sworn."

Walsh nodded to signal his understanding. Black Davey started writing.

Twelve names were called out and those who answered to them were sworn in. Walsh had made no objections. What's the point anyway? Black Davey put his pen and paper back in his pocket. Only Simon saw it. No-one else seems to think to check these days.

Kate Holloway stood up and gave Simon a look before smiling at the Jury.

"Members of the Jury," she said slowly, "the Defendant Daniel Walsh stands charged on an indictment containing only one Count. He is accused of possession with intent to supply a drug of class "A" – heroin, in this case."

She paused to let it sink in.

"Not a hugely serious case, you might think. But this is not just a case of a few wraps of heroin to sell on the street. No – this, as you will see later, is far more...large-scale. Daniel Walsh, the Crown says, was found to be in possession of over a quarter of a million pounds' worth of heroin."

The fact that one of the Jurors gasped didn't help. At least, it didn't help Simon or Walsh. Kate was happy enough with it of course, and she went on for a good twenty minutes before calling her first witness. Well, why not make a play of it?

Kate's first witness was probably her star witness. The Scenes Of Crime Officer. Everyone calls them SOCOs. Kate went first and Simon listened out for leading questions. The only way he was going to get one up on Kate here was if she asked a leading question to which he could object. He had read this guy's statement and it was watertight. Kate stood up.

"Could you state your full name please?"

"Carl Andrew Saunders."

"Thank you. And do you work?"

"Yes I am employed as a scenes of crime officer with Northumbria Police."

"Did you make a statement in this case?"

"I did."

"Why did you make a statement?"

"Er...because I was part of the investigation."

It sounded like a stupid question. But it wasn't. Kate had avoided asking a leading question and in doing so, she had avoided criticism from Simon and humiliation in front of the Judge and Jury.

"You were involved in the investigation?"

"Yes"

"Of what?"

"Well, of Danny Walsh being, like, you know, a heroin dealer."

Simon recapped it in his head. Kate had not led this witness at all. They were all his own words. And so far, Saunders had said that he was investigating Walsh. And that he was a heroin dealer. This is not looking good. The Jury have probably made up their minds already.

Kate went on.

"So, were there any conclusions to be drawn from this investigation?"

"Well, a few parcels of heroin were found in his car."

"How many?"

"Er, I don't know to be honest..."

Oh this might help me, thought Simon.

"...they were all piled up on top of each other in the footwell and seat of the passenger side."

Or it might not.

"So there were several?"

"Yeah, several."

"More than ten would you say?"

Oh alright Kate, don't rub it in.

"Oh yeah, definitely. More like about thirty. You can see them on the photos."

Kate smiled. "I was about to ask you about that. Which photographs do you mean?"

"The photos I took of the interior of the car."

Kate proudly handed six copies of the photographic exhibits to the Usher who walked towards the Jury box.

"Your Honour, the Jury will see the witness' photographs. Perhaps they can share one between two?"

"Yes Miss Holloway. Do I already have these?"

"They should form part of Your Honour's bundle, yes."

Kate gave the Jury a few moments to look through the exhibits that they had just been handed.

"Mr Saunders, are these the photographs that you took of the interior of the Defendant's car?"

"They are, yes."

"We'll hear later from another witness who will say what is contained in those packages. For now, though, would you wait there? There may be some questions from my Learned Friend."

Simon remembered what Donald Ramsey had told him the first time he watched a Crown Court trial. Always ask when. And always ask why.

"Mr Saunders, I just have a few questions for you. I won't keep you long."

"OK."

"Did you make a note of the time you arrived at the scene?"

"I did, actually, it was 6.32am."

"And what prompted you to go to the scene in the first place?"

"What do you mean?"

"I mean why did you go to the scene? What made you decide to go there?"

"Well, I didn't decide to go there, I was told to go there."

"Oh I see – by whom?"

"Well, by Sergeant Whelan."

"Oh, so it wasn't your idea?"

"What?!"

What is this guy talking about??

"Now I know you can't speak for anyone else, but what I *can* ask you is this – what is the procedure for SOCOs to attend scenes of alleged crimes? What happens from the commission of the alleged crime to you being on the scene?"

"Well we just get told to go there. Er…like, we just get a message through from control. Or sometimes we get picked up if there's other officers going."

"I see. So how did you get there on this particular morning?"

"I drove there myself."

"You drove there yourself," Simon paused. Because he was trying to think of some decent questions to ask. And when you can't think of one, you keep talking.

"And you say you arrived at 6.32am?"

"Yes."

"And how long did it take you to get there?"

"About ten minutes."

"I suppose it must have been quiet at that time of the morning?"

"Yeah, there wasn't really anyone else on the road."

"So who was there when you got there?"

"Er…well there were a couple of cars. Sergeant Whelan

was there…and about four or five other officers."

"And what were they doing?"

"Well, just waiting for me really."

"Was Danny Walsh there?"

"No, they arrested him later that day."

"How do you know there were four or five officers if they were just sitting in their cars waiting for you?"

"Hey, I never said they were in their cars."

"What – so they were all standing outside of the cars?"

"Yes."

"Oh, I see."

This might go somewhere now…

"Where were they standing?"

"Around Walsh's car."

Now Simon found himself in an interesting position. He realised, as he was on his feet asking this witness a series of questions, that the photographs that he had taken were all of the heroin. It hadn't occurred to him until now but he suddenly realised that there was no photograph of the car before the heroin was seized. Before the windows had been smashed and the door forced open. This was a major hole in the evidence. Just a few more questions should do it. Then I can ask the Judge for some time to discuss matters with Walsh before going on.

"Mr Saunders, when you arrived on the scene, was the car secure?"

"Er…no, the window was smashed in so that the Officers could seize the heroin."

"Who had smashed the windows?"

"Well, the Officers."

Now then. This is interesting. Heart beating faster now. Keep cool. Just ask the question.

"Did you see them smash the window?"

"Well, no, but…well, I wasn't there when they smashed it."

"Mr Saunders, if you didn't see them force their way into

the car, how can you say that they did so?"

Simon looked over at the Jury. Just briefly, but for long enough.

"Well, I can't I suppose."

"No, you can't can you?"

Saunders said nothing. He hadn't done anything wrong. It wasn't his fault. But Simon was going to jump on this point and Saunders knew it.

Simon looked up at Her Honour.

"Your Honour, I wonder if perhaps this is a convenient time for the members of the Jury to take a short break. I appreciate that the witness' evidence should not be interrupted in this way, but I must take instructions on a small matter."

It was no small matter.

"Yes, Mr Silver, I follow. Ladies and Gentlemen, if you would like to follow the Usher out of Court, you can take a short break."

The Jury left the room. And Her Honour rose. Now Simon could have a word with Walsh behind the door to the cells and ask him something important. He turned to Shelley.

"I'm going to have a word with Walsh behind the door ok?"

"Oh right, I'll just wait here then."

"Well, no, I need you to come with me."

"Oh, sorry, I just thought you meant, like, for me to…"

She was as nervous as Simon had been. He remembered the feeling. He still had it when in the company of judges and silks. He smiled at her. And tried to bridge the impossible gap between understanding and patronising. It can be easy to be both, even when you don't mean to be.

"It's ok – I have to take some fairly important instructions and I need a note of what's said, especially with this bugger!"

They walked through the dock and the door was opened to the back of Court for them."

Walsh looked fairly indifferent. But he was sitting down

with his hands linked together which made Simon assume that he was at least interested.

"OK Danny?"

"Yeah. How do you reckon it's going?"

"Well," said Simon, sitting down beside him, "that's what we need to talk about."

"Oh?"

"You've heard what the guy's said about you. Heroin dealer etc. etc."

"Yeah, it's fucking bollocks that is," replied Walsh, who then looked to Shelley and apologised for being rude.

"I know it is, Danny,"

He didn't know.

"But the thing is, he's also said that the coppers had already broken into your car when he got there."

"Aye I heard him say that. See? Told you I was set up! They obviously put the stuff there."

"Well this is why I've asked for time to speak to you. I need to know from you what your instructions are."

"What d'you mean?"

"Well, if you want me to put the case in terms of being set up by the coppers then you have a decision to make."

"Aye but you know I've been saying I was set up the whole time."

"Yeah, but who are you saying set you up?"

"Well who did you think I meant?!"

"I'm just making sure, Danny. It's a funny business when you're standing up asking questions. There's no time to start wondering what your case is – you have to be dead sure. Especially with this sort of thing."

Walsh was clearly getting angry now. And perhaps losing his faith. But it didn't last long. And if it did, it didn't really show. There was a reason why Walsh had got to where he was, in terms of the underworld. He was a calm professional. Well, he lost his temper every so often but he became professional eventually. And his mind now turned to what he had to do. No point in wallowing. There was a job to do. He looked to Simon.

"So – what do you need instructions on?"

"OK, I need to know whether or not you want me to run this case as a police set-up."

"Well aye, course I do!"

"Hang on, Danny, there's more."

"Sorry, go on."

"You need to know that if I allege this set-up, then I am casting what they call an imputation on the character of a prosecution witness."

"So what? They're all lying bastards."

"Danny, look, if I do that then the Jury will find out about your previous convictions."

"Why's that? Are you going to tell them, like?"

"No, I'm not, but the way it goes, if you slag off a prosecution witness, call them a liar or suggest they have set you up then they effectively get to do the same back to you by telling the Jury you have got previous form."

"Aye, but I've only got a couple of burglaries and an assault."

"I know, but that makes you dishonest – they can use that against you."

"I don't give a fuck. I want you to take the piss. I'm not going to just sit here and have them call me a drug dealer when I'm not one. I've been set up Mr Silver and I want you to call every single one of these coppers fucking liars."

"OK Danny, but are you happy enough to let me do that even though your convictions will go in?"

"No bother. Just get on with it. I want to see them all shown for what they are."

Simon looked at Shelley. And down at her paper to see

that she had made a decent note of the conversation. She had. And his back was covered.

"OK Danny, that's all I need from you."

The Court reconvened. The Jury came back in. And Simon actually had something to say now. He had a defence. And one which, hopefully, would have a bit of credence. Juries don't believe that the Police set people up. They are unconditionally honest aren't they? Of course they are. Walsh had no proof. Simon had his suspicions of course, but then he wouldn't bet his life either way. He knew what Police Officers are capable of. In truth, most of them are good people. Especially the ones who never get promoted. But it only takes one to bend the rules and suddenly everyone starts claiming Police set-up. And they are usually wrong to do so. But then, sometimes they are right. The question of whether that was right in *this* case remained to be seen.

Carl Saunders came back into the witness box and Simon stood up to meet him.

"Mr Saunders, I am proposing to recap the last few things we talked about before the short break. Would that be helpful?"

"Yes please."

"You said that you arrived on the scene to find a group of four or five officers standing around Danny's car."

"Yes."

"And you said they were waiting for you."

"Yes, they were."

"Well, forgive me, but why wait for you? What do you add to the investigation?"

Simon had insulted Saunders. Hopefully that would make him lose his temper.

"Well, *with all due respect*, I add a lot to the investigation."

Always better to get people angry. They let things slip.

"I don't mean to offend you Mr Saunders, I'm sure you are a vital part of the investigation, especially with your camera."

"Yeah, well, maybe my job isn't as good as yours mate, but I wasn't born with a silver spoon in my mouth was I?"

"A *Silver* spoon?" asked Simon, smiling.

Saunders had to smile too.

"You know what I mean…"

"I do. Mr Saunders, don't be offended by my question, it wasn't meant to insult you. I asked it for a very good reason. The reason is this : you said earlier that the windows were smashed when you got to the car."

"Yes, I did. They were."

"And the photographs that you took are of the interior of the car only."

"Yes."

Simon breathed in. Crunch time. No going back.

"Is that usual practice?"

"Well…I…I don't know."

"You don't know."

"I mean, it's…I don't know."

"I asked you earlier whether, since you didn't see the officers smash their way in, they might not have done."

"True."

"So how do you know that the drugs weren't planted there?"

"Planted? Who by? Here, there's over a quarter of a million there – who's going to waste that on setting Danny Walsh up? He's not *that* big time!"

"No, he's not is he? In fact, he's nobody. But that's not what the Police think is it?"

"I have no idea – I just take the photos."

"But you know that they've been after him for years don't you?"

"Yeah, they have – he's a drug dealer."

"But up until now, they couldn't find any evidence on him could they?"

Silence. So keep going.

"In fact, there has been so little to pin on him that this time, you all thought you'd invent something yourselves. A little crime creation. Isn't that right?"

"Don't be ridiculous."

"When you arrived, the car was intact wasn't it?"

"No, I've told you already, the windows were smashed in by the officers."

"And once you got there, the officers *then* smashed the windows."

"No."

"And planted the heroin inside."

"No way – like I say, why waste all that money?"

"Heroin that was in fact made up of packages seized over the years from other raids. Heroin that should have been destroyed."

"No."

"But was kept for a rainy day."

"Ridiculous."

"Was it a rainy day Mr Saunders? Or did it brighten up once you all knew you could put Danny Walsh behind bars and get away with it?"

"You're dreaming."

"That's why you only took photographs after the windows were smashed in isn't it? Because the drugs weren't there to be photographed before you planted them."

Silence. Simon sat down.

Kate did not re-examine the witness for long. She just gave him a chance to deny what Simon had put to him. And then she relished in applying to Her Honour Judge Kristensen for Walsh's previous convictions to be put before the Jury. She allowed the application. Simon could not challenge it. The Jury were not particularly taken aback. They had lunch on their minds. And because it was almost one o'clock, Her Honour released them for the short adjournment.

★ ★ ★

Simon left the Court with Shelley. He offered to buy her lunch. Not because he was trying to impress her. If anything, he wanted to make sure that her note of Walsh's instructions were up to the job. They were. And she had brought her own lunch anyway.

Billy Cameron approached Simon with the offer of a cup of coffee. He too probably had more than coffee on his mind, as Simon had done in offering Shelley some lunch.

"Do you mind sitting in here?" asked Billy, "I know it's not the Advocates' lounge, like!"

"It's fine," Simon replied, "and anyway, how do you know what the Advocates' lounge is like?!" he laughed.

"I'll tell you later," Billy replied. He was not smiling.

"Er…OK," said Simon, following Billy into the public canteen.

He sat down with Billy and was soon joined by the others.

"You don't mind if I smoke do you?" asked Houdini.

"Not at all," Simon said, and paused before adding, "I'm not fucking royalty you know!"

"Well, you're not one of us either," replied Stobbsy.

For some reason Simon was offended. He wanted them to like him. Why didn't they consider him to be one of them? But then, why did he care? Why would he want to be thought of as a criminal? But were they criminals? He had reason to suspect so, but then again he couldn't name a single thing they had been convicted of. Maybe they were of good character. Unlikely? Perhaps. But he had no proof. He wanted them to say he was one of them, maybe not involved in their business, but at least someone they thought of as a friend. Someone to confide in. They could see that his face had fallen.

"Here, man, don't get upset – I'd swap lives with you any day!" said Black Davey.

"Would you?" asked Simon, "why exactly?"

"Well, the money for one thing. And people don't look down their noses at you. They respect you, take you seriously."

Black Davey had perhaps summed up the reason for his own chosen path in life. He craved only respect and the means to live comfortably. And not to be thought of as a second-class citizen. And it was nothing to do with his colour either, it was all about the area he came from. Full of the unemployed and the substance-addicted. That's what you hear anyway. Some people lock their car doors when they drive through such areas.

"Look," said Stobbsy, the person with perhaps the biggest chip on his shoulder, "I'm not trying to be funny with you right? But we don't belong in your society and you wouldn't last five minutes in ours."

More valid social comment.

"But I'm not like the rest of them. Don't put me into a category right? How do you know about where I grew up?"

"Where did you grow up? Same place as me?"

"Well, no, I didn't."

"Exactly."

Simon was offended. And not scared to say so. So while we're all being honest...

"Oh that's really nice that is! I like it how I'm the only fucking Barrister not sitting through there reading the Times, but I'm the only one you would say this shit to!"

Stobbsy looked taken aback. And he stared into Simon's eyes with raised eyebrows

"If you've got something bugging you, Stobbsy, then I'm sorry, but I can't help where I grew up. At least I haven't wasted the chances I've been given. It would be worse if I just fucked about wouldn't it? That should piss you off more."

Stobbsy said nothing for a long moment. Oh God, Simon, what have you done? Imaginary concrete sets very quickly when faced with this lot.

Stobbsy sighed.

"Aye, I know. Sorry, mate, you're right. I'm just pissed off about everything today."

Now then. I was scared for a moment. And now I'm having a real conversation with a real villain.

"Tell, you what, come to the club tonight and I'll buy you a pint," he went on.

Yes please.

"OK."

"Aye, and maybe I'll tell you how I know about the Advocates' lounge!" laughed Billy.

Simon smiled. He couldn't think of anything to say. He was loving it.

"So how do you reckon it's going Mr Silver?" asked Cautious Terry.

"Call him Simon you twat! He's not fucking royalty!" laughed Stobbsy.

Simon laughed too.

"Well, it's like I told Danny, we're up against it. But at least we're taking the piss a bit."

"Aye, you're doing a good job Simon," said Billy, "I'll use you if I ever get caught!"

* * *

The Court was assembled once again at just after two o'clock. And Kate called her next witness, Police Constable Alan Wright. He was one of the annoying officers who got into the witness box, took the oath without reading from the card

66

and announced who he was before being asked to do so.

"Constable, have you made a statement in this case?"

"I have, Your Honour."

He was also annoying in that he addressed all of his answers to the Judge. Why they do that no-one knows.

"Could you please tell the Court of your involvement in this case?"

"Well, I received a radio message to attend Drake Street as there was a report of a car with heroin hidden in it Your Honour."

"And did you see such a car?"

"I did, Your Honour, yes."

"Do you know whose car it is?"

"It is registered to Danny Walsh."

Oh, he's stopped saying "Your Honour".

"How do you know that?"

"Because I was the Officer who ran the PNC check."

"For the benefit of the ladies and gentlemen, could you explain what a PNC check is please?"

"Yes, it stands for Police National Computer, it's…like a database…with information on it like car registration and that sort of thing."

"Thank you. So how do you run a check?"

"Well, you just speak to control on the radio and give them the vehicle registration number and they check it on the computer."

"Does it take long?"

"No, about ten seconds."

"Impressive."

No, Kate, it's worrying. Not impressive.

"And you ran the check on this number plate?"

"That's correct, Your Honour."

Oh he's doing it again now. Dick.

"So when you arrived at the scene, were you alone?"

"Well, I was in company with PC Cheung."

"But were you the first on the scene or were there other officers there too?"

"No, no, it was just PC Cheung and myself."

Myself? That is another of Simon's bugbears. PC Cheung and myself... arsehole.

"Could you tell the Court what you did on arrival at the scene?"

"We both got out of the car and approached Walsh's vehicle."

"Did you know it was his vehicle at the time?"

"Well, not for sure at that exact time but once we saw the heroin inside I went back to our vehicle and ran a PNC check."

"So you saw heroin inside the car?"

"Yes, well, packages of something which turned out to be heroin. We didn't know from just looking at it."

"Why were you suspicious of it then? Why run the PNC check?"

Oh come on, Kate, leave some questions for me will you?!

"Well, when we received the call from control we were told that there would be heroin in the car. We got there and saw some packages inside and so we just radioed it in."

"I'm not criticising, Officer, don't worry. Now, this is an important question. Were the windows broken when you arrived at the scene?"

"The windows?"

"Yes."

"Well, no...why?"

"Don't worry about that. Could you wait there? my Learned Friend may have some questions."

Simon stood up. He did have some questions. Not as many as he had before Kate had made sure that all angles were covered. This case was hard enough without her ruining it by being brilliant.

So what was there to ask? Kate had established that this

man was the first on the scene. She had established that he went there because there was heroin in the car. She had established that the car belonged to Walsh. And also that the windows were still intact on arrival. So the only thing to focus on was this Police conspiracy to plant drugs.

"Officer, you say that when you arrived the windows to this car were intact?"

"That's correct."

"That's simply not true though is it?"

"What? It is true!"

"And how can you prove that to the Court?"

"Well, I can't, 'cos I never took the photographs…"

"No, you can't prove it can you?"

"Well, the SOCO took photographs of the car."

Leave it hanging…

"Who smashed the window, Officer?"

"PC Cheung."

"And why?"

"Because Sergeant Whelan asked him to."

"Sergeant Whelan?"

"Yeah, our Sergeant."

"And you saw him do this did you?"

"Well, yeah, I was there with him."

"So he smashed the window?"

"Yeah."

"With what?"

"A hammer I think."

"A hammer?"

"Yeah."

"That's a standard-issue item, is it?"

"Well…no…Sergeant Whelan had the hammer and he passed it to PC Cheung."

"Where did he get this hammer from?"

"I don't know."

"So he could have been carrying it in his pocket?"

"I suppose so."

Kate stood up.

"Your Honour, forgive the interruption, but this witness cannot give evidence as to where another person may or may not have been carrying something."

"Yes, Miss Holloway, I quite agree. Mr Silver?"

"I won't push the point, Your Honour."

It's OK, I've planted the seed. Save the rest for this Whelan character, whoever he is.

"So what happened after PC Cheung smashed the window?"

"The SOCO took photos of the heroin."

"And what happened to the heroin after that?"

"It was seized."

"By whom?"

"Well, we all carried a few packets each, considering there were so many of them."

That didn't help.

"Officer, is Danny Walsh a drug baron?"

"Well, I wouldn't say he was a drug baron, not really."

"No, he isn't is he? So what is his involvement in the drug world then?"

"Well he's, like, number one in the area. The top man in the local chain."

"The top man in the local chain...so what's the top man in the local chain doing in possession of all of this heroin? Don't you find that strange?"

"Not really, no. Why?"

"Well, doesn't the boss have people who work underneath him?"

"I suppose so."

"And yet he leaves it all in his car on display?"

"That's how arrogant he is. He likes to show us how unstoppable he is."

"But he isn't unstoppable is he? He's on trial now."

"Well, yeah, 'cos we caught him."

"Did Danny Walsh ever touch any of the packets of heroin?"

"No idea. He must have done though."

"Could you explain why there are no fingerprints on the packets?"

"He must have been wearing gloves."

A fair point. Can't really argue with that.

"So let's recap a while. You say that Danny Walsh, the top of the local drugs chain, as you put it, who must have people working for him, leaves a quarter of a million pounds' worth of heroin on display in his car, because he is so arrogant and wants to show you that he is unstoppable?"

Silence.

"Officer, that doesn't make sense does it?"

"Well…"

"Does Danny Walsh have any convictions for dealing drugs?"

"I don't know."

"Would it surprise you to know that he has no previous at all for drug dealing?"

"Well, I suppose. But then maybe not, cos he's probably had people take the wrap for him."

Simon looked away from the Officer.

"Do you call that evidence? 'He's probably had someone take the wrap for him'…come on Officer, let's stick to evidence shall we?"

More silence.

"The truth is, Officer, that Danny Walsh has no previous convictions for drug-dealing because he is not involved in dealing drugs, isn't it?"

"He is involved."

"Then why have you never caught him before?"

"I don't know why."

"Come on! He leaves heroin lying around for all to see! Even Inspector Clouseau would have had him banged up long before now!"

"Maybe that was the first time he left heroin lying around like that, I don't know."

"What actually happened that night is this. You arrived on the scene in the company of several officers. Someone smashed the window and you all placed the heroin into his car to set him up."

"Are you serious?!"

"Oh yes, Officer. Because in truth, that's the only thing that makes sense isn't it?"

"Why would we want to set him up?"

"Because, like you say, you've not been able to catch him yet. So you all made sure this time, didn't you?"

"Come off it – anyway, everyone knows he's a major drug dealer!"

"But you said earlier he wasn't a drug baron. Why change your mind now? Because I've found you out?"

"He's not a drug baron. But he is a major dealer."

"What's the difference?"

"Well, let's just say, he has someone above him."

"Oh, and you have evidence of this do you?"

"Well…no."

"Did you interview Mr Walsh?"

"Yes, I was there during the interview, along with Sergeant Whelan."

"And did you ask him about this supposed boss of his?"

"No."

"Why not?"

"Well, why would I? It's not relevant."

"The fact is, Officer, he has no boss, does he?"

"I know different. Come on, everyone knows it."

"He has no boss because he is not involved in the heroin

trade is he?"

"He is."

"But you have no evidence that he is. You haven't produced any have you?"

"No, apart from the drugs in his car."

"Drugs which you, along with others, planted there."

"No."

"Thank you."

Simon sat down. Nothing more to say. Simon had put his case. And made a few decent points.

Kate re-examined.

"Officer, did you plant heroin in the Defendant's car?"

"No, I certainly didn't."

"Did anyone plant heroin in his car?"

"No."

Someone did. So Danny would have Simon believe.

The Jury heard no more evidence on day one. It was not the most efficient trial Simon had ever been involved in. Only two witnesses in a day. But then, they had started late. Tomorrow, he would be cross-examining Sergeant Whelan. Maybe he should go straight home and prepare his cross-examination. But then, maybe not. Maybe he should go to the club for the pint that Stobbsy had promised him.

* * *

It was just after six. Simon walked into the club still wearing a suit, but with his tie and collar off. He still looked out of place. He hadn't been here before but he knew how to find the place. There were few people there. Just the five men, a barman, some women sat at a table, and a few other men he didn't recognise. He recognised the type though. Short hair, faces scarred with pock-marks, Paul Smith jumpers. We all know the type in truth. People wearing smart clothes but finding it hard to disguise their battled appearances. They all looked far older than they actually were.

He was greeted by a cheer from the Firm, which made the women look over to him, and made the other men look at each other questioningly.

"Get the man a drink!" shouted Stobbsy, putting his arm around him. Stobbsy had clearly had several already.

Billy passed Simon a bottle of lager and didn't ask for any money for it.

"Come on, Si, I want you to meet some people," said Stobbsy, grabbing Simon's arm and leading him towards the other group of men.

"Lads, this is Danny's brief – he's fuckin' class."

They looked at Simon for a moment, all sizing him up. One of them spoke.

"I've heard about you," he said, putting out a hand for Simon to shake, "name's Kirby."

Simon had heard of Kirby too. But he didn't say anything. In fact, he had heard most of the names he was to hear over the next minute or so.

This was a rush. Pure and simple. Simon was on a natural high. Talking to these people was exhilarating. But Simon was a natural analyst. He asked himself why he found it so exciting. The answer was quite simple. They were people you heard about but never met. They had reputations. Names like Kirby were bandied around the Robing Room, big names who established Barristers represented. And looked down their noses at those of Simon's age and experience. But now Simon was the special one. He was in the inner sanctum. They had let him in. He was welcome. And he just knew that his Practice was going to explode from this. They would all want him to represent them. He was obviously trusted by the Firm. Maybe they were warming to the idea of him being one of them.

The drinks came thick and fast from there. And before long, Simon had taken off his jacket and joined Stobbsy and the others at a table. He was comfortable now. Like he belonged. It was becoming more natural. It was about nine o'clock now. Still early. Still time for more drinks. People started to wander into the club now and the lights had since been dimmed, though Simon hadn't noticed. He sank back into his seat and held another bottle of lager on his chest with his hand clenched around it. He was more confident in his company now. He was talking louder and more freely.

"So Billy! What's this about the Advocates' Lounge then?!"

He checked himself. What kind of a thing to ask was that? But Billy didn't seem bothered.

"Oh aye I forgot about that!"

"What you doin'?!" asked Cautious Terry, looking at Billy.

"He's alright, man!" Billy replied, waving his hand loosely at Cautious Terry. He looked to the others. "Terry's even more cautious now than he was before Fivers fucked off!"

They all laughed. Even Simon, though he didn't really understand the joke.

"Aye, this Lounge business. Well it was all Fivers' idea really," he said, looking at Simon.

"Oh yeah – Fivers. I remember you told me about him."

"Aye well, he was, like, the ideas man, you know? Anyway, he had this idea right? He wanted us all to, you know, like, go straight and that. So he wanted to set up this company so we could all tidy up the money a bit. Anyway, Danny told him to fuck off 'cos, you know, Danny's a tight-arse, like. There's no way he would pay a Solicitor to set up a company for him, or get, like a financial, like, I don't know – whoever it is who sets companies up. Anyway, Fivers said we could just do it ourselves."

Simon was listening intently. Billy was letting his mouth go. But no-one except Cautious Terry seemed to object to it. And so he listened, not because he was gathering information, but because he was genuinely interested in the story that one of his new friends was telling him.

"So we were all in Court one day, right? One of Kirby's lads was up for a commercial burglary. Anyway, Fivers reckoned that there was a library in the Court and he thought maybe he could find out about how to set up a company from a book."

The Firm were all starting to smile now. Where was this going?

"We all told him to shut the fuck up, cos he always had stupid fucking ideas, Fivers. But he was dead set right? So Stobbsy told him he was calling his bluff and he said, well, Stobbsy, you tell him."

"Aye I told him to borrow my car and go home, put a suit on and just walk into the library and pretend he was a brief! And he fucking did, the daft twat!"

"Did he get caught?" asked Simon.

"Did he fuck," said Billy, "nobody batted an eyelid, man."

"Anyway," continued Billy, "see that lad over there next to Kirby?" He pointed over to the group that Simon had met earlier.

"Yeah"

"Well, he was the one up for the burglary right? And anyway, the only witness they had was this twat who went QE, you know, like Queen's Evidence."

"Of course he knows! He's a fuckin' brief!"

They all laughed again. Even Billy, though he was the butt of the joke.

"Alright, alright. Can I finish the story now? OK, so anyway, Fivers went into the library and had a look about. And then he got a bit bored and fancied a bit look around the rest of the place. So he wanders in to the Advocates' Lounge and pours himself a cup of coffee. Still no-one says anything to him."

Simon was not in the least surprised. People are far too

self-involved in that place to notice the odd gangster helping himself to a drink here and there.

"So then, he sits down and starts reading the paper right? He even starts talking to a couple of the other briefs, telling them that he's doing, like, work experience. One of them even wished him good luck! So then he has a wander about the Robing Room, pretending to read the court lists right? And then, so he says, it just came to him."

Simon raised his eyebrows. Was this going to be a punch line or a troubling climax?

"He noticed that one of the windows was open. And he looked around, and he noticed that the whole room was full of windows that you could open. He tried a few. They all opened right? And so he looked out of them. And so he came running upstairs to where we all were. He looked dead excited about something.

Simon had never really taken much notice of the fact that you could open the windows in the Court building. But when he thought about it, he realised that the only windows that could be opened were those in the Robing Room. Fivers must have noticed that too. And Simon could almost predict the sort of thing that was coming.

"So, anyway, he tells us all about the windows and he reckons he's got this great idea. And to be honest, it was a corker of an idea. 'Cos, right, the trial was going to start sometime that day. They were still sorting stuff out in Court, like pleas and that. And we were dying to have a quiet word to the lad who had grassed on Kirby's mate Stevie, you know, to stop him giving evidence."

Simon knew exactly what a quiet word was. And it probably wasn't just a word – there would probably have been a bit of action involved as well. And he wanted to hear more. He wanted this group to have succeeded in committing what was, after all, an offence. He wanted the end of the story to pan out in such a way as to make the grass retract his statement. Or give evidence in Court that didn't match his statement. He looked over at Stevie. He was standing here in the club, right now. He mustn't have been convicted. But was it because he was innocent? Or was it a lucky verdict? Or was it that Fivers had helped the Firm to pervert the course of justice somehow? Armed only with the knowledge that the windows in the Robing Room can be opened. Simon's heart quickened as he waited for the story to conclude.

"I'll say one thing for Fivers, right, he was a fucking genius. Honestly, man, the ideas he had. Out of this world, I'm telling you. He, like, thought things through dead quick you know? He made plans up in his head. Left the likes of Houdini here standing!"

They all laughed at Houdini. All except Simon. He wanted to know more.

"What happened next?" he asked.

"Fivers asked us all if any of us had a gun in the car outside. Stobbsy had one. And he got him to give him his keys so he could go and get it."

Hang on, a gun? First of all, how the hell do you get a gun through the security checks at Court, and second, why are they telling me they have guns? Maybe they really do trust me.

"Fivers had it all mapped out in his head. He asked Stobbsy if he could borrow his car to drive to this fishing shop up by the Football stadium. We all thought he was taking the piss but he was deadly serious. He wanted one of us to go with him and so I said I would go."

A fishing shop? What's that all about? What's that got to do with the Robing Room, a window, Court security and sneaking a gun into Court? Oh hang on, I see where this is going. Oh my God, this really was genius. This was real courage. More so than making a daring application to a Judge. Or asking a witness a question that might yield a make-or-break answer. No, this was what balls really were.

"So we drove up to the fishing shop, Fivers and me. He pulls up outside and gets me to go in and buy some fishing wire and a cheap knife. I tell him to fuck off cos there's no way we'll get those into Court, the knife would set the security thing off. 'Cos then, right, at that time, I thought Fivers was going to sneak the fishing wire into the Court and, like, wrap it round the grass' neck or something. But it turns out he's got other plans."

Simon was dying to know what these plans were. This was the weirdest story he had ever heard.

"I went in the shop and got what he asked for. And then we started to drive back. On the way, though, Fivers asks me to cut the wire into lengths of about 2 metres right?"

"With the knife…" said Simon, the plan dawning on him.

"Aye, so I did that right? And we got back to Court and he tells me to stay outside with the gun in my pocket and he'll go in. And then, while we're sitting in the car, he drops his trousers!"

Everyone laughed again. Billy was laughing too, while trying to talk.

"Aye! I know! I didn't know what the fuck was going on! Then he says, give us the lengths of fishing wire"

Stobbsy couldn't resist a poor joke.

"See?! That's why he dropped his pants! I always told you he was after your length!"

They all laughed, despite the fact that it wasn't even funny.

"So anyway, Fivers feeds the wire down both of his legs and over the arsehole bit of his underpants, pulls up his trousers and gets out of the car. So, right, the wire is hanging down both of his legs, inside his trousers. And he walks into Court. Straight through the security checks and upstairs. I'm waiting outside with the gun, now realising what the whole daft thing was about."

Simon realised now too.

"He must've gone into the toilets and knotted the lengths of wire together and then stuffed it into a ball into his pocket. 'Cos after about five minutes I heard a voice from an upstairs window. He'd even had time to go and buy a bar of chocolate to weigh the wire down with, cos he chucked it out of the window and held on to the wire from the window. I knew what I had to do. I stood there, gun in my jacket pocket and this bar of chocolate dangling beside me. So I took the chocolate off and walked round the corner so nobody could see me. Then I tied the gun up with the wire and walked back to where I was. I looked up at Fivers and he winked at me as he started to pull the gun up on the wire. Fucking genius. So I just walked into the Court eating a bar of chocolate looking normal as anybody!"

This was true genius. Who would have thought of that? Simon must have been in the Robing Room thousands of times. And he had never noticed whether the windows were open or closed. And even if he had, he wondered whether he would have considered it a security risk.

"We all met back up outside the Court where Stevie was on trial. And the next thing we needed to do was find the grass. We knew he would be in witness support. But we also knew that he would need to go to the toilet at some time. So we hung around by the witness support bit of the Court. Just an area screened off. So they have to use the public toilets. Dragged on a bit that did, remember lads?"

"Aye, took him fucking ages to need a piss!" laughed Black Davey.

"Anyway, *eventually*, right, he wanders into the toilets. We all walked in, except for Houdini who stood outside the toilets so no-one would come in. I had the gun and we cornered the little bastard. Stobbsy and Davey held him up against the wall while I got the gun out and showed him that it was loaded."

Simon couldn't help thinking that he now didn't want to hear the end of the story. It was fine while it was a cheeky tale to tell. But now it had become sinister. But there was still a part of him that wanted them to shoot the grass. To punish him. To assert themselves as being untouchable. Part of Simon wanted to go beyond the evil that these men represented and take pleasure in it. The same part of him that was disappointed the day they arrested Ronnie Biggs.

"So I was just standing there, dead calm, looking at the gun, loading it and unloading it a couple of times, just playing with it, like. And the grass stopped struggling. I walked up towards him and just held it to his head. Little fucker starts to piss himself. And I say to him 'look at the mess you've made you daft twat!' and then I go all serious and tell him that we're all going to remember that he died pissing himself. And he starts to cry."

Go on. Do it. Kill him.

"Then I take the gun away from his head. And I look at him, pretending to be upset for him, like pitying him you know? And then I say 'now you know what we can do to you'. And he nods. And I tell him that if we can get a gun into Court then imagine what we'll do to him after he gives evidence. He comes up with the idea of retracting his statement! Police wouldn't have it at first, but then he told them that he had made everything up and that he was actually the one responsible for the burglaries. That's the only reason he got bail, the fact that he was going to give evidence against Stevie. And so they let Stevie go, and the grass got remanded! Fucking hilarious!"

Simon was laughing. He even cheered. Partly because he was impressed at the story. Partly because he felt involved with the Firm.

*   *   *

81

A few more drinks and it was after ten. Almost bed-time for someone part-way through a trial. And Simon still felt that the night was still young. And he was with his friends. Maybe tomorrow would miraculously be cancelled. The whole world would stop for him, so that he could enjoy himself with what were perhaps the most genuine people he had ever met. And they were genuine. They had nothing to prove, after all. What they said was not just hard talk. It was hard fact.

They always tell you not to give clients your phone number. They can ring you at Chambers if they really need to. Or get in touch via the Solicitor who sent you the work in the first place. But not by ringing you directly. They always warn you about that. And Simon had always heeded such warnings. But, as is perhaps always the way of things, a woman changed all of that. Her name was Melissa.

All four of Simon's new best friends saw his eyes follow Melissa as she walked into the club. None of them were particularly surprised to see his jaw drop.

"Fucking hell, who's she?"

"That's Melissa," said Stobbsy, looking around at the others, "she used to be Danny's lass."

That pretty much put a lid on any likelihood of getting anywhere with Melissa as far as Simon was concerned. That, and the fact that she was clearly out of his league. In his head, of course, they were already married. He would be a fool to mess around with someone like her though, she would laugh in his face for asking, and then Danny would find out. Danny would probably have something to say about Simon muscling in on his woman. But then, Stobbsy did say 'used to be'.

"So they're not together now?"

"No, the daft twat gave her the bullet!" said Houdini, "must be fucking mental!"

That was about right.

Simon studied Melissa from across the room. Perfect legs,

perfect chest, perfect skin, hair, face etc etc. Perfect. Be careful.

Terry had so far seemed a little uneasy about letting Simon into the fold. But he seemed more comfortable with him now. And he made Simon's heart jump a little when he spoke next.

"It was a while ago now, she's been single ever since Danny."

"Why's that?"

"Why do you think?" he asked, laughing.

"Well, I don't know…"

"Who would want to get involved with her? What if he wanted her back?"

"Well, if they're not together then why would he care? She can be with whoever she wants can't she?"

"Doesn't work like that, mate. Besides, why do you think she still comes to the club? She likes to be part of the scene, that's why. She likes to be associated with Danny and all of us, and what we do. She likes to jump the queue, she likes people to know she's in the posse, like. Know what I mean?"

"You mean, she just likes the image, just likes being seen to come in here?"

"Aye, and she's hanging around waiting for Danny to take her back."

"And will he?"

Terry laughed again.

"Will he fuck! She's nowt to him. He never even mentions her name. He lets her come in here cos she's nice to look at, but that's about it."

Simon looked over at her again. She was standing at the bar, being served, even though there was a queue and she had only just walked in. It was clear that Simon was taken. Billy noticed it straight away.

"Fucking look at him!" he laughed, "here, don't bother with her, Simon."

"Why? Because of Danny?"

"Fuck Danny, man, he wouldn't give a shit. Just don't bother with her. She's one of these, you know, 'intelligent' types, likes fucking ballet and that."

"What's wrong with that?!" asked Simon, laughing.

"Well, man, you want a lass that's, you know, a bit thick. Women are for shagging not fucking talking to! Isn't that right lads?"

They all said 'aye' and took swigs from their bottles at exactly the same time. It couldn't have been rehearsed any better. Simon thought it was absolutely hilarious, and since he was in the company of friends, he didn't hide the fact.

Melissa was on her own. Of course, she was known to pretty much everyone in the room, but she had come in to the club alone. Such was her status as part of the furniture that she could do something like that, go out alone but be able to guarantee that she would know several people inside the club. She turned around from the bar, having been given her drink, which Simon noticed that she made no attempt to pay for, nor was she asked to do so. She seemed to pause for a while, looking around. Her eyes passed Simon's, noticing that he was transfixed by her, but pretending not to. It was the group with whom he sat that interested her anyway. Walsh's closest friends. Colleagues perhaps. She wondered how the trial was going. Out of interest really. She had no desire for Walsh himself, only the status he brought to her. And perhaps she was really just scanning the room to see who was lined up to take over from Walsh if he was convicted. She needed to make sure her position was still open to her. So who was this new guy in a suit sitting with Walsh's friends? Was he worth getting to know?

She stayed where she was for a while longer, sipping from her drink occasionally. Best not to make it look too obvious. And when the time was right, she made her way slowly over to the table where five gangsters and an unknown suit were sitting. Nice and slow. Remember, these people can welcome you, or they can tell you where to go.

Simon watched her walking over. He looked away as his heart started to beat faster. He took a swig from what turned out to be an empty bottle and made a big deal about putting the bottle back on the table, concentrating very hard on something he had probably done about fifty times already this evening. Beautiful women made him nervous. And right now, he was very nervous.

He pretended to be listening intently to some rubbish that Houdini was talking while Melissa arrived at the table. She didn't sit down straight away. Billy stood up immediately to greet her and they both turned their backs to speak to each other about something that Simon assumed must be regarding Walsh.

Billy put his hand in his pocket, removed something and passed it to Melissa. They turned round, Billy resumed his original seat and Melissa walked towards Simon's side of the table, pushing her hands upwards towards him ushering him to move along.

"Shift up," she said.

He did. She sat down.

"Melissa, this is Simon Silver, Danny's brief," said Billy.

She was impressed. She didn't appear so.

"Hi Simon," she said, without looking at him.

She removed a small, flat box from her purse and placed it onto the table. She opened it up and proceeded to pour out a quantity of cocaine onto the table, lined it up and bent over the table to take it in, appearing almost desperate to do so. Simon knew that Billy had given it to her, but he refused to believe it. They were not drug dealers, these people. Simon had been specifically instructed about this by Danny Walsh. For a moment he became very aware of where he was, who was there with him and what had just happened. This was not good. He immediately chastised himself for being so backward. Most of his income was derived from drugs anyway. And, justifying it to himself in that way, he abandoned his self-awareness and concentrated on today's "most beautiful woman he had ever seen".

It was 11 o'clock now. It was really time to go. But this place closed at 2am. And that was the closing time for the public. Simon knew that he could stay longer than that. The Firm did, after all, own the club anyway. But he wanted to go now. Melissa had spoiled the evening. Now he was nervous. It was fine while he was sitting with the men. But now she was here, everything revolved around her. He could not speak in the way he had been speaking earlier. What would she think of that? Would he appear too clever? What if he dumbed it down a bit – would she prefer that? Why should she? She was "one of those intelligent ones" according to Stobbsy. And while Simon searched for an answer, he remained silent, looked bored and came across as arrogant.

"So… a Barrister eh?" she said, out of the blue.

"Yeah, more fool me!" he replied. He always said rubbish like that. He wondered why he did it. Now the conversation will be predictable. She will say something about how good the job is, he will say something along the lines of 'yeah I suppose so' and then there will be a deathly silence. They will both part company and he will go home and sleep alone. It was the same every time. But this time it was different. This time, it made him sit up and actually have a conversation.

"Well, if you don't like it, you should get a different job," she said, looking away.

No-one had ever said anything like that before. Simon liked it. And they started to talk in such a way as to suggest they had known each other for years.

"Well, it's a very lonely job you know."

He did not know why he said that. She was intrigued. He was talking personally already. She turned back to look at him.

"Lonely? Really?"

"Yeah, it's pretty busy."

"But you must know loads of other Barristers?"

"Well I suppose so, but it's a very superficial environment. People are never really themselves."

"What – you mean they put on an act?"

"Yeah – exactly. And you play along with it. You have a laugh. But you only ever tend to see them at work. They hardly ever socialise outside of Bar events, which are just like being at work anyway, except with wine!"

"Oh, I always thought it was like a big clique."

"Well it is I suppose, but a false one. It makes it easier to get through the day, don't get me wrong, you know, having people to joke around with, but there aren't many who you would invite round to your house."

"That's really sad!"

"To be honest, I hadn't really thought about it until tonight. You know, sitting here with people I probably shouldn't be sitting with. But it's so genuine with this lot, you know? There's no falseness."

"I know what you mean. You always know where you are with them. Do you know what else? They never seem to talk about each other behind their backs either. That's because they say whatever they want to say to each other's face. And they're comfortable enough to say it."

Careful now. A few drinks. An invitation to be honest to each other. Heart going faster and faster, adrenaline flowing like mad. It's times like these when you consider getting carried away. So don't. He didn't. But, surprisingly, she did.

She moved closer to Simon and moved her head to whisper into his ear.

"That was quite an honest conversation wasn't it? You wouldn't usually say stuff like that straight away would you?"

"Well, no, probably not."

Oh God, don't kiss me. Then I'll want to marry you.

"So why did you?"

"Well, since we're being honest, I thought you might get bored if I was superficial."

"Well, you would be right," she smiled, "but I'm not bored am I?"

"I hope not."

Kiss me.

He could feel her cheek brush against his. He knew it was deliberate because she did it slowly. Oh God.

"I always wished for a tall dark stranger to take me away from all of this," she whispered.

It was clearly the cocaine. Or the alcohol. Both, in fact. And Simon knew not to believe that this was real. It was late at night, ideas always seem better at this time of night. He knew that she was just playing him. But he yearned to give her the benefit of the doubt. There was no doubt. But he created some. Just enough so that he could play out the fantasy too. Tall dark stranger? He certainly fitted the description. It was a load of rubbish, but it was making him feel excited. And he was dying to think of something to say. Something sexy. Something she would respond to by whisking him out of the club right now and introducing him to her bedroom. But there was another issue here. And it diminished all of the fervour he had started to allow to get the better of him.

"What's the story with you and Danny?"

She looked away. Clearly, she was unimpressed.

"Melissa?"

"Why does it always come back to that? To him?"

"Because he's my client and I'm going to see him tomorrow."

"So? He doesn't own me!"

"No-one owns you, Melissa. But if he thinks that he does, then he will act like he does. And I will be on the receiving end. Even though he's wrong."

"Everyone's so fucking scared of him! Why?!" she was getting too loud. Billy could hear what she was saying. And Simon was beginning to worry.

She got up. As did Simon.

"Where are you going?"

"To the bathroom. Is that alright?"

Simon raised his palms to her in defence. He sat down and looked at Billy.

"Bit of a live wire, her! We told you not to bother didn't we?!"

"I just asked her about Danny and her," said Simon, clearly anxious, "and she went all weird on me."

"I know, I heard. Don't worry, man. Anyway, we're not Danny's spies you know. She's gorgeous, you're a bloke. Danny doesn't go after every bloke who talks to her!"

Simon noted with interest that Danny didn't go after *every* bloke who talked to Melissa.

She came back to the table after a few minutes. Simon was pleasantly surprised to find her sitting beside him again. She didn't say anything for a moment or too and Simon filled the silence by pretending to be interested in what was going on around him in the club and sipping from another drink with more frequency than he usually would. The silence filled, it was Melissa that broke it.

"Simon, look, I'm sorry for going off it."

She looked like she really was sorry, too. Usually Simon would assure whoever apologised to him that they needn't worry. That it was ok. Even when it wasn't. But Melissa had been honest enough with him to happily show her frustration and so he felt no need to stick to his usual method of backing down just to keep the peace.

"You can't just shout at me and then say sorry. If you're going to do that, maybe you should think about not shouting at me to start with."

"Don't get clever with me, Simon, that's the trouble with people like you."

"No, the trouble is, Melissa, that everyone can hear you shouting, but no-one except me gets to hear you apologise."

She liked the fact that they were talking like this. The false argument continued for a while, until such time as they were both able to talk about something else. Before long they were laughing again. And shortly after that, she started flirting again. By then, Simon didn't care whether it was chemically-assisted or not. He was as completely taken as Melissa appeared to be.

She left for the bathroom again after a while. Simon was now back to sitting with the boys again.

"You're in there, son!" shouted Billy.

Simon played it down.

"No, no, she's off-limits, Billy."

"Is she fuck, man, go for it," he laughed.

"You told me not to go for it an hour ago!"

"I'll say anything, me!"

Simon was not at all convinced. In fact it made him self-conscious and very aware of the time. Just after midnight. It really was home-time now. And he would have to leave the car overnight. Which meant getting up even earlier in the morning to make sure he could get into town in time to buy a parking ticket. Melissa was coming back over now. She sat down beside him and he was sure she was sitting closer than before.

"Melissa, look, I really should go home you know. I've got a big day tomorrow and I need my wits about me."

She sighed.

"Actually, I might head off too," she said.

What did that mean?

"Oh, right," said Simon, pretending not to be intrigued as to what she meant.

"Yeah," she said, picking up her bag, "come on, I'll walk out with you".

She stood up, as did Simon. He looked at the group, who all seemed very interested in what was going on.

"Lads, I'm heading off."

"OK Simon, we'll see you in the morning," said Stobbsy.

Simon and Melissa walked out. They got to the main door and she linked arms with him. He felt like he was on fire. Was this going to go somewhere? Hopefully. But hopefully not at the same time. She was beyond attractive. But she was off-limits, let alone out of Simon's league. Maybe that's what made him so excited.

Stobbsy and Billy looked each other in the eye on seeing this. They didn't need to say anything – the look in their eyes was enough. They both got out of their seats and followed Simon and Melissa as they walked out of the main door. They stopped momentarily as they reached the main door themselves. Stobbsy looked up at Billy, as though to seek instructions.

"Just poke your head outside," said Billy.

Stobbsy watched Simon walk with Melissa to a taxi rank. They stood arm in arm. Pushing it a bit isn't he? They seemed to be talking. Stobbsy had no idea what they were saying.

"I suppose you have to be up early tomorrow?" she asked him.

"Yeah," laughed Simon, "I have to come in and move my car in case some bastard puts a ticket on it!"

He was starting to talk like they did now.

"Oh."

Silence.

"I was hoping you might come back for a coffee or something."

A coffee is rarely a coffee. No-one even likes coffee that much. Well, certainly not so much that they would extend their night just for the taste of coffee. There's always more to it than that. And Simon was dying for a coffee. He looked at her almost longingly. It was one of those moments. No need to be coy about it. Quite simply, he wanted her there and then. But she was Danny Walsh's ex-girlfriend. And it was late.

"I would have loved to, really I would. But I really can't."

"I know."

There was more silence while both of them wished for a taxi to appear and save them both from an uncomfortable time. Perhaps not all that uncomfortable, though. She did, after all, still have her arm linked in his.

They didn't need to wait long. She released herself from Simon's arm and it was then that he realised that the night was definitely over. But she kissed him on the cheek. She was just as disappointed as he was. This was beyond exciting. Yesterday he was thinking about starting a trial. Now he had been out with his client's friends and got very close to his ex-girlfriend. An interesting 24 hours to say the least. He should have gone home and enjoyed the fantasy. 24 hours in this sort of situation is 24 hours too long. And it was about to extend to 48 as she looked him in the eye.

"Come again tomorrow, won't you?"

Careful what you say, Simon. If you start something now, it means committing to a totally new life. Remember what happens in the films. Stop this liaison before it starts. Can you do that? Can you tell her that you won't be coming back tomorrow?

"Yeah, I'll see you tomorrow."

"Bacon tastes good..."

Vincent Vega in *Pulp Fiction*, 1994

(dir. Quentin Tarantino © Miramax Film Corporation)

The world felt different the next morning. On the positive side, Simon was buzzing from the previous night. It had been exciting, hearing the stories and meeting the moll. But on the negative side, he was tired, hung over, late and regretful. There's a reason people sleep on things. The cold light of day can lend the most telling perspective to a question. The question was whether Simon should really have been at the club last night. And whether he should have told Melissa he would be there again tonight. The answer was clearly 'no'.

It was perhaps this fear that kick-started Simon's day. He got into the city centre far earlier than was necessary, moved his car while probably still over the limit, and walked along the river to find somewhere to get a bacon sandwich. Not a very Jewish thing to eat but, well, it tastes nice so who cares?!

He walked past Vapour, the club he had left only five or six hours ago. Typically, the pavement around the club was decorated by flyers and vomit. There were even some drops of blood leading off in the direction opposite to Simon's route. He wondered why there was blood on the pavement. Someone could have had a nosebleed or something. Yeah, right.

He remembered, as he passed the club, where he and Melissa had stood and parted company hours earlier. He wondered what she was doing right now. Asleep, no doubt. Waiting for tonight to come so she could carry out her daily routine of socialising. Maybe that was unfair, perhaps she too had a job. She didn't need one though. She rarely had to pay for anything. The men that she met saw to that.

He thought about the story he had been told the night of Danny's plea hearing. He imagined Mick and Millsy standing outside the club on the night that Danny had bought the club. He wondered what had happened to them after Fivers had stuck the boot in. They hadn't said. Maybe the blood outside on the pavement was a clue. Well, perhaps more an indication of the sort of thing that *could* have happened. It was about two years ago when Fivers first got involved with the Firm.

Was Simon involved now too? He started to really regret last night now. What the hell was he doing? Why do night-time ideas seem much better than they do in the morning? If anyone had seen him last night then this could well be his last case. Paranoia? Not necessarily. It just doesn't do for Counsel to be seen socialising with gangsters. But Simon could still justify it. These were not his clients. Only Walsh was. And *he* wasn't out last night. He was safely tucked away in Durham prison awaiting day two of his trial. So in truth, Simon had done nothing wrong at all. Or so he told himself. You can bend the rules. You can twist things to suit you when you want to. Just like Simon does every time he eats a bacon sandwich and imagines his father chastising him for it.

*   *   *

This morning was going to feature Sergeant Whelan's evidence. Simon had done nothing overnight to prepare for it, but in all fairness, he was only continuing from yesterday. He walked into the Robing Room and put on his collars, wig and gown without speaking to anyone in particular. Kate wasn't in the building yet. Nor, in fact, was Shelley. Perhaps now would be a good time to go and see Walsh. Talk to him about what was going to happen today. And perhaps also what had happened last night.

Walsh looked as fresh and de-loused as he had the day before.

"Morning, Danny, have a seat."

"Did you go to the club last night?" he asked, with a smile on his face.

Shit. What does that smile mean?

"How did you know?"

"Stobbsy said you might be going. You look worried, Simon."

"No, it's ok. I did go, yeah. Stayed for a fair while actually."

"Well I hope you're up to the job this morning!"

Simon laughed.

"Don't you worry about that, Danny! I'm in fine form."

That wasn't strictly true.

"So did you meet Melissa?"

Oh God. He knows everything.

"Er, yeah. That's one of the reasons why I've come down to see you so early to be honest."

"She's a canny piece her eh?"

"Well, yeah, she's...she's very attractive."

"Aye," sighed Danny, "pity that didn't work out. Still, birds are birds aren't they? They always get upset when they find out you're seeing other people!"

"Is that why you split up?"

"Aye." Danny paused. "Do you fancy a bit yourself like?"

"Well, no, but...I just..."

"Get stuck in man, Simon. Have a bit of fun. You work too much."

That was certainly true.

"Seriously? You wouldn't mind?"

"Here, man, what's mine is yours. I'm not posh like you

lot, you know. Where I come from people share and share alike."

"Oh right, well, I mean, that's assuming she would have me."

"Don't be daft, man! She'll take anything that's going! The question you have to ask yourself is whether or not you would have her."

"Well I don't want to tread on your toes."

"Tread on my toes...honestly, man. I couldn't give a fuck. Think of it as a present from me to you for all your hard work!"

"OK, well we'll just see how it goes."

"Simon, can I ask you something?"

"Yeah, course."

"Are you scared of me?"

"Scared?"

You know you are, Simon. Don't try to hide it.

"Aye, do I scare you?"

"Well, we get on pretty well don't we? I mean, I've heard stories about you. But your friends have all been very welcoming."

"Never mind them, what about me?"

"Well, I wouldn't want to cross you. But then, I don't tend to cross people anyway."

That sounded pretty wet. So Simon took the risk of saying something else as well.

"Then again, Danny, you need me don't you? I don't suppose I need to be all that scared of you."

"Aye, true enough! But what about after the trial?"

"Well, if you get the result you want, what have I got to be worried about?"

"Nothing, mate. If I get the right result."

Nothing was said for a long few seconds. Was this a threat? This guy tended not to make threats. But then, what could he do in a cell other than make threats? Perhaps here in the cells, a threat was as good as a beating on the street.

It worried Simon a little. So it should, given the stories he had heard, ranging from social tittle-tattle to almost horse's mouth stuff like he had heard last night. But last night he had continued to subconsciously consolidate a new way of talking to people. Genuine people demand frankness. And he felt able to talk to this notorious man in such a way as to suggest that he was nobody.

"There's nowt like putting your lawyer under pressure is there?!"

Danny laughed.

"That's what I like about you Simon. You're honest. Not like the rest of the posh boys and girls!"

Simon smiled.

"Simon, fuck off upstairs and get yourself a cup of coffee. I'm going to get the daft lads here to make me a cup of tea. Come back down in a bit."

"Alright, I'll see you in a bit, mate."

Mate? This really *was* new. And very exciting.

* * *

"Hi Mr Silver," said Shelley.

"Oh, hi Shelley – you ok?"

"Yeah, thanks. Bit tired though. Went out last night."

"Well, don't let on, but so did I! Do you want a coffee?"

"Ooh, yeah, thanks."

"Anyway, you don't look that tired," said Simon as they sat down.

"Well, I only stayed 'til about 11. My friends all went clubbing but I had to be up early for this trial!"

Take note, Simon.

"Yeah, well that's probably a good idea, Shelley."

"Do you go out in the town?" she asked.

"Sometimes. Not all that often though. You never know who you might run into."

Hypocrite. Take a sip from your coffee so she can't see that half-smile on your face.

"Yeah, God, imagine bumping into a client in town!"

"Or someone you've prosecuted."

"Yeah, that would be worse wouldn't it?"

"Depends if you got them sent down I suppose."

"Doesn't Danny Walsh own a club in town?"

"Yeah, do you know Vapour on the Quayside?"

Please say no.

"No, I don't think I've ever been there."

Thank you.

"Oh look, here's Kate. Excuse me a minute Shelley."

"OK."

"Kate, hi."

"Hi Simon," replied Kate, without looking at him. Oh it's like that is it? Might as well just stick to business then.

"Anything we need to talk about?"

"Don't think so."

"Oh, OK. See you upstairs then."

"God, she's a miserable one, she is," said Simon, sitting down.

"You can say that Mr Silver, I have to mind my 'p's and 'q's!"

Simon laughed.

"Is that why you keep calling me 'Mr Silver' instead of 'Simon'?!"

Shelley looked embarrassed.

"I was just being polite."

"Shit, I'm only messing! Don't be offended."

"Well, I'm not offended as such – it's just, you know, with my dad and all…"

"What do you mean?"

"Well, he sends a lot of work to your Chambers. I don't

want to look like I think I can just wander around here and call people by their first name."

"Oh. I didn't think of it like that."

"It's OK."

"No it's not. Sorry for being rude."

She looked up at him and smiled. And Simon noticed for the first time how attractive she was. Maybe it was because they had had one of those honest conversations that Melissa was talking about. Ah, Melissa...

* * *

"Legal for Mr Walsh please," said Simon, through the intercom that linked through to the cells.

He and Shelley were ushered in.

"Alright boys and girls?" said Danny, walking in and sitting down.

Shelley smiled a hello and Simon started talking.

"Right, Danny, this morning we've got Sergeant Whelan's evidence. I don't know who they're going to call after him. We'll probably get through a couple of witnesses this morning and then have a lunch break."

"Aye, now this Whelan fella, what's the deal with him?"

"Well, he doesn't say a great deal more than the other two we heard yesterday. They just like to fill the place with coppers to make you look more guilty."

"Bastards eh?" said Danny, looking at Shelley.

She smiled in agreement.

Simon could predict a comment coming from Danny to the effect that Shelley wasn't much of a talker. So he decided to speak first, if only to rescue her.

"Yeah, so I'm going to cross-examine him in pretty much the same way."

"Aye – try and make him cry if you can, mate."

"That would be nice wouldn't it?! Thing is, he's quite pivotal, Sergeant Whelan. He's the one who was in charge when they seized the drugs in your car. So I'm going to come at him from the stitch-up angle like I did yesterday. Hopefully we can make him flounder about a bit."

"Here, if you can prove that he stitched me up then will that make them drop the case?"

"If we can prove it, yeah. But I don't know how likely that is."

"Well, you either can or you can't Simon."

"Danny, you know me by now, I like to do this job without taking anything for granted. You just never know what might happen."

As it was, Sergeant Whelan was thinking about just that while he sat in the Police room upstairs. You just never know when people can spring a surprise in Court.

* * *

David Whelan was about to be called to give evidence in his first case as a Sergeant. He wasn't nervous about giving evidence. But he was nervous about the trick he was about to pull. A few months ago he would never have dreamed about doing what he was about to do today. But time spent with Detective Inspector Jim Lowry had taught him about how to bend the rules. In fact, it was more like he had been taught *to* bend the rules, rather than shown how to. Either way, that was what was going to happen this morning. He knew he was going to face criticism for it. But that was a price worth paying. Walsh's convictions were in now. The Jury knew a bit more about him because he had alleged set-up by the Police. But the Police hadn't set him up. And Whelan was about to prove so. And that was one hell of a reward. The price? Being criticised by the Court. And how far would that go? Nowhere. A slap on the wrists. And in all likelihood, a chance at another promotion sooner than Whelan would have had if he had played by the rules.

"Sergeant Whelan, you're on," said the Usher, poking his head out of the Court.

"Thanks," he said, getting up, straightening his jacket and following the Usher into the waiting courtroom.

He was handed the Bible, which he took in his right hand.

"I swear by Almighty God that the evidence I shall give shall be the truth, the whole truth and nothing but the truth".

"Could you state your name and rank for the Court please?" Kate asked.

"Sergeant 347 Whelan, currently stationed at Newcastle West Police Office, Your Honour."

Oh God, he does it as well. "Your Honour". Why?!

"I daresay this is not at issue," said Kate, almost to herself, "were you the Officer in charge of this case?"

"I was, Your Honour, yes."

"How did you come to be involved in the case?"

"Well, a call was made to the control room and I was sent out to investigate."

"To investigate what?"

"Well, the heroin that was in Danny Walsh's car."

"Was there heroin in Danny Walsh's car?"

"Yes, there was, Your Honour."

"Pause there please. How did you know that it was Danny Walsh's car?"

"Because it was registered to him."

"And how do you know that?"

"Because he doesn't deny it."

A good point. Maybe he should have.

"But were you aware that it was registered to Daniel Walsh on the morning in question?"

"I was yes."

"How did that come about?"

"One of the PCs who got to the car first must have rung it in."

"What do you mean by 'rung it in'?"

"Well, run a check on the PNC. The, er, Police National Computer."

"Sergeant Whelan, when you arrived at the scene, was anyone else there?"

"Yes, the two PCs who beat me there."

"And who are they?"

"Alan Wright and Michael Cheung."

"What were they doing?"

"Waiting for me I suppose."

"Did they say anything to you when you got there?"

"Yes, Alan said that this was the car and pointed through the window at the bags of heroin."

"Sergeant, this is very important, when they pointed through the window, was the window broken or intact?"

"It was intact."

"Did you seize the heroin?"

"I did, yes."

"How did you manage to get it out of the car?"

"I asked Michael Cheung to smash the window."

"Thank you. Can you wait there please? There will be some questions from my Learned Friend."

Simon stood up. Convictions already in. Might as well have a pop at the coppers. It's a laugh. And clients like it. Just start it off with a non-question.

"Sergeant Whelan, you were the Officer in charge of the investigation weren't you?"

"That's correct, Your Honour."

"You don't need to refer to me as 'Your Honour', Sergeant."

"I was referring to the Judge."

"Well, would you be kind enough to refer your answers to

the Jury please, since they are the tribunal of fact here."

"Well, we are told to address our answers to the Judge."

Simon held Sergeant Whelan's gaze for a moment.

"Would you do it anyway please? Just for me?"

Her Honour cut in.

"Is this really important Mr Silver?"

"Your Honour, civilian witnesses are asked to address their answers to the Jury, I see no reason why the Police should be any different. They are, after all, no more honest than civilians."

"That's getting pretty close to casting an imputation, Mr Silver."

"With the best will in the world, Your Honour, I am saying that this officer is no more honest than an honest civilian witness. To suggest otherwise would be to cast an imputation against civilian witnesses wouldn't it?"

Her Honour Judge Kristensen sighed.

"Just get on with it please."

Well, it was worth a go. Anyway, Danny was smiling, which was half the job done.

"Sergeant, be honest, who put the heroin in Danny Walsh's car?"

"I presume that he did."

"I am suggesting otherwise."

"That's your business."

"What I am in fact suggesting, Sergeant Whelan, is that you or your officers, or both, planted the heroin in his car in an effort to set him up."

Whelan was counting on the fact that Silver would think that.

"That's not true. Not true at all," he replied. His heart started to beat fast now.

Walsh's heart rate had increased too. Simon was about to have a real go at this guy. And embarrass him.

"Have you seen the photographic exhibits in this case, Sergeant?"

"I have, yes."

"They are quite revealing aren't they? Quite damaging?"

"Oh yes, very much so."

"In fact, they show that heroin was left on the passenger seat of Danny Walsh's car."

"They do, yes."

"That heroin was placed there by you, Sergeant. Or by one of your officers."

"No, it wasn't."

And now for the kill. Apparently.

"Then please could you explain why the photographs of the heroin inside the car are all taken after the window was smashed?"

And now for the surprise.

"That's wrong."

Simon reached for the bundle of photographs.

"Would you care to look at the bundle? Or would you like to tell the truth instead?"

"I am telling the truth," said Whelan, putting his hand into his pocket.

He pulled out what looked like a piece of paper and held it in his left hand.

"Here's a photograph of the heroin inside the car before the window was smashed," he said, knowing just how devious he was being, awaiting criticism and loving every second of it.

The Jury saw it. And looked to Simon with looks on their faces as though to say that their minds were now made up. Walsh would have fallen over, were it not for the fact that he was sitting down. Instead he battled with the realisation that the Police might not have set him up at all.

"Your Honour, there is a matter of law on which I seek a ruling," said Simon.

"Yes, Mr Silver, I thought there might be," replied the Judge, before sending the Jury out for a cup of coffee.

* ★ *

"Your Honour, I must regretfully apply for a re-trial. We have all been surprised by this photographic evidence which, I might add, comes far too late in the day. And it seems clear to me as to why. This is a clear tactical ploy by the Police to ensure that the Jury hear the Defendant's previous convictions, which they now do of course. They are therefore prejudiced and ought to be discharged."

"Miss Holloway?"

"Your Honour, the Sergeant's revelation is a surprise to me too," she said, looking at Simon as though to reinforce the point that it really, honestly, *was* a surprise.

"Do you oppose the application?"

Kate looked at Simon again. This time her face said 'I have to'.

"Your Honour, I do oppose my Learned Friend's application. Knowing of the Defendant's previous convictions, which do not include drug convictions, makes, in my submission, no material difference to the trial at all. Had the photograph been served in the proper way, then I anticipate that there would have been a conviction anyway, irrespective of the defence of set-up and irrelevant previous convictions."

Oh, they're irrelevant now are they?

"I take that point, Miss Holloway."

Unbelievable.

"I have to say, Mr Silver, I do object to the way in which this has come about, but I don't see that it would have made any difference to the outcome of the trial at all."

In fairness, Simon could see her point.

"Your Honour, this is an abuse of the Court process."

"It may well be, Mr Silver, but in truth, what difference would it have made if you had had the photograph earlier on?"

Probably none.

105

"Your Honour, my cross-examination would not have included attacks on the character of the Police witnesses. It appears that they are more sly than dishonest in this case."

"Yes, and I take *that* point too. But how could the Jury come to a conclusion other than that Mr Walsh is guilty?"

"He could still have been set up, Your Honour."

"How exactly?"

"I have no specific instructions on that, Your Honour."

"No, I daresay you don't."

Shit. What else is there to say?

"Your Honour, the Jury are still prejudiced by the fact that they know of Mr Walsh's previous convictions."

"But are they? There are no drug convictions, as Miss Holloway says."

"He has convictions for dishonesty, Your Honour. The Jury could read something into that."

"I don't think so, Mr Silver. Being caught with the heroin in his car would be the fact upon which the conviction was based, not a few thefts and burglaries several years ago."

Trouble was, this was a fair point.

"I have to say, Mr Silver, I am not minded to discharge the Jury."

"Then I have another application to make."

"Oh?"

"I would ask that Your Honour exclude the photograph from the trial under Your Honour's discretion under section 78 of the Police and Criminal Evidence Act. It is clearly more prejudicial than it is probative."

No it isn't, though. It proves the whole case.

"Miss Holloway?"

"Your Honour, to do that would be to say that the evidence is worthless. This case now clearly turns on that single photograph. Now I accept that it should have been properly exhibited, but it proves beyond any doubt that the heroin was in the Defendant's car before the Officers smashed the window. If it prejudices anything, it prejudices the Defendant's right to get away with a crime. But that's all."

That was well put, in all fairness.

"I am going to rise to consider this."

"Court stand!"

Simon looked at Kate.

"Simon, I honestly didn't see that coming. I'm not like that."

He wasn't convinced and she could see it.

"Do you know what pisses me off? Nothing will happen to Sergeant fucking Whelan for this."

Simon noticed how much he sounded like Danny Walsh.

"I know, you're right. It's shitty. But I had to oppose your applications, you know."

"Yes, don't worry about that. Anyone would have done the same," he said, dismissively, casting doubt on how sincere he was being. Now he had to go and speak to Walsh.

* * *

"Fuck," said Danny, as Simon and Shelley walked into the holding area behind the Court.

"That's about right, Danny."

"My head's properly battered now. Who the fuck set me up?"

His head was in his hands now. And Simon remained standing, just in case Walsh got excited.

"It's not going well is it?" asked Danny. He knew the answer.

"No, it's not. We'll just have to hope the Judge excludes the photograph."

"She won't though, will she? She's got her fucking orders to make sure I get sent down."

"Usually I wouldn't believe that sort of thing. But I'm

thinking differently now that she didn't discharge the Jury."

Simon paused. He too knew the answer to the question he was about to ask. But he had to ask it.

"It's not too late to plead guilty, Danny. You'll still get some credit."

Walsh looked up, slowly.

"Are you fucking stupid or what? I've been fucking set up!"

He looked almost as though he was about to stand up and set about Simon for daring to suggest something so controversial. Shelley started to get a bit worried. Simon, on the other hand, was starting to know how to deal with Danny's sort.

"Hey – I have to tell you or I'm not doing my job properly. You say keep going and we keep going. But you know that you're going to be convicted now."

Danny sighed.

"Aye, I know," he said, and paused. "Fuck it, let's take the chance eh?"

"Definitely keep on with the trial?"

"Well aye, crack on."

"OK, Danny."

* * *

The Judge returned with a ruling at 11.30. It was not a ruling that made Danny Walsh a happy man. The trial was to continue now. The Jury would see the photograph of the heroin inside the car before the window was broken. The question now was how the hell it got there. And Simon had no clear instructions from Walsh as to how to play the trial on that basis.

"Your Honour, in the light of that ruling, I need to take instructions," he said.

"I think it's more likely that you need to advise on plea, Mr Silver," replied the Judge.

"Your Honour, I can tell the Court that the plea of Not Guilty is to be maintained."

"Then you are in a difficult position aren't you? I daresay you need some time," she said, looking at the Usher, "it's 11.30 now, the Jury can be told to wait until, say 12 o'clock when I will have you back in Court to update me Mr Silver."

"Grateful, Your Honour," said Simon.

The Judge rose, the Usher went to update the Jury. And Simon told Danny that he would see him downstairs in the cells.

"She is fucking corrupt, she is," said Danny as he barged into the conference room and sat down.

"She seems keen for you to plead guilty, I'll give you that," replied Simon.

"Well that's not going to happen, Simon. I'm not pleading to something I haven't done."

Now that the Police had a photograph of the intact car containing the heroin, Simon was not convinced of Walsh's innocence. How had it got there without someone breaking the window? Perhaps the answer to that question was one for Walsh to answer, rather than for Simon to ponder.

"Right, Danny, what I need from you now is this – how do you want me to run the rest of the trial?"

"What do you mean?"

"Well, are you still going with the set-up defence?"

"Of course I am!"

"OK – fair enough. What we need to think about now though is how we are going to counter the Prosecution case. What can we say about how the heroin got to be inside the car?"

Walsh sighed. He had no idea.

"What can I say? I didn't fucking put it there, I know that much."

"But we can't blame the Police now can we?"

Shelley had not spoken yet. She had been too scared. But she did have a thought to share.

"Just because they didn't smash the window doesn't mean that they didn't put the heroin in the car. Could they not have found a way to get inside the car without having to damage it?"

It was worth a go.

"Keep going Shelley," said Simon, "how could they have done that?"

She stayed silent. She felt like she shouldn't have said anything. In fairness, she was closer to the truth than she realised.

"Seriously, Shelley. There might be something in that, as long as it is plausible."

"Well, is the car alarmed?" she asked, looking to Walsh.

"Aye. But people know not to steal my car."

"OK, but how do we know they didn't prise the door open and disable the alarm?"

"I suppose we don't," said Simon, a little frustrated not to have thought of that, "there's no comment from any witness about the state of the door."

"Go with that," said Walsh.

Yeah. Why not?

* * *

David Whelan was brought back into Court at just after midday to complete his evidence. Simon stood up to meet him.

"Sergeant, it appears that I was wrong to suggest that you smashed the window and planted the heroin in Danny Walsh's car."

"Yes, you were."

"Well, I'm very sorry about that. Because, in fact, you didn't smash the window at all – we can all see that from the photograph."

"Yes."

"The truth is, you didn't need to smash the window when you could just as easily prise the door open and engineer this little ploy of yours with the evidence that you withheld – isn't that right?"

"Ridiculous. No way."

"How long have you been after Danny Walsh?"

"Me personally? Not long."

"No, 'you' as in 'you the Police force'?"

"A fair while, I suppose."

"And so far, no joy eh?"

"That's right – he has managed to hide his drug empire for almost twenty years."

"Drug empire? You mean that he controls the local heroin market?"

"Local? Try national."

"Danny Walsh controls the national heroin market does he?"

"Well, maybe he doesn't control it as such, but he's definitely up there."

Simon pretended to look through some papers.

"It's funny, Sergeant, I can't seem to find a reference to that in your statement. Perhaps you could point me to it," he said, holding out the statement and making the Usher wonder whether or not he needed to pass it to the witness.

"It's not in my statement."

The Usher sat back and crossed his legs.

"Why not?"

"Because I didn't think it was relevant."

"Really? But it seems relevant enough now that you are giving oral evidence."

"Look, everyone knows about Danny Walsh and his involvement with the drug trade. I didn't write in my statement that I am a human being. That's an accepted fact too."

This guy is obviously no pushover. But, no need to let everyone know that you think so. Keep at him.

"It is not an accepted fact at all, Sergeant. You have absolutely no evidence that Danny Walsh is involved in the national heroin trade have you?"

"Not on me, no. I gave you what I had in my pocket. That's evidence enough isn't it?"

This is going to go nowhere. He's got an answer for everything. Just put your case and sit the hell down.

"No, Sergeant. That is evidence that there was heroin in his car."

"Well, that's enough for me. There's no heroin in my car. Or yours. And we aren't on trial are we? There's a reason for that."

Never answer their questions.

"The reason is this, Sergeant. You were put on this case because you have never been involved in trying to catch Danny Walsh before. A fresh pair of eyes to keep the vendetta going. You prised open his car door..."

"No."

"...planted heroin inside the car..."

"Rubbish."

"...closed the door and then photographed the heroin inside..."

"No."

"...and after that you smashed the window to draw attention away from the door because no-one would think to look at the door if they could see that you smashed your way in."

"Absolutely not."

Simon sat down.

Kate had no re-examination and the Judge had no questions either. In fact, she didn't even castigate Sergeant Whelan for his dirty trick. Her mind was made up. And in fairness, why wouldn't it be? Take the law out of the equation, remove the lawyers and sometimes you are left with a painful truth – the evidence speaks for itself and there is nothing that you can do about it.

"I can't believe that copper!" said Stobbsy.

"I know, mate, I'm fucking incensed," said Simon, joining his friends in the canteen.

"How do they get away with it?"

Simon had his head in his hands now.

"I don't know – it just makes you wonder why you bother trying you know? How can you take on the Police when they get away with absolutely everything? If that had been me fucking magicking up evidence, I would have been referred to the Bar Council for breaching the codes of practice. That fucker's punishment will be free drinks and a promotion."

"Here," said Billy, "listen, mate. We all know it's not your fault. Danny knows it as well. He might not look like it, but he does."

"Actually, he's been alright so far, Billy. I would be a hell of a lot more pissed off than he seems to be."

"Well that's good – he can be a bit intimidating at times."

It seemed like even Danny's mates were frightened of him.

"So what's this afternoon then?" asked Houdini.

"Just continuity stuff really," replied Simon.

"What do you mean?"

"Well, you know, we have to hear from everyone who was there the night the Police set Danny up."

All eyes suddenly shot to Billy. And for an instant, Simon wondered whether they might all have been in on the set-up. Maybe it wasn't the Police after all. Maybe that's why they were here, keeping an eye. Maybe that's why they were being so nice to Simon.

"Well I'm going to the club if it's just more coppers," said Houdini.

"You'll fucking stay here and support Danny," said Billy.

He didn't appear to be joking either.

Or stay here and make sure Danny's brief is still alleging *Police* set-up? Simon couldn't get the idea out of his head.

Simon spent the afternoon putting his case to more Officers. It was the same allegation each time. And it was met with the same reaction every time. Simon wondered whether he was barking up the wrong tree. Maybe that look that everyone gave Billy in the canteen was an indication that the Firm itself had set him up. Could it have been them?

Simon convinced himself that they couldn't possibly have done it.

The thing is, of course they could. If it wasn't the Police, then even if the lads didn't have access to that much heroin, they could certainly have rustled up the money to get it. And they would surely have known where to go to find it, connections being what they are with such people.

Sometimes, the evidence speaks for itself. The lads were scared of Danny, or so it seemed. They had money. Access to his car, perhaps. Plus, they seemed to be having a great old time of things at the club as well, like the cat was permanently away and they were enjoying the play-time that it afforded them. And they were clearly keeping an eye on Simon. Seeing him in Court all day, entertaining him at night. Giving him unrestricted access to Melissa.

But sometimes, in the face of the evidence, we decide to conclude otherwise. Because it suits our purpose. Maybe the Police really *had* set Danny up. Or maybe Danny really *was* guilty. Either way, the lads couldn't have been responsible. Because if he thought that they *were* responsible he would tell himself not to go out to the club with them tonight.

And he couldn't possibly do that, because that would mean not seeing Melissa.

* * *

Simon further convinced himself, fairly quickly, after having entered the club that night that he was wrong about the Firm setting Danny up. The reason was simple. On the table, as he approached the lads, he saw a piece of paper. As he got closer, he could make out a list. And once he got to the table and stood beside it he saw that it was a list of names. Some of the names rang a bell. The reason was that he had heard them the previous day. They were the names of the twelve Jurors in the Walsh case. The group was obviously thinking of ways to get to them before they started deliberating over the verdict. The trial was going badly. It always pays to have options. And if the Firm *had* set Danny up, they wouldn't want to frighten the Jury into finding him not guilty. Nor would they want to speak to the Jury to make sure they convicted Danny. The Police, after all, would be taking care of that side of things. So the Firm *couldn't* be behind it. A relief, to say the least – represented by the image of Melissa in Simon's head, smiling at him, pleased that they could still see each other.

"Boys," said Simon, making himself at home by sitting down. "What's happening?"

"We're just talking about Newcastle, mate," said Billy, taking the piece of paper and folding it up, hoping that Simon hadn't noticed what was written on it.

"Do you reckon Newcastle is a violent town, Simon?" asked Davey, trying to divert attention from the list of names.

"I don't know, Davey," Simon smiled, playing along with the game, "the thing is, I see loads of assault cases at work but I hardly ever see any bother on the streets."

It was a non-conversation. But a conversation at least.

"There's never any bother in here," said Davey.

"Well, except when people like Millsy wander in," Simon suggested.

"Aye, true enough, Simon! God that was funny as fuck that night…"

Funny wasn't the right word really. It was fairly brutal. Then again, Millsy had had it coming after what he had done to Fivers.

"Tell you what, though, Simon," said Davey, "it depends what you call bother. I mean, there's always going to be a bit of pushing and shoving in the town you know? People out on the drink and that."

"Yeah but people pushing each other doesn't really count as violence," said Simon.

"Aye, I don't just mean *actual pushing*, I mean like, you know, proper fist-fights and shoeings."

"Well that would count as violence, yeah!"

"You see plenty of that here. Well, I say *here*, I mean outside, you know? But that's not what I mean by violence. I mean, like, murders and that. And, like, proper GBH and stuff."

"Well, yeah, I suppose you don't hear about many murders and stabbings compared to other places in the country."

"See, that's what I think. But Newcastle has a reputation as being a rough town, you know, like, nationally."

"Yeah, that's true. People hear 'Newcastle' and they think football, lager, fighting and tarts!"

"Aye, and it's not always like that," said Houdini.

Everyone was silent . Everything Houdini said made him sound stupid. And then they all laughed.

"Here, what the fuck you all laughing at?" he asked.

He got no reply.

"Right, fuck the lot of you," he said and headed for the bar.

They continued to laugh.

"Mind, Davey, you do hear some horror stories," said Simon.

"Aye, true, ever hear about that fella Joe MacRae?" asked Davey.

"God yeah – I read about that in the paper," replied Simon, "it freaked the town out for a while, that did. Apparently it was some random attack. The poor bloke is in a wheelchair for life now."

"Want to know what really happened?" asked Davey.

Maybe it wasn't a random attack after all.

* * *

Walsh had deemed the visit to be beneath him. He didn't need to deal with things like this anymore. His position meant that someone else could do it, while he attended to other things such as counting the money, meeting with other members of the supply chain, administering a beating to someone who had crossed him personally, even just taking his daughter to the park. He sent Billy Cameron instead and allowed him to take whoever else he needed so as to help sell the policy to the as yet unwitting client.

Joe MacRae heard a noise outside his office and was immediately irritated by it. His business was growing nicely. He had bought himself a new car a few days earlier. People were starting to hear of him. More clients. More money. More exposure. And the growth of his business meant that his staff were working to the bone. And now they were making a noise. He got up out of his chair and walked around to the front of his desk, heading for the door to see just what was going on. He didn't quite get that far as Billy Cameron burst through it. He could have opened it. But he had opted instead to barge through it, causing it to become dislodged from its housing.

Seconds before, MacRae had been sitting at his desk calculating his weekly expenses in silence. Now he was standing near the door of his office faced with a man whose entry had more than surprised him. He fumbled for words – he was angry, self-defensive, but also scared to death.

"Who…who the fuck are you?!"

Billy pushed him to the floor without much effort.

"Fucking hell, mate. Looks like you need to sort that door out. It's just about hanging off its hinges," said Billy, "Have you seen the state of it?" he asked his companions who had entered the room behind him.

He looked to MacRae who was still on the floor. He pointed at him.

"I'm serious, mind. It's a plight. You'll need to get it fixed, you could get into all sorts of trouble. Health and safety and all that."

MacRae didn't know whether he should get up or stay where he was. Billy closed the door as best he could, given that it was more a piece of wood now than a door. MacRae rose nervously. He knew that he was in trouble for something, but he had no idea what. He hadn't annoyed anyone that he knew of. Who were these people? Why were they here?

"Have a seat," said Billy.

MacRae walked back around his desk and sat down as nervously as he had got up from the floor.

"What do you want?" he asked, and in doing so felt that he might suddenly have angered the men. His heart jumped. His choice of words had not meant to convey that he was being territorial. But it was said now and while he felt it an injustice to be made to feel bad for asking, he was still scared.

"Well that's a fair question I suppose," said Billy, calmly.

He was loving it. Angry, then calm. Always messes people up.

"This is just a sales call really. We would have phoned, but it's always better to meet people face to face, know what I mean?"

MacRae found himself nodding in agreement.

Billy went on.

"Now Mr MacRae, you don't need me to tell you how risky the business world is. Staff can let you down, suppliers can leave you high and dry."

Here it comes, MacRae thought.

"And sometimes even your premises are at risk – you know? Of course you know – you're a sensible bloke. Got a good head for business so they say."

Yes, now I know why they are here.

MacRae seemed to calm down now. Now that he knew where he stood. It was almost a relief that he was sitting down facing a man that was part of a protection racket. At least he hadn't been mistaken for someone else. Someone who might have pissed these men off for running drugs or prostitutes on their turf. No, he was just a regular businessman who was on a list of successful people. People with money to throw around. It was almost like a sign of status – confirmation of success in the eyes of others. But in all fairness, MacRae wasn't a regular businessman. He had ideas. He had an imagination.

"Now I see you have an intruder alarm. Sensible. And the gates outside look pretty sturdy."

"They didn't stop you getting in."

Billy laughed.

"No, they didn't did they?! But one thing you haven't really thought about is what to do in case of fire. I mean, just imagine the whole place getting burned down. That would be a right royal pity, that would."

MacRae raised his eyebrows in agreement, but in apparent submission too.

"How much do you make in a week do you reckon? 3000? 5000?"

"More like a thousand."

Billy looked at MacRae with sudden anger.

"Don't take the fucking piss. I reckon you must be making

three grand a week here. Maybe even more. So don't fucking lie to me."

MacRae was silent. He had no idea what to say to that. This man was unpredictable.

But silence wasn't a problem since Cameron kept talking anyway.

"What do you reckon, lads?" he asked his friends.

"I think somewhere around three grand," replied Stobbsy.

Billy turned to MacRae.

"See? He thinks three grand as well. So there it is. Now on the basis of that I want you to pay five hundred pounds per week for the insurance against fire."

No chance. Not in this lifetime.

"OK," replied MacRae.

Billy felt like he had won. And so he saw no point in hanging around talking.

"I'll see you next Monday then," he said as he left the room, "get this door fixed."

★ ★ ★

MacRae's door had been fixed. His office looked tidier too. And he didn't look as scared as he had done a few days earlier when Billy had first met him.

"Mr MacRae!" announced Billy, as though pleased to see an old friend. He walked over to MacRae's desk. "So – have you got our money?"

Good, he said the word money.

MacRae looked him in the eye.

"No," he said.

Billy's face changed. He no longer conveyed happiness.

"No?"

"That's right, no. I changed my mind."

Billy put his hands on his hips. One of the men from the

last occasion left the room quite routinely and seemingly without purpose; the other one produced a pistol from under his coat.

Good, they've got a gun.

The man that had left the room returned soon after. He was dragging one of the secretaries in with him, pulling her along by the hair which inspired her to try to walk as best she could to limit the pain he was causing her.

Billy turned round to her and punched her with force in the face. She fell to the floor, screaming.

Good, he punched her and she's screaming.

The man with the pistol bent down and held it against her head as he turned his head to face MacRae. She was struggling for breath as she lay there, almost hyperventilating.

This was going pretty well, thought everyone in the room, except the secretary of course.

MacRae saw the opportunity to tactically concede.

He stood up and raised his palms towards Billy.

"OK, OK, I'll pay, just let her go."

Billy looked at MacRae with a certain fury.

"Sit down," he commanded, "and get her out," he said, without turning his head to face the colleague to whom he was speaking.

The Secretary was thrown out through the new door and she continued to cry as she got to her feet and headed for the bathroom for no reason other than that she felt safer there, as though the men wouldn't be so rude as to go into the ladies' toilet.

Billy still had his hands on his hips.

"So?"

"I haven't got that sort of cash here. I'm sorry. It's just that we don't deal with cash that much. Our orders tend to be on the internet and over the phone."

Billy believed him. And rightly so. But he had given MacRae plenty of notice to arrange for the cash to be there.

"But you knew that we were coming – why would you insult us? Can you put fires out yourself?"

Now he had said the word fires too. Brilliant.

MacRae bowed his head.

"I'm sorry. I'll have the money for you by next Monday."

"No, no, Mr MacRae, I want the money tomorrow."

Shouldn't be a problem.

MacRae feigned a look of helplessness. And then he sighed.

"Alright, I'll go to the bank and get it."

Billy cheered up.

"See? It's not hard to arrange is it? Don't you feel safer now? It must be a relief for you."

Billy and the two men turned to leave. As Billy walked through the door he turned back to look at MacRae. He smiled at him. And then he resumed the angry look as he punched one of the panels on the door with such force that it went through. As if to tell him that he was big time, with a gun or otherwise.

Another door needed. But why not add criminal damage to the list of offences today? Threats, violence, damage. All MacRae needed to do now was hand over some cash.

* * *

This time, MacRae watched out of the window and saw Billy coming. But there were only two of them this time. Billy, and another man who he immediately recognised. Danny Walsh. Almost a celebrity. Certainly the stuff of legend. The type of person who, if you were stuck behind in traffic, you kept a distance from. And then told your friends when you next saw them. Someone who had a reputation and a following. And someone who engendered fear. There was no room for fear today. MacRae had to keep a cool head. But he was nervous enough without Walsh being here. It was almost like a state visit. He was just a man. A criminal. A gangster, though. He deserved the title too. MacRae felt a rush of adrenaline. Was he going to manage to pull this off?

Walsh was a calm man. That was what scared most people. The truth was, he had nothing to prove. He had already proved it and gossip relieved him of the burden of continuing to do so. There were so many stories. Murders organised by him, robberies he was supposedly responsible for. He was big time. He didn't need connections. He *was* connections. The top of the ladder. If someone threatened you and mentioned his name alongside that threat, then you believed them. It was their business if they wanted to dare to take the risk of naming him if they weren't connected to him. If they were just full of talk, he would find them. And show them just how unconnected they were. So the only people who mentioned his name were those who could rely on it.

But then Billy hadn't mentioned it. And there was a reason for that. Threats are for children and the unconnected. At the top of the tree, people don't make threats. They don't tell you what they are going to do to you "in a minute". They just do it. Their reputation makes the threats implicit, so much so that they don't need to make them. In this game you find out if you have offended someone after you have been punished for it, assuming that you are still alive. That is just the reality of it. It keeps a handy cloud above the head of the rival but more than that, it denies him the chance to talk to the Police.

It was almost worth the money just for MacRae to have the rest of his life to tell the story of when he met Danny Walsh. He would still be telling the story when he was eighty, standing at the bar in a pub. Or so he thought.

Billy and Walsh walked into the office. MacRae had already gone into his own office where he now sat, waiting for them to come in. The top of his desk was completely clear, save for a pile of fifty-pound notes. And a small package, neatly wrapped up and tied with shiny ribbon.

"I see you've fixed the door," said Billy.

"Well, it was getting old. Wear and tear and all that," replied MacRae.

Billy smiled.

Walsh looked at Billy.

"Is this him?" he asked with a straight face which gave the impression that he was annoyed. It was a tactic of sorts. He could have asked MacRae himself. Anyway, of course it was him. Billy had spoken to him. It was just a way to make MacRae feel belittled. Like the irrelevant chancer that he was. And it worked. He was taken aback. And he felt like a schoolboy faced with the school bully. With no chance of a teacher coming in to save him. No, he was very much on his own. But it didn't matter. MacRae had a plan and he was convinced that it was going to work. He was going to show Walsh that he was no soft touch. That while he might think the local businessmen and women were easy to manipulate and frightened enough to maintain their silence, he was not like that at all.

Walsh leant over the desk. He waited for MacRae to look him in the eye. And smacked him in the face.

"That's for wasting my fucking time."

MacRae had felt harder punches before. But this one had the sting of an ever-present threat attached to it. He was bleeding now. And he took a handkerchief from his pocket and pushed it against the resulting cut under his right eye.

"Now fucking pay up so I can get back to work."

It was MacRae's moment now. A week ago he was a successful businessman. His mother was proud of him. He was living a real boy's lifestyle, with wealth that impressed women into bed. And he wanted things to stay like that. He liked his life and he wanted to hold onto it. His imagination had stepped in at this point, acting in tandem with his instinct for survival, and helped him come up with a solution to the problem he faced standing in front of his desk. He picked up the pile of notes.

"There you go, Mr Walsh," he said as he handed it over.

Walsh would have gone there and then, had he not seen the package on the now otherwise empty desk. MacRae saw Walsh's eyes pick it out. And they slowly rose to meet his.

"What's that?"

"That's for you as well. A gift."

Silence.

"Go on, you can open it."

Walsh looked at Billy, who shrugged his shoulders as he picked up the package.

He held MacRae's gaze as he unwrapped the paper to reveal a video-cassette.

He dropped the paper casually onto the floor and held the cassette in the air.

"What the fuck is this?"

Now then. Can you remain calm? You are about to threaten a man who cannot be intimidated and who can hurt you more than you can hurt him. Maybe not though.

"It's a tape of yesterday," said MacRae, looking at Billy now.

Walsh was an old master at confrontation. And he remained totally calm.

"Go on," he said softly.

"That's a copy for you. It shows you assaulting my secretary, damaging the door and threatening to burn down my premises unless I pay you five hundred pounds per week. The other copy is in a deposit box at the bank. And I've left it in my will to the Chief Constable of Northumbria Police. "

He stopped wiping the top of his bleeding cheek. And from somewhere, he gained a confidence that surprised everyone in the room, not least himself.

"So you make fucking well sure that you die before I do," he said, looking to Billy.

Even the sentence sounded good. Like something a gangster would say. Maybe Walsh would say something like that. Maybe he would respect MacRae for talking his language. It certainly appeared so.

"I don't expect to see you here again. And I don't expect my business to be interfered with. In fact what I expect is that you make sure it is protected at all costs."

He was still nervous. But he was an aggressive negotiator in business and he liked the thrill that this sort of conversation gave him.

Walsh looked at MacRae, the corners of his mouth turned down and his eyebrows raised as he nodded to him.

It was almost like a stand-off. No-one said anything for a few long seconds. Walsh smiled. Perhaps out of respect. Perhaps recognising that MacRae was not a pushover.

Hopefully, but MacRae would have felt it more a victory if Walsh had not just turned and left the office without returning the five hundred pounds.

*   *   *

Walsh was absolutely raging. Even Billy was frightened of him when he was like this. It was not a physical fear. If the two came to blows then Billy would, in truth, have little to worry about. But Walsh still frightened him. His reputation was not an inherited one. He had got it for a reason. The reason was that he was the ultimate loose cannon and he acted arbitrarily when he was under pressure. He knew no rules and trusted only himself. Billy had arrived at the industrial estate with him in good spirits. But for the whole journey back, Billy was not entirely convinced that he was safe.

"Danny, have I fucked up?" he said eventually, this giant yet timid man.

Walsh sighed.

"No…I'm just pissed off at the whole thing. There's no way you could have known he was taping you." Walsh punched the steering wheel and it made even Billy jump.

Billy knew that Walsh was annoyed. And while he believed him when he said he didn't blame him, he knew that he had to come up with a decent way to sort the situation out, otherwise he would have more than simple failure to worry about.

"Ferocious, aren't I?"
Vincent Hanna in *Heat*, 1995
(dir. Michael Mann © Warner Bros Inc)

They were getting nowhere. Walsh was obviously going mad at the whole affair, MacRae's arrogance seemed to have flicked a switch inside his head. The audacity of the little bastard really got to Walsh and he was taking it out on everybody else. And more than that, he was losing focus.

Walsh usually had the ideas. Then people chipped in with alternatives, or improvements. But he hadn't even suggested anything yet. He was hardly speaking to anyone. He just stood by the bar, knocking back vodkas and looking more and more dangerous with every drink. He muttered from time to time, smashed a few glasses and shouted various profanities at nobody in particular.

Everyone except for Walsh was sitting down at a table, pretty much waiting for Walsh to turn around and talk to them. They had arrived in dribs and drabs and the face on each person as they came in said the same. What's going on? What's he doing? Is everything alright? What's happened? Billy turned to Fivers, who was sitting next to him.

"He's fucking losing it, he is," he said, making a special effort to say it quietly in case Walsh heard. He was in no kind of reasonable mood.

Fivers looked over at Walsh and spoke.

"Danny? Everyone's here now."

Billy's eyes widened as he shot him a glance as if to ask what the hell he was doing.

Walsh turned round slowly to face Fivers.

"You what?"

He looked like he was going to explode.

Fivers knew that he might. He was unprofessional. He was unpredictable. But he also knew that Walsh was like everyone else in the world; if you look them in the eye and speak to them with confidence, but without patronising them, you can talk your way out of anything.

"Danny, I'm just saying, we're all here so you can tell us what's happened if you want."

Walsh turned back around and finished his drink in the same manner in which he had drunk each one so far. And then turned again to face the group. His Firm.

"I'll tell you what's happened, Fivers. This is what's happened. I am in a world of fucking shit, that's what," he pointed at Fivers, "and I don't need you being funny".

There was no point in crawling. Or apologising. This was just Walsh's way of maintaining control of the meeting since he had been prompted by Fivers to speak. He wasn't going to do anything so Fivers was not concerned at his tone towards him. Walsh remained standing, even though there was a spare seat at the table.

"The Joe MacRae problem needs sorting," said Walsh.

Billy knew who Joe MacRae was. So did Stobbsy and Houdini. No-one else had heard of him. Fivers certainly hadn't, but then he was hearing new names all the time these days. Who was Joe MacRae? A local rival? Or someone from another city who was trying to break the Newcastle underworld? Well, if you don't know something, you ask.

"Who is Joe MacRae?"

Walsh looked at Fivers. And then at Black Davey and Cautious Terry who, though they had not asked, appeared to want to know too.

"He has an internet business in Sunderland," replied

Walsh. "Quite a wealthy bloke. And up until yesterday, we were going to do alright from him."

Walsh smiled. It looked like a grudging smile. The sort of smile where you have to admit to yourself that even though you have been caught out by someone, you respect the person for having done it in the way in which they did. He went on.

"He's a clever lad, I'll give him that. Billy went round to sell him a policy and when he went back, MacRae wouldn't pay. Then Billy got a bit excited and pulled a gun on some tarty secretary who worked there."

Billy started to feel nervous. It sounded like praise. It made him look pretty favourable in the eyes of the firm. But he felt criticised too. What if Walsh were to pull a gun on him, there and then in the bar? It wouldn't be the first time he had done that sort of thing.

"So I went back again with Billy and then MacRae, the little fucker, handed me a videotape which he said was a tape of Billy threatening the tart and trying to make a sale."

No-one could believe it. The Joe MacRae problem. But more than that, they couldn't believe that there was a Joe MacRae *problem*. They would have expected MacRae to have been dealt with there and then. Maybe Walsh was losing his bottle. Maybe that's why he looked so pissed off here in the club. They soon found out why MacRae was still alive.

"He told Billy and me that he had changed his will and left another copy of the tape to the Chief Constable of the Police, so that we would have to leave him alone."

Fivers was impressed. He would have come up with a plan like that if it had been him in MacRae's position.

There was a pause before Walsh spoke again. And when he did, the firm saw a side to his personality that they had never seen before.

"So, basically, lads, I am stuck for what the fuck to do."

And so was everybody else. Fivers too, until he got some

more information. Then he came up with a blinder of an idea.

Fivers had an organised mind. He was focussed. He sorted out problems one at a time and then put the solution together to see if it worked as a whole. This one seemed to. And since no-one else seemed to be saying anything he thought he might as well approach Walsh with his idea.

"Danny, I was thinking, right?"

"Oh aye? This should be a laugh. Stick to selling tac, Fivers!"

They all laughed. They didn't mean to direct it at Fivers as such. But it was an excuse to lighten the mood.

Fivers knew his place. At the bottom of the pile. And he felt very strongly about it because he didn't deserve to be there. He knew that you have to work your way up. But why this slowly? Why wouldn't they take him seriously? His mind was far more sophisticated than any other in this room. Why couldn't they see it? He bowed his head a little as if to give up.

"Alright man, Fivers, don't be a baby about it. What did you want to say?" asked Walsh, laughing.

"Well I was just thinking that there's only a problem if he dies. There's no problem as long as he's alive."

Walsh looked at him sternly.

"That's right, Fivers, but while he's alive he gets to keep five hundred quid a week that should be in my fucking pocket."

"I know. I'm just getting to that."

Walsh folded his arms, which Fivers took to mean that he should go on, which he did.

"Well first you need to do something to him to make him go and retrieve this tape from the bank. He'll have to know it was you. That'll make him want revenge. So he'll go and retrieve the tape and you can, you know, arrange to intercept it. Cos, right, without the tape he'll have nothing on you and you'll get your money."

131

"That sounds nice and simple, that does. Life's not like that though, is it? And by the way Fivers, don't say 'retrieve' – you're not posh."

"OK Danny, I'm just telling you what I think generally. I've got some specific ideas as well."

"Go on," said Walsh with a smile that he shared with everyone else.

Fivers did go on. And as he did, they stopped smiling. Even Walsh was impressed. He laughed out.

"Fucking hell, Fivers! You're as sick as me!!"

Yes, but more organised, Danny. With more passion and less to prove.

"Alright so he got shot in the foot - what is it, like, a big fuckin' deal?"
Tommy DeVito in *Goodfellas*, 1990
(dir. Martin Scorcese © Warner Bros Inc)

Fivers had quite a shopping list. His plan was well thought out. Cautious Terry could have taken the day off that day because every potential flaw had already been addressed. And it was more imaginative than Walsh had ever been. Fivers was older now than Walsh was when he became prolific. But this had only occurred to Fivers. Walsh did not think in such a way. He was the boss and he always would be. And he dealt with anyone who had any talent whatsoever by putting them down, never praising them. Perhaps that was his way of letting Fivers know not to get too clever. It would never work. He would only ever be second-in-command, and probably not even that. There was no way the rest of the group would take Fivers' orders, but Walsh had given the green light to the whole plan and so the firm didn't question what Fivers suggested they do. He couldn't boss them around. The question of who did what would have to be decided by them. There was no point in assigning jobs because simply put, Fivers was a meaningless kid who had created the perfect plan. He got no recognition from it. If anything, they were more wary of him now. Someone with a brain. What might he do to them if the desire took him?

First on the shopping list were some details of MacRae's company. Fivers needed to know a great deal. It meant finding out the names of all of those who worked at MacRae's and also those who were contracted to him but weren't office based. There might be no such people, but an answer was needed either way. He needed details of where they lived, where they socialised. He needed to know about all of MacRae's accounts. Which bank had MacRae deposited the video at? Which branch? Was there even a second copy? He couldn't be bluffing could he? No. Was he? Come on, no-one would take that sort of risk. There was no disputing the fact that Billy, Stobbsy and Houdini had been caught on tape – they had all seen it. Why would he give the only copy of the tape to Walsh? He must have made another one. But what if he had made more than one? He might have put one into a box at his personal bank. Maybe MacRae's personal bank was different to his business one. There were too many questions. But there was a way to answer them. Walsh still had five hundred pounds from MacRae. He could take it back to him, talk to him, size him up. See if he could find out how many tapes there were. Fivers had this angle well and truly covered. The plan was immense. Over the top maybe. Certainly the hardest five hundred pounds per week that the Firm had ever earned.

So the first tasks were assigned like this. Walsh was going to take back the five hundred pounds. Fivers would go with him, as his driver for the most part, but also as someone else who could witness the conversation. It was his plan. He knew the sort of things he would be listening out for. The two of them would have a look around the place, check the entry and exit points. Stay until it closed and follow MacRae home. That paved the way for Stobbsy and Houdini to wait outside the building and watch to see how many people came out, make a note of how many there were, what they looked like. Then, when everyone had left, they would stay and keep a look out for any interested boys in blue. Cautious Terry and Black Davey would then break in to the building and look around for company details, bank statements, staff rotas in order that they could know everything about the place. Fivers was thorough and no-one had even asked Cautious Terry for an opinion. He was relieved in a way, if anything went wrong at least it would be Fivers' fault. In truth though, he wasn't particularly worried anyway. It seemed like a flawless plan.

*　*　*

MacRae's heart jumped when he saw Walsh coming up to the door of the building. He was in his office standing by the window, thinking. That was his privilege now that he was successful. He delegated tasks to those he employed, while he talked on the phone to big clients, worked out every penny of his tax-allowable expenses or just stood by the window looking out at girls from other offices walking past. That's what he was doing when Walsh came up the path with another man MacRae had never seen before. And women were no longer on his mind once he saw Walsh and whoever it was that he was with.

Why were they here? Had Walsh not heard what he had said to him? Was he here to make threats? Maybe he should call the Police. But they would be gone before the Police got here. His heart raced now. They were at the door. And soon they would be barging through the door. Gangsters don't need to make appointments.

MacRae sat down and linked his hands together, resting his elbows on his desk. It made him look more confident. But in truth the real reason for doing so was because he was too nervous to stand up without shaking. That was their power. Them, and others like them. They engender such fear, more than they know. The people whose lives they touch lose sleep. They look over their shoulders. They ring their wives more often, just to make sure everything is alright. They pick their kids up from the school entrance rather than from the gates or up the street. Through fear. Fear based on myth in reality. But you hear stories. Kidnaps, ransoms, beatings. You see it on the news. In films. You don't think about it until you have occasion to meet these people. They change your life without having been invited to do so. And they make you sit down rather than stand up because you are tormented by unrealistic though imaginable eventualities. And it makes you nervous.

Walsh walked in first, followed by Fivers, who closed the door behind him quietly. Almost politely. A rouse? The gangster equivalent of good cop, bad cop? That's what Billy Cameron had done. It messed with MacRae's head – he couldn't be sure of exactly what was happening. But he still spoke.

"Mr Walsh," he said. That's all he said. He just acknowledged him.

Walsh walked up and climbed onto the desk, sitting cross-legged on it and faced MacRae. He sat there silently for a while. And then smiled as he looked MacRae in the eye.

"Got a business proposition for you," he said.

What? Now he wants me to get involved with him? MacRae wanted nothing to do with this. If that's what he meant. That must be what he meant. He had lost out on the protection money, or 'insurance policy' as Billy had dressed it up. Now he wants to go into business with me? To do what? Sell drugs? Weapons? Use the building at night for prostitution?

"What kind of business proposition?" he asked.

"Well, Mr MacRae," said Walsh, reaching into his pocket and making MacRae's heart pound in doing so, "it all depends on whether you want this back."

He put the five hundred pounds on the desk.

"I don't understand."

"Come on MacRae, we've made the effort of coming all the way back over here just to return your money to you. You should be happy."

For some reason, MacRae felt able to talk to Walsh. He was so notorious that even MacRae didn't really mind appearing weak and human in front of him.

"Well to be honest Mr Walsh, I'm finding it a bit tough to be happy at the moment. How do I know you're not just putting me on?" He was visibly nervous now.

Walsh looked round at Fivers. And then back at MacRae.

"You don't, I suppose. But that's fair enough. I'll just take the money back."

He picked it back up. But he held onto it rather than putting it back into his pocket.

"Mr Walsh, look, from my point of view, right? it's just, like, a bit strange to see you back here with my money," he managed.

"We're both businessmen Mr MacRae. I'm not going to just *give* you it back."

Thought so.

"What do you mean?"

"Well, I want to buy something from you."

This was getting too much. The riddles. You don't imagine conversations like this when you go into business.

"Buy what? There's nothing I sell that costs that much," he said with a clear look of confusion.

"I know, I'm offering you more money than it's worth."

What?

MacRae said nothing and so Walsh went on.

"They only cost about a tenner in the shops, you know. And I'm offering you five hundred quid."

MacRae still looked vacant. He was thinking a million thoughts but looked as though he was thinking nothing at all.

"Videos, Mr MacRae. I want that second video."

And this was the test. He was nervous now. He found himself in that child-like position where you're so scared of a situation that you let the truth come out. Because as Fivers pointed out to Walsh when he introduced this plan to him, if MacRae took the money, that meant that he had made more than two copies. He would take the money back but still have his trump card. The second copy was worth far more than five hundred pounds to both Walsh and MacRae. The three men in the room knew that. It was worth 10 years in prison. And there was no way MacRae would want to give it up, if he really had made only two copies. If he held onto it, he held on to Walsh. He bought his own freedom.

He was scared to say it, but he did. Because he knew how valuable the second video was. And he knew that it was his protection. His own insurance policy. And he smiled as he spoke, though only slightly.

"But Mr Walsh, we'd all be back to square one. I'd have my money back but I'd have given up the video. No deal, sorry."

Walsh showed no emotion. And MacRae went on.

"I can see you're worried about it. That's why you've come here. But I don't know you, Mr Walsh. I only know your reputation. And if it's accurate then I would really rather keep hold of the video. If I gave you it, how do I know you wouldn't just come back and torch the place?"

"A fair point," said Walsh with a smile, "I would probably think the same thing myself."

"It won't ever get seen you know. Not unless something happens to me. I'll keep my word. I know you're connected. I know that something would happen to me if I turned the video over to the Police. I just want a quiet life you know?"

"Nothing will happen to you," said Walsh, climbing back down from the desk.

He stood up and faced MacRae, holding out his hand as he did so.

"You're a tough man to deal with," he said, smiling, as MacRae shook his hand.

Walsh and Fivers left the office. MacRae sighed. But he

was buzzing. He had won. He watched them walk out of the main door and down the path.

Walsh looked at Fivers.

"Small office eh?" he asked.

"Yeah."

"Won't take long to find what we need."

"No, shouldn't take too long."

★ ★ ★

Walsh never drove cars. He got others to do it for him. Fivers was driving today. And when MacRae came out of the office Walsh's mobile rang.

"Stobbsy?" he asked.

"Aye, he's locked the place up,"

The phone went dead. They never spoke for long, even on mobiles. The less they said, the less people could hear.

Walsh looked at Fivers, who started the engine and drove towards MacRae's premises.

MacRae had treated himself to a new car this year. And Walsh seethed at it. A brand new DB7. Walsh had enough money for one of course. But, unlike MacRae, Walsh couldn't be seen to spend that sort of money. They let MacRae drive on for a few seconds, let a couple of cars get in between them and then set off to follow him.

At the same time, Cautious Terry got a call from Stobbsy.

"Reckon it's dark enough yet?" asked Stobbsy.

"Aye," replied Cautious Terry. And if Cautious Terry thought it was dark enough, then it was. Simple as that.

It was almost time. Terry called Walsh.

"Terry – small place, not many rooms. Won't take you long," said Walsh.

"OK."

He hung up. And joined Black Davey outside of the car.

* * *

It was a small office. Trouble was, the windows were pretty small too and it wasn't easy to climb inside. They managed, though, after a while. It had taken a little too long for Terry's liking and Davey bore the brunt of his cautious nature as he kept telling him to hurry up and find what they were looking for.

"Have you found it yet?" he whispered, though loudly.

"No, man, for fuck's sake, I'll tell you if I find it."

"Hurry up!"

"You hurry up! You're supposed to be looking as well!"

"I am, you twat."

All they needed was a clue as to where the company banked their money. They needed more than bank statements though, as Fivers had reminded them, they needed details of the branch where the company account was opened. That way they would know where the video was likely to be kept.

They both searched through filing cabinets and boxes, careful to leave the things that they touched exactly as they found them. The office needed to appear completely normal and give no suggestion of having been interfered with. It was over ten minutes before Davey found the bank statements and his elation was met by Terry's fears that they were taking far too long. He was so wound up that he called Stobbsy.

"What's the matter?"

"Can you see any Police?"

"No, why?"

"Cos I don't want to get caught in this fucking office, that's why."

"Terry man, I'm sitting in the car outside for fuck's sake, I'll tell you if anyone turns up."

"What if you can't see them coming until it's too late?"

"Jesus! Look, Houdini's standing up the road, that's the

only way you can get into this estate. Don't worry – he'll see them coming before I do anyway."

Terry hung up. And called Houdini.

"Alright Terry? Found owt yet?"

"Let us know if you see any Police."

"Er...aye, I know."

"Right, but keep a good look out eh?"

"I'm not fucking thick you know!"

He hung up.

"Terry, here's what we need. Bank statements and a staff file with names and addresses in," said Davey, walking towards Terry.

"OK, right, we need to write the details down in case we forget. Fuck, what if we get it wrong? we'll have to come back again tomorrow night. Jesus, Davey, hurry up and write it down. Can you find a pen?"

"Terry, man! Stop flapping about! Honest to God, you're a fucking nightmare you are!"

Davey casually switched on a photocopier and took copies of the documents.

"See? Easy. No need to wet your fucking pants."

"OK, let's just go."

They crawled back outside and got into the car.

"Fuck! Terry, I forgot to switch off the photocopier!" shouted Davey.

"Oh Jesus!" he shouted, utterly panicked.

Davey started laughing.

"You're a daft twat, you are, mate."

"So you did switch it off?"

"YES! Jesus..."

* * *

Stobbsy had seen them climbing out through the window

and started the engine straight away. He drove up to the top of the road to collect Houdini and headed off for the club. They had arranged with Davey and Terry to meet there afterwards.

Terry drove with Davey in the passenger seat, heading for Vapour for the group to reconvene. Davey glanced through the documents he had copied.

"Lloyds TSB in Grey Street – that's where the statements come from. That must be where the video is," he said.

"Well, maybe, but you never know for sure do you?"

"What do you mean? That's the branch where the company account is!"

"You're probably right, Davey. I'm just being…"

"Cautious," interrupted Davey.

"Aye."

"Hey, look at this – it's got MacRae's address here as well. I'll ring Danny."

He dialled Danny's number.

"Danny it's Davey. We got the info no bother. But, look, we got his address as well so you can stop following him now if you want."

"Cheers, see you back at the club then."

* * *

They met up back at Vapour within the hour. To the uninformed, these were just six people having a drink in a club. No-one looking at them would imagine where they had just been. Following the owner of a successful internet business. Breaking into his office and copying company documents. These were professional people in every sense. They were, with the exception of Terry of course, unfazed by what they had just done. It was the sort of thing they had done countless times before. Breaking into a property was not exciting. Perhaps that's why they never made mistakes. It was effectively part of a day's work.

"So," said Danny, "what's next then?"

Was this question for Fivers? He wasn't sure. Of course, it was his plan and so he was the obvious person to decide how to continue it. But even now he still didn't truly feel part of the fixtures and fittings and he had to wait until he was assured of everyone else's silence before daring to speak without being specifically asked to do so.

"Well," he said, looking around, still checking that he wasn't treading on toes, "the next step is to familiarise ourselves with the staff."

"Familiarise…" said Danny, "who the fuck says that?"

They laughed.

"Alright, alright, never mind the piss-taking," he said, with more confidence than he felt comfortable displaying, "do you want to hear what I think?"

"Aye, go on then if it'll stop you crying," said Davey.

They just didn't appreciate him. That's what got to Fivers the most.

"Davey, let's have a look at that staff information that you got," said Fivers, holding out his hand to receive it. He read through it, which didn't take too long.

"Right, looks like there's only four people who work there, apart from MacRae," he announced.

He took the ensuing silence as an invitation to keep talking.

"So I reckon the best bet is to get a photograph of them, coming out of their house or whatever. Then we'll know who they are."

"Can we not just watch them go into work? That would save us the bother of waiting for them to come out of their houses," said Terry, the now-deposed king of plans.

"We could, but how would we know that they were staff? They could be MacRae's clients."

Oh.

"I suppose…" said Terry.

"Why do we need to know about the staff anyway?" asked Danny.

"I just think it's best to know everything," replied Fivers, "but more than that, we need to know who is the most likely person to go and retrieve the video. If it's being held in the company account then it would have to be someone from the company who went to sign for it."

"Aye, that's assuming that it is in the company account though, Fivers," said Billy.

"I know, but at least we can say we've checked it out," Fivers insisted.

"Fucking waste of time if you ask me," said Danny.

"He's right, Danny, you only know it's a waste of time once you know for sure that it was wrong," said Terry, of all people.

Danny looked surprised.

"When did you two start kissing and cuddling?!" he asked.

"Danny, I'm just saying, it makes sense, that's all," said Terry, almost bowing his head.

"Alright, fair enough, don't cry," said Danny. His way, perhaps, of admitting that he was wrong without having to actually admit it and still maintain an air of being in charge.

"Now, Fivers, what if it's held in his personal account? How will we find that out?"

"Well, that's another plan, Stobbsy."

"Well, tell us then."

"OK, once we've got to know the staff a bit, we can think about having a look round MacRae's house. Find stuff out about him."

"Fucking hell, Fivers, how long is this going to take?" asked Billy.

"It'll take as long as it takes to get it done properly, Billy," said Fivers, with a hint of anger, "I've got something else planned for after that. And we don't want anyone to be able to link us to it. Then we'd all be living in Frankland for the next ten years."

★ ★ ★

MacRae's business partner was a woman called Heather Ramsey. She was a woman the same age as MacRae and Fivers theorised that they had perhaps met at school or university. Or it could just be a coincidence that they were the same age. She lived at a house not far away from where Fivers lived, even though it was a far more exclusive area, tucked away somewhere in between a perimeter of housing estates ranging from very normal to downright uninhabitable. It was Fivers' job to stake out her house and get a photograph of her.

Fivers didn't have a car of his own. Stobbsy lent him his after Danny had, perhaps predictably, told him to fuck off if he thought for one minute he was driving the Jaguar without Danny in it. He pulled up outside her house around 7 o'clock in the morning and found that he didn't have to wait too long for her to emerge. He got three or four snaps of her from varying angles as she walked out of her house, unaware that she was being watched. Fivers let her drive to the bottom of the road before starting the engine and driving home to continue his night's sleep. Seven o'clock is far too early to be up and about, especially when your body is used to the night-shift pattern of the underworld.

He turned up at Vapour in the early afternoon and met up with the rest of the Firm. It was his idea, seconded by Terry of course, to use a digital camera from which the photographs could be uploaded onto a laptop computer, which Danny had reluctantly agreed to buy for the purposes of the job, moaning that it just wasn't worth going to the expense just for some arsehole who wouldn't pay five hundred quid a week not to get burned down. It was worth the while, as he was reminded, since getting "surveillance" photos developed somewhere in town might arouse suspicion, and he changed his mind in the usual way – insulting Fivers and making the others laugh at him.

They were all agreed that Heather was a real beauty when Fivers uploaded the photographs.

"You would!" shouted Houdini when he saw her.

As it turned out, MacRae *was*. And that was one of the reasons why the plan worked.

Stobbsy's job was to get shots of Joan Hendrie, the typist. Davey had the task of securing shots of Amy Harrison, the tarty secretary who Billy had assaulted in MacRae's office. The only other employee was a young lad called Jonathan Barlow, the receptionist, who Houdini had the job of photographing.

They took it in turns. One stakeout per day to keep things simple. By Friday, they were ready to watch them all come in to work.

*   *   *

They had to take two cars in order to park outside MacRae's office and watch his staff arrive at work. Terry wasn't happy about taking two cars, and in truth neither was Fivers. It did look a bit more suspicious. But then again, there was little choice but to take two cars, since they all had to be able to identify the workers and wouldn't all fit in Danny's car at the same time.

"Why are we doing this again?" asked Houdini.

"Because we need to know their faces," said Fivers.

"Aye, but why?"

Fivers sighed. Why didn't they get it?

"Because if the video is stashed in the bank under the

company account then one of the people from the company will go and get it. And when we are waiting outside the bank, we'll see them go in. We'll be familiar with their faces from all the bank customers that go in and out that day."

"Fivers, why the fuck will they go and get the video from the bank? He's left it there on purpose in case anything happens to him."

"True, and he'll want to get revenge on Danny for what I've got planned next."

"Oh aye, this daft plan of yours."

"It's not daft, Houdini, it's the only way we can be sure of getting the videotape back."

"Aye, so *you* say."

"Just watch for them coming to work will you?"

Houdini was the only person that Fivers felt comfortable talking to like this. Probably because he was essentially as thick as mince.

They had all seen the photographs and recognised the staff as they came in to work that morning. Heather, Joan, Amy and Jonathan. Fivers was satisfied that everyone was ready to move on now, probably because they all kept moaning about how it was cold, early and a waste of time. The next step was finding out MacRae's personal bank account details. And pure chance allowed the group to do that.

* * *

Fivers had spent that particular afternoon at home watching daytime television with his mother and drinking endless cups of tea. He hated daytime TV but it was nice to sit down with his mother, even though they didn't really talk all that much.

It got to about 8 o'clock and Fivers' mother was watching some ridiculous show about DIY.

"Mam, turn this off will you?"

"No, I'm watching it!"

"Mam, it's shite, man."

"Shut up, anyway I'm thinking about getting the bathroom done."

"Are you going to do it, like?"

"Well, no, I can't do it can I? I can't reach up to the ceiling."

"Well, why do you need to know about DIY if you're not going to do it yourself?!"

"It's no good asking you to do it for me though, is it? You're too bloody lazy!"

She meant it. He was, in truth. Around the house at least.

"It doesn't need doing. Turn it off, man, watch something else."

"There's nowt else on."

"Well aye there is, there's a film starting on Channel 4."

"I'm not watching that shite."

Fivers sighed. There was silence.

"Mam, do you want another cup of tea?"

"Aye, go on, I will"

Fivers walked into the kitchen and put the kettle on.

"Mam, have we got any biscuits?"

"You what, love?"

"Have we got any biscuits?"

Silence.

"Mam?"

"What?!"

"Have we?"

"No, you'll have to go to the shops."

"Fucking hell…"

"Don't you use language like that in my house! I've told you about that!"

"Sorry mam."

"Adam, get us twenty tabs while you're at the shop."

He resisted the temptation to curse under his breath this time.

"Aye…"

He left the house.

The shop wasn't far away, only about a ten minute walk. And there's always something to take your mind off the walk in that neighbourhood. This time, it not only took Fivers' mind off the walk, it made him pull out his phone and make a call.

"Danny, you'll not believe who I've just seen going past my road."

"Who?"

"Fucking MacRae!"

"What?! Past your house?"

"No, no – on the main road just by the shops."

"Oh aye? I wonder where he's going."

"I don't know. He's going up towards the A1 though."

"Can you still see him?"

"Aye – there's a bit of traffic building up cos of the roadworks."

"See if you can see where he goes, Fivers."

"Aye, I'll walk up."

"Don't let him see you!"

"Don't worry I won't."

Fivers walked up towards the temporary lights.

"Oh, the lights have gone green Danny. He's driving off."

"Bollocks. Never mind, mate."

"Oh hang on, he's turned left."

Fivers paused.

"Hey – guess who lives up that way!"

"Who?"

"Heather whatyoucallher. Heather Ramsey."

"Oh aye?"

"Danny, are you busy?"

"Not really, why?"

"Well, it might be worth driving up to her house and seeing if he's parked up there. I'm just thinking. If he's shagging her then that'll mean he sometimes leaves his house empty."

"Ooh, I like it. I'll drive up now. Wait on the road and I'll pick you up."

* * *

Danny arrived inside ten minutes. Sure enough, MacRae was parked up at Heather Ramsey's house. Across the road from the house sat Danny Walsh, with Fivers in the passenger seat.

"Course, it might just be business," said Fivers.

"It might, but you never know. Tell you what though, mate, can you see a light on? I can't," said Danny.

"Do you think I should wander up to the door – see if I can hear anything?"

"Aye, go on. In fact, go round the back if you can."

There was no obvious noise from the front door as far as Fivers could tell and so he decided to look from the back. He jumped Heather's back fence and slipped through into the back garden. There was a dim light in one of the upstairs rooms and, rather than risk walking into the garden and turning the security light on, Fivers shimmied up the drainpipe and onto the garage roof, leaving him around a metre from the room where the light was on. There was little noise from traffic. This was a quiet estate. And he didn't have to concentrate too hard to hear Heather moaning louder and louder inside the room. She was obviously enjoying MacRae's company. He must be a bit of a tiger. That would soon change though.

Neither MacRae nor Heather had any idea that while they were in the throes of passion, someone was standing less than a metre from the window, listening in. They had had no idea about being followed and photographed either and neither had the other members of staff. Fivers thought about that as he jumped back down from the garage roof and walked back to Danny's car. It gave him a real buzz to think like that. Being involved with Danny Walsh was generally a buzz. He enjoyed even the skulking around that he got to do.

"Aye, he's giving it to her," said Fivers, getting back into the car.

"Dirty bastard!"

"What – like you wouldn't?"

"Course I would!"

They laughed.

"Anyway – I see you've got your wing mirror sorted," Fivers said.

"Aye, at fucking long last! Barnsey sorted it in the end. Took a while though, there's not many of these babies about!" said Danny, looking around the interior of his car.

"How long have you been waiting like?"

"Pffff…a good few months. Eventually, this fella's at a round-about in his XK8 and some daft twat drives into the back of him, full speed just about. Nasty crash apparently. The front was alright, but the back was knackered, like. Had to be written-off."

"Poor lad eh? Losing his car like that."

"Fuck him, I get a new wing mirror," said Walsh, blandly.

Typical Walsh, really. Fivers wondered why he should expect anything less.

"Right," said Danny, starting the engine, "I'll drop you back at the house."

"No, just drop me at the shops – I only came out to get some tabs for my mam."

"No bother."

Fivers walked back into the house, around an hour after he left.

"Where the hell have you been?"

"Sorry mam, I saw someone I knew."

"Give them tabs here."

* ★ ★

Fivers was still buzzing from his quality detective skills. In fact, he pretty much volunteered to be the one who broke into MacRae's house to sift through his bank details. The others weren't really having it because Fivers didn't have much burglary experience and so it was eventually decided that he *could* be the one to break in as long as he was supervised by Stobbsy, who was once something of an expert in that particular trade. He hadn't burgled a house in fifteen years, truth be told, but it's one industry that tends not to change much over the years.

Houdini kept an eye on Heather's house a few nights later and watched MacRae park up outside and go in. He called Fivers and Stobbsy straight away and told them that this was their cue to break in to MacRae's house since he was going to be, for a while at least, otherwise engaged.

MacRae did have a personal account, nothing particularly surprising there. But it was helpful to note that it was at the same bank as the business account. It would have been a fair guess and simple assumption would have meant avoiding the risk of being caught burgling the guy's house. Then again, they only knew that it was obvious now that they had burgled the house. Fivers maintained that it's best to cover all angles although he was still criticised for wasting time. It was now almost two weeks since Joe MacRae's videotape revelation and Danny was getting restless. He didn't like plans. He liked to get on with the job in hand rather than wait around. He was too impulsive for Fivers' liking. Hot-headed. That attitude risked trouble for Danny Walsh, though in the last twenty years, no-one had dared to challenge him about it.

They sat, as they usually did, in Vapour, talking through the MacRae problem.

"Right then Fivers, the fucking man with the plan, tell me we can go and get that video back."

"Not just yet, Danny, there's something else."

"Oh for fuck's sake! What the hell is there left to do?! Jesus, I'm sick of hanging about for this twat."

He meant Fivers. And Fivers knew it.

"Actually, Danny, I think this is the bit that you'll enjoy."

"Oh aye?"

"Yes, this is the bit where you get to hurt MacRae."

"Oh, go on then," said Danny, suddenly enthused.

"Right, we know so far that MacRae has a personal bank account and a business one. We know the name of the bank, the branch – everything," said Fivers.

He paused before going on, perhaps trying to make the story more interesting. Or perhaps waiting for some acknowledgement that the group had gained information that was very difficult to get, through his own genius. None came, so he went on.

"We also know that there are five people working at MacRae's office and we know where they live. MacRae lives alone – we know that cos the house was empty when he went to see his fancy woman. And we all know that she is a nice bit of skirt as well!"

They all laughed. But for the wrong reason.

"What do you know about that you twat? You've probably never seen a pair of tits in real life!" shouted Danny, causing more laughter to erupt from the members of this easily amused Firm.

Fivers bowed his head.

"OK, anyway," he managed, "the next step is to do something to MacRae that will make him want to get back at you Danny. To do that, he will probably use the video."

"Probably? Don't fucking say 'probably', Fivers, not after the effort I've been to in the last two weeks!"

"Well, we have to make sure that it's something big. Something life-changing. And we have to make sure that he knows you were behind it."

"What sort of thing are you thinking about?" asked Billy.

"I was thinking about hurting him, Billy. Badly."

"Oh aye? Sounds like a laugh," said Danny, clearly eager to exact any revenge that he could.

"The thing is, we all need to make sure that we are elsewhere when it happens. It can't be any of us that does it."

"How the fuck is that going to work like?" asked Danny.

"I know how, Danny," said Billy, almost immediately, "in fact I know just the man. Let's give Mental Kev a ring."

"Who's Mental Kev?" asked Fivers, amused at the name, for now at least.

"He's a mate of mine. We used to work together," said Danny, "now he's kind of, like, freelance."

* * *

Kev Wardle was in the middle of a debt enforcement when his mobile rang.

"Hang on," he said, to a man covered in blood as he answered the call.

"Hello?"

"Kev?"

"Depends."

"Kev it's Danny Walsh."

"Fuck me! How's tricks mate?"

"I've got some work for you."

"Oh aye," said Kev, kicking the man in the face, one hand holding his phone and the other holding a baseball bat which he rested on his collar bone.

"Can you come to the Quayside?"

"Well, not at the minute mate, I'm working."

"Where are you these days anyway?"

"Down in Birmingham."

"Fucking hell, Birmingham?"

"Aye. Tell you what, I'll ring you back in a minute right?"

He looked to the man cowering on the floor.

"Now what was I saying? Oh aye, we were talking about you paying up. Now, look, that was a mate of mine on the phone and he's kind of cheered me up a bit so I'm going to leave you for now, right? Now keep them payments up ok? And go and wash your face."

★   ★   ★

"So who was this 'Mental Kev'?" asked Simon.

"Well, remember when we all used to work for them other people when we were younger?" asked Davey.

"Yeah."

"Well, Kev Wardle was well in with them."

"What – so you used to work for him?"

"Not exactly, he worked *with* us, *for* them."

"So did he go to prison when they did?"

"No, he was never charged. Fair enough, like, cos neither were we. No-one really knew who we were then."

"So what happened to him?"

"Well, don't tell Danny that I said this, right? But basically, Kev is the only person that Danny is scared of. And when Danny took over, for some reason or other, he let Kev do his own thing."

"So, what, was he, like, muscle for hire?"

"Aye I suppose you could say that. He's about 50 now, but he's still fucking huge! There's no-one I know who would want to take him on!"

"I can't imagine Danny being scared of anyone."

"Well, Kev has something on him, we reckon. From the early days. He's always kept Kev sweet. It's not like they argue or anything. They're good mates, you know? Kev does work for Danny every so often and Danny makes sure that he gets well looked after."

"So where is he now?"

"No idea, mate. Like I say, he does his own thing. Truth is, he doesn't go in for the lifestyle, he's not bothered about money and status. He just likes to hurt people! If people didn't pay him, chances are he'd probably do it for free anyway!"

Simon laughed. He would not usually have done so.

"So what happened after Danny rang Mental Kev?" he asked, still laughing.

"He came straight up to Newcastle and met up with us all. Didn't really take to Fivers at first, but once he heard about Fivers' plan, he was dead pally with him."

"Oh yeah – what was the plan anyway? I still don't know."

"Right. Well…"

* * *

Kev Wardle walked into Vapour, having been told about the place, and where it was, over the phone on the way up from Birmingham. He was impressed. He didn't announce his presence – he just walked in and stood by the doorway, looking around.

"How!" shouted Danny.

"Hey, this place is alright isn't it?" asked Kev, shaking Danny's hand.

"Never mind that, how the fuck are you?!"

"I'm alright, mate. Not bad. How's business?"

"Getting there. See that Jaguar outside? That's my little girl that is."

"Aye, I crashed into it when I drove up."

"You better not have."

"Why's that, like?"

They began to wrestle, like the little boys that some would perhaps suggest that they were. Though not to their faces.

Danny was, of course, soon on his back shouting at Kev to let him go.

"Bastard…" he said, getting up.

"Where's the rest of the lads then?" asked Kev.

"Over here," said Danny, pointing to the table where the Firm sat.

"ALRIGHT LADS!"

Several 'alright Kevs' were muttered. And once Kev had looked around the group his eyes came to rest on Fivers.

"Who's this then?"

"That's Fivers," said Danny, before Fivers could introduce himself.

"What school does he go to then?" asked Kev, laughing.

The others laughed too. Any chance to have a dig. Or agree with the one man who dared to put Danny Walsh on his back.

Kev looked to Fivers.

"Well? Stand up for yourself then!"

"What's the point? You look like you've made up your mind."

"Oh aye? Clever bastard this one," he said, looking at Danny, "he'll not last long."

Fivers was beyond embarrassed. If only Kev knew about Fivers' plan. Then he would see how seriously to take him. Maybe now was the time to tell him.

"Right, let me change your mind then," said Fivers, standing up.

Kev doubled back.

"Look at him – coming at me! Don't hurt me *please*. Here, lads, do you think he'll make a move?!"

"I'm not going to make a move. You would win. I know my limitations. But, Mr Wardle, I also know my strengths."

Kev stopped.

"Oh aye?"

"I don't want to tread on Danny's toes, but since we're talking I might as well let you in on why Danny asked you up here."

157

"Fivers, you're getting a bit ahead of yourself," said Danny, sternly.

"No, it's ok Danny, let the little fucker speak."

"Mr Wardle, we have a problem with a man called Joe MacRae…"

By the time Fivers was halfway through the story, Kev was sitting down at the table. He was intrigued. Especially when Fivers told him that the job he was being hired for required the use of a sword. Kev hadn't used a sword for years.

"Hang on, mate," said Kev, "before you tell me any more, I'm going to get a drink. Do you want owt?"

He asked only Fivers. No-one else.

"Aye I'll have a bottle of lager."

"No bother – Houdini, go and get us a bottle of lager each will you?"

Kev was impressed by Fivers. He had courage. And imagination. After that, they got on like a house on fire. Danny wasn't happy. He still thought Fivers was a jumped-up little shithouse who didn't have the brains he was born with. He was wrong to think that, and more wrong still to let it be known that he thought as he did.

* * *

Mental Kev had a house down in Birmingham. Fivers was initially a bit anxious about imposing on Kev in the way that he was about to, but to him it *did* make good sense. Hopefully, Kev would agree.

"So hang on son, you're saying I have to drive back down to Birmingham, leave my car there, travel back up on the train, *with a fucking sword*, do the job and travel back down?"

"Er, yeah. Sorry."

"Fucking hell. Well, I'm not paying for the train tickets, I'll tell you that right now."

"Don't worry, we'll sort that out."

"Is that right?" asked Danny, with his arms folded.

"I'm not paying for fucking train tickets, Danny. No way."

"Why the fuck do you want him travelling up and down the country Fivers? Can he not just do it tonight?"

"No, cos we are still here. We need to arrange to be somewhere else."

"This is costing far too much, this is."

Fivers lost his temper for the first time. He stood up and pointed at Danny Walsh.

"You can think about the fucking cost when you're sitting in prison! You'll have fuck all else to do while you're in a cell for 23 hours a day!"

Danny stood up. It started.

He grabbed Fivers' arm and pushed it away.

"Don't fucking point at me you little shit. And don't ever shout at me."

Everyone else bowed their heads and looked away. They didn't dare look at each other. Everyone except Kev, that is, who just looked relaxed as he took swigs from his bottle of lager.

That would have been it, had Fivers not kept it going.

"I'm sick of you whinging on about how much this costs! You want it done right, you do what I suggest!"

"You're getting close to a fucking smack, Fivers!"

"Why? Eh? All I ever hear is you and these fuckers taking the piss all the time! If you don't want me here then just say. I'll go and get another job! But I swear to God, Danny, if all you're worried about is money then do the job a different way! Just don't involve me in it! I've got absolutely no faith in you at all. You might be a hard bastard but you've got fuck all upstairs!"

That's what did it. That last bit. Danny launched himself over the table and landed on Fivers. He banged Fivers' head against the ground several times and punched him again and again in the face. After a minute or two, Kev came over and lifted Danny off, whispering something in his ear that no-one else heard. Danny walked away.

Fivers was in a bad way. He was only a young lad and he had no chance against someone like Danny Walsh. His face was covered in blood as he lay on the ground, moaning. Kev lifted him up, hoisted him up onto his shoulder and carried him across the dance floor and into the back of the club.

Fivers had an idea about what was coming. This guy was called Mental Kev for a reason. And he didn't really wonder why the rest of the Firm followed him with their eyes. They all thought that this was the last time they were going to see Fivers alive.

As it turned out, Kev sat Fivers down on the toilet, ripped off some toilet paper, wet it and began to wipe the blood from his face.

"Ooh, you're not going to pull for a while!" he said as he did so.

"I never do anyway," laughed Fivers, though it was a half-laugh. His face was too painful for a full one.

"Try not to say owt for a bit, mate, cos you're still bleeding. Try and keep your face still."

Kev finished wiping Fivers' face. He used almost a full toilet roll, such was the state of his injury.

"Right, now I've got something to say," he said.

"OK," said Fivers.

"Now, I could have stepped in the minute Danny went for you, but I didn't. And there's a reason – you were in the wrong there. There's a kind of, well, think of it as a code. Never undermine the boss in front of other people, right?"

"I know," sighed Fivers.

"And for fuck's sake don't point at the bastard, he hates that!"

Fivers half-laughed again. Kev smiled.

"OK, now just remember the lesson. This is how much it hurts when you step out of line. And if it wasn't for me, you would be lying in a hospital bed. So don't forget it. I'll not point at you cos I'm not a hypocrite!"

Another half-laugh.

"Do you think I'm wasting everyone's time with this plan?"

"I'll be honest, it is a bit over-the-top, and a bit expensive. But it does seem sensible. Maybe a bit *too* sensible, mind you. But I'll go along with it. You seem to have thought it through."

"It makes sense in my head," said Fivers.

"And in mine, mate. In fact, I think that Danny is pissed off cos he didn't come up with it. He's a bright lad. Fucking genius at times. But this plan of yours is better than any I've heard him come up with. And I think that's why he went for you. But look – don't let on that I said so ok? Don't show him up, cos I won't step in for you again."

He meant it.

* * *

It didn't really matter what day it was. MacRae seemed to have a fairly well-established daily routine that involved working, going round to Heather's house, going home and getting up for work again. He was seeing more and more of Heather these days. They had been seeing each other for years in truth, but lately it had become more of a permanent arrangement. He saw other women, of course. But not as much as he used to.

Kev had driven back down to Birmingham the night before and he was taking a mid-afternoon train up to Newcastle. It was due to arrive around seven o'clock which gave him time to get a taxi to Heather's house, in the nice quiet estate where she lived, and wait. He was tired though. Driving long distances always made him tired. It didn't help that he was also quite nervous. He had done this sort of work before, but not in the same way. Fivers' plan had meant that Kev had to sit on a train for a few hours which gave him time to think. He didn't usually have to do that. Things tended to be done without much preparation for the most part. He got a call, got an address, went round, had a word and went home. He thrived on the spontaneity of it – no time to think meant that he didn't have time to imagine the mistakes that he might make.

He sat on the train, having walked on carrying a bag, shaped to carry a fishing rod. He had to look the part and so had also worn a wax jacket and old trousers. Fivers had made sure that Kev knew a little bit about fishing in case someone started talking to him on the train. He could now tell such a person that he was going to meet some friends up in Carlisle and go off fishing various tarns. He wasn't from the North-West and had never fished there so he would be excused, and not look suspicious, for not being able to supply the name of the places that he was going to. Fivers had also taken the ridiculously cautious step of making sure that Kev knew the names of a few different fish, should the conversation arise. All of this because no-one could think of a way to carry the sword without it looking like a sword. Kev almost hoped that someone would ask him about where he was going, talk to him about fishing, if only to justify having done so much revision! Good kid, though – Fivers. He thought things right the way through.

There were few people in Kev's carriage. Probably due to the time of day. He had managed to secure himself a table seat and so far, no-one had ventured to join him. He could relax. Maybe get some sleep. No-one would look in the bag would they? Maybe they would. God, maybe someone might steal the bag thinking there was an expensive rod inside which they could get a few quid for. Not going to risk that. Stay awake instead.

How can you stay awake when you're tired? And on a

boring train journey with nothing to do but get excited at the thought that the trolley would be coming round soon? Kev looked out of the window for a while. And then he started to hear noises. Off and on. They didn't bother him to start with.

On the table seat on the other side of the carriage, a young lad about Fivers' age was sitting. Slouching was more appropriate. He coughed every so often. It wasn't a problem as such. Not to begin with. From time to time he would snort loudly, clearing his nose from the inside. Even that didn't trouble Kev for a few minutes. But he kept coughing. Real gutteral coughs. And he made no effort to conceal his coughing, or snorting. Ignorant fucker.

Kev had grown up with people like this kid. Animals. At least Kev had had the good sense to get involved in organised crime. At least that showed a level of breeding more advanced than this little shit. A real surly little bastard. Coughing more now. Each one was like a drip on the forehead. And Kev started to predict the next cough. And the next snort. Maybe there was a pattern to it. Christ, could he not just go and blow his nose?!

He was getting restless now. He really wanted to say something. Maybe he should go and sit somewhere else. Adrenaline rushes kept coming with each cough or snort and Kev did well not to rise to the temptation of telling the kid to go and sit somewhere else. He usually would have, but today he wasn't supposed to be here. He was supposed to be in Birmingham, where he lived. He couldn't do anything to attract attention to himself. He had to stay quiet.

But the kid was doing it more and more. Kev took it personally now. He made a bet with himself that no-one on any other carriage on this train was having to endure this barrage of annoying sounds. This kid just didn't realise he was being such an annoyance. It wouldn't occur to him. Kev looked at him. The kid was totally oblivious. In fact, he coughed again.

That's it, I'm tired, I'm bored, I'm fucking annoyed. No, stop there, you can't do it. It might put the plan in jeopardy. Sit somewhere else. Why? I sat here first. I'm quite comfortable. There might not be any more table seats. Why should I move for this runt?

The lad went to the toilet. This was Kev's chance. No-one would see. He could follow him up to the toilet, barge his way in before he locked the door and set about him. Repay him punch for punch for every cough and snort of the last half-hour. Kev got up and walked a few paces behind the kid. He knew he shouldn't. Someone might steal the bag. But he needed to.

The kid walked into the toilet. Now! No. Go back to your seat. You know it's a stupid idea. Don't mess the plan up. Anyway, Fivers had suffered for his imagination. Kev went back to his seat, gathered up his fishing bag and walked to the next carriage. The kid stayed in the toilet, doing what he was doing. He would never know that Kev had almost followed him into the toilet to leather the shit out of him. He coughed a couple of times, did up his trousers and went back to his seat.

Kev was proud of himself. He had done well not to go crazy. He congratulated himself all the way up to Gateshead and, as the train was about to pull into Newcastle, he joined the rest of the carriage in looking out of the window just as the bridges across the Tyne started to line up. Everyone seems to do that. Kev smiled. He didn't know why he ever left this town.

He took a taxi from outside the central station and headed up through the town to the main road near the estate where Heather lived. It was eight o'clock. The plan was to wait until nine and if MacRae didn't show up, Kev was to get a taxi back into town and find a hotel for the night, where he could stay and wait to try again the next day. He didn't have to.

Fivers had pointed out to the group that the bus stop at the end of Heather's street was a convenient place for Kev to stand and wait without anyone wondering why he was there.

Better than waiting outside of her house. He would look suspicious. This way, he was just a bloke waiting for a bus to come. He had two large carrier bags in one of the pockets of his wax jacket. In one hand he held his fishing rod bag. In the other he held a mobile phone.

MacRae's car stood out among the other cars. Not many people have DB7s. And Kev could see it at the temporary lights, the number plate partially obscured by two other cars that sat in front of it. He began to walk up Heather's street, taking his phone out of his pocket and dialling a friend of his in Birmingham. He looked towards the DB7 to make sure that it was the right one. It was.

"OK, now mate!" he said.

His friend on the other end of the phone started the engine of Kev's car and drove at a steady 50 miles per hour along Birmingham's Bristol Road, a road where traffic was restricted to only 40 miles per hour. He made sure that he maintained his speed through a speed camera and once he saw the camera flash twice, he headed for the next roundabout where he turned full circle and headed back to Kev's house, where he left the car and went back to his own house. Kev could expect a speeding fine now. But face no accusation of being anywhere near Newcastle at 8 o'clock that night.

Kev was still walking up Heather's street. Just a few more houses and he would pass MacRae's destination. He slowed his pace now to make sure that that didn't happen. Not just yet. He needed to see where MacRae was going to park first. Timing was everything. It had to be done right. MacRae was driving up the street now – Kev could hear the purring sound of the engine coming up behind him. He overtook Kev and pulled in on the right-hand side of the road, a few houses down from Heather's house. Perfect. He would be getting out in a few seconds and he would have to meet Kev coming the other way before getting to the entrance to Heather's house.

Kev took the fishing rod bag from over his shoulder and had one last look around just to be sure there was no-one else around. There wasn't. This street was like that. It was as though no-one lived here. He removed the sword from the bag and walked up towards MacRae's parked car holding the sword down his right-hand side. MacRae stepped out of his car and into a puddle. Oh well. Could be worse.

Kev was only metres away from him now. He let MacRae walk past him. He even smiled at him. As soon as he was past, Kev turned around, using the momentum he had gathered to allow him to swing the sword hard into the lower legs of Joe MacRae. It sliced through them like butter and he fell backwards screaming in agony, his feet and calves standing quite neatly on the pavement. Blood was streaming from just below his knees where Kev's sword had cut. He was making noise now. Time to go.

Kev put the sword back into the bag and lay it on the floor. He took one of the large carrier bags from inside his wax jacket and placed MacRae's lower legs inside, tying the top of the bag tightly. He placed this bag into another bag, picked up the fishing rod bag and swung it back over his shoulder.

He looked down at the helpless man on the pavement, the man who would now never walk again. Blood still pumping out of his lower leg stumps. Still screaming.

"Danny Walsh sends his regards," said Kev, before making off down the street in the direction he had walked up.

He didn't have to wait long to flag down a taxi. Plenty of them around, given the time of night. Good job, too. The Police were on their way. Some nosy neighbour had already made the call. It didn't matter.

"Quayside, mate."

The starting fare was £2.40. Fucking disgrace.

All the way to the Quayside, Kev's heartbeat never quickened. It was all just routine. His mind was already on the return journey. One thing had troubled him about that. If, for some reason, anyone thought to look at CCTV from the Station, they would see Kev arrive and then return within a few hours. He would have no explanation for that.

Fivers had, of course, thought about that. The problem only existed if someone were to look at the CCTV. The cameras couldn't be helped. They were a permanent feature. The thing to change would be Kev.

Kev walked along the River Tyne to a point just before the Arena. It was dark there. He swung the bag hard and released it into the river. Happily, it was heavy enough to sink almost straight away and Kev had managed to land it pretty much in the middle of the river. No chance of the tide going out to reveal Joe MacRae's legs in a bag on the mudflats. Not that anyone would ever think that it was anything other than a bag. There are all sorts of things in the Tyne.

He walked back up towards the station. But he went the back way. The quiet way. Where there is scarcely a non-derelict building to be seen. No-one bothers to go there, unless they fancy trying to avoid rush-hour traffic by taking a shortcut. So by the time early evening comes about, there is simply no-one to be seen.

Fivers, knowing this, had left Kev a bag, hidden nicely in a bush. It contained a few important items, but more importantly, was large enough to fit the sword in. Kev took off the jacket that he was wearing, placed it in the bag and replaced it with another coat of an entirely different length and colour. He put on a cap, which Fivers had also left him, zipped up the bag and walked up to the station. There was a train to Birmingham in about half an hour's time. Time for a quick pint and then he could go home.

Kev walked onto the train and placed his bag on the overhead rail. He removed his jacket and sat down at the only table that wasn't already taken up. There was someone else sitting opposite him, but Kev wasn't too bothered. He was probably just going to go to sleep anyway.

"Alright?" asked the man, shuffling in his seat even though he was not in anyone's way.

"Knackered," replied Kev, "been away fishing – supposed to be relaxing!"

"Fishing eh?"

"Aye."

"Whereabouts?"

"Up Carlisle way."

"Oh aye?"

"Aye, went to a few different places. Don't ask me the names though, cos I can't remember! Good rainbow trout area round there, you know."

★ ★ ★

"They didn't put that in the papers, eh?!" laughed Davey.

"No," said Simon. He couldn't decide whether he was impressed or repulsed. Probably both. These people clearly had no qualms about ruining lives, as long as it was to their own benefit. Better, then, to be on their side rather than the side of the opposition. What must Joe MacRae have gone through? What must he still be going through? But, perhaps more importantly, what happened after that? Did they catch Kev? Did they get the video back?

Simon looked to Davey.

"So what happened to Kev? did he ever get caught?"

"Did he fuck. He's still working down Birmingham way as far as I know. Last we heard of him, he rang Danny up and asked him for the money to pay his speeding fine. He got twenty grand for the job as well – Danny would have moaned about that and told Kev to pay the fine out of the twenty grand but, you know, this is Kev we're talking about. People tend to do what he says – even Danny."

"What about the video then?"

"Simon, my throat's drying up – go and get a couple of bottles from the bar and I'll tell you the rest."

Simon put his hand in his pocket for some money.

"Simon, man, just go behind the bar and help yourself for fuck's sake," said Billy.

He felt more like a member of the Firm now than ever before. They had stopped being polite to him. And they were sharing dangerous secrets with him.

He grabbed a few bottles of lager and returned to the table.

"So then. The video," he said.

"Well," said Davey, taking a swig from his bottle, "not much to tell you really. Fivers' plan was so good that the next bit didn't cause us too much bother."

* * *

Heather Ramsey had found MacRae outside of her house. Initially she had heard screaming but had not reacted to it. After a while, she began to get curious and peeked out of the window. She couldn't see MacRae's condition at first. She thought perhaps he had been attacked, or maybe even had a heart attack. He did work an awful lot.

When she found him she vomited. No surprise, perhaps. Anyone would, in that situation. She sobbed her way through a 999 call to the Ambulance and Police services but was told that emergency vehicles were already on their way. They allowed her to travel in the ambulance with him and she stayed with him all night even though the morphine that had been administered had had the effect of sending him to sleep soon after arrival.

She woke up beside him to the sound of her mobile phone ringing. She ought really to have turned it off, being, as she was, in a hospital. But no-one took too much offence at it given the circumstances. It turned out to be Joan, ringing to ask where MacRae was since the three members of staff were all standing outside of the office, freezing, waiting to be let in.

She gave them all the day off but did not tell them exactly what had happened. They would find out on the news eventually, because MacRae could offer no explanation as to who had attacked him. In truth, he did not know his attacker. But he knew who had sent him. And MacRae had, as Fivers predicted he would, his own plan of action. He wasn't going to tell the Police anything yet. Not until he got the video.

Fivers had gone on and on about the fact that no-one could be sure as to which account MacRae had used to deposit the video. The answer was obvious once they realised. Yes, it was the company account and Heather was the only person who could sign anything to retrieve it. So she would be the one who went to collect it. Danny was not a happy man. He said it had been a complete waste of time gathering all this information on MacRae because any fool could have guessed that it would have been in the company account, for the simple reason that MacRae was not married and had no-one who could go and sign on his account. Fivers pointed out that even then, he could have given someone per pro authority, and that the truth comes as no surprise once it's known. Danny had to concede. Well, perhaps not concede, but at least he didn't smack him about this time.

One member of the Firm waited outside each of the branches in Newcastle city centre. It was not an easy job to begin with, it required a lot of patience. And it was made worse by the fact that MacRae hadn't told Heather about the video until the day after the staff had been surprised with a day off. So they waited all day without her having turned up at all. They were, of course, looking for any of the staff at this point, for all they knew, any of them could have been sent to collect the video.

On the day that MacRae asked Heather to collect the

video, she went immediately to do so and Fivers saw her go into and come back out from the branch that he was watching. Fivers was still made to feel like he had to explain himself endlessly, that it had all been a waste of time, but the important thing was that Heather had the video. Perhaps it had been obvious, but not at the time. No-one seemed to get that point.

The problem then became one of remaining covert. In all likelihood, Heather's house was being watched by Police in case she was in any danger herself. She didn't help her cause at all by driving back to the hospital as soon as she had picked up the video. Stobbsy was watching the branch nearest to the one Fivers was watching and he had a car, so he followed her all the way to the multi-storey car park at the Royal Victoria Infirmary.

He smiled when he saw the sign that read "no responsibility will be taken for damage to vehicles, howsoever caused". That tended to suggest that there was no CCTV in the car park. He smiled even more when he noticed her putting the video into the boot of her car. He called for the rest of the Firm to assemble at the site and make sure that all the car park staff were out of the way. They were all there within minutes.

As Heather walked into the room where Joe was lying, watching mid-afternoon television, she had no idea that her car was being broken into. Stobbsy, for his part, had begun his criminal career by stealing cars and selling them on. He was quite an accomplished car thief. Of course, breaking into cars is easy – it's only difficult when you don't want to leave any trace of having done so. You have to leave that to the real professionals – the ones with imagination.

Fivers' plan was a total success. And, for once, they acknowledged the fact, eventually anyway. They had the tape. MacRae was totally unarmed. And Fivers woke up with a sore head the next morning. And not because Danny had hit him this time. They had to place an extra order for bottles of lager the next day, such was their celebration.

"So that meant that Fivers was back in Danny's good books then?" asked Simon.

"Aye, for the time being," replied Davey, "I'll tell you about that another time mate – I've had enough storytelling for one night!"

Simon didn't mind at all. After all, Melissa had just walked into Vapour and listening to another story would mean not talking to her.

She stood at the bar, as she had done the previous night. This time, she acknowledged the fact that she had seen Simon and she waved at him in a particularly cute and appealing way. He raised his bottle of lager at her in a perhaps less than appealing way, but then Simon never was very good with women.

She came over. Simon knew she would. And the anticipation of her doing so had made him nervous and self-conscious of the usual minor details – was he sitting down in a good way? What is a good way? Does it really matter how you sit down? Should he stand up to greet her? Oh for God's sake.

"Hi gorgeous," she said, sitting down next to Simon.

What do you say to that? What would Simon usually say? He thought about it, but remembered that last night they had talked honestly. It made him make an effort to relax, if that's possible.

"Gorgeous eh?" he said.

That was no good. But she didn't seem to mind.

"Yeah, gorgeous – is that alright?" she asked, playfully.

"I suppose it is," replied Simon, bending over towards her and whispering in her ear, "as long as you don't mind me saying that you are the most beautiful woman in the room!"

"Well no, I don't mind that at all, as it goes!"

"How long have you been here?" she asked him.

"About an hour or so."

She feigned disappointment.

"So you're not bored enough for me to tempt you away yet?"

Oh yeah? What was this?

"Well, I'd better let you finish your drink at least."

She laughed. It was a good enough answer in the circumstances. She knew how difficult his position was. But she also knew the position she wanted him in.

"Maybe I should drink it down all in one!"

"Maybe you should!"

Simon was now sitting almost sideways on the bench-style sofa with one foot on the floor and the other resting on the end of the sofa, his knee against the back of it. His left arm rested on the top of the sofa and his left hand rested against his head. In short, he was making himself at home and he became very aware of the fact. Maybe the lads would have problems with that. He turned to them.

"Melissa, go and get us a few bottles eh?" said Billy.

She put her drink down, sighed and stood up.

"The things I do for you lot…" she said.

"Simon, what the fuck are you doing?"

This worried him. Maybe he was getting carried away. Maybe he should behave himself. God, why was he even here? In the company of his client's associates?

"What do you mean?" he asked. He knew what they meant.

"She's fucking gagging for it! Take her home and stop making us all feel sick!" said Billy.

Oh, so they didn't mean what he thought.

"And by the way, Simon, your patter's shite," said Stobbsy.

"Is it fuck!" shouted Simon.

They laughed.

"Here, what did we say last night? Stop fucking talking to her and just get her into bed. Make hay while the sun shines!" said Davey.

The sun *is* shining, thought Simon. In fact, she is making it shine. Simon didn't dare say anything like that though. They would rip him to bits! But the thought was there all the same.

Melissa returned to the table carrying a few bottles of lager. She sat down and picked up her own drink. No-one said anything. Simon was dying to think of any question at all that began with "So – " but nothing came. And now the lads were staring at him, willing him to get down to business and enjoy himself. He still needed final clarification from them as to his personal safety, if anything, and so looked to Billy, who he saw as the ringleader, or perhaps Danny's closest thing to a personal representative, with a look on his face that said "Really? You don't mind?"

Billy looked back. His look suggested "no, now go for it!" and so he looked back at Melissa.

"So – you finished that drink yet?"

"Nearly," she replied.

"OK."

"Simon?"

"Yeah?"

"I know I shouldn't say something as ridiculous as this, but I'm going to say it anyway."

"OK?"

"Your place or mine?" she smiled.

"Whichever's the closest," he said with a smile to equal hers.

"Have no attachments. Allow nothing in your life that you cannot walk out on in 30 seconds flat if you spot the heat around the corner."
Neil McCauley in *Heat*, 1995
(dir. Micahel Mann © Warner Bros Inc)

Two days ago, a lot had changed. In the morning, he had watched as Davey had sat in the public gallery, taken a piece of paper and written down the names of the Jurors in the Walsh case.

That night he had met a girl called Melissa for the first time while socialising with Walsh's friends at a club owned by him. And yesterday, the case against Danny Walsh had become unsinkable. He had been out again with Walsh's friends and gone back to Melissa's house with her to spend the night, No surprise for Simon, then, that when he walked into the Robing Room on the morning of the third day of the Walsh trial, Kate Holloway approached him and told him that one of the Jurors had been threatened over the telephone the previous night. And no surprise that Simon feigned shock at this revelation. Clearly, the trial going as badly as it was, someone involved with the Firm had made the threat. But Simon wasn't going to say so.

Counsel were called into Her Honour Judge Kristensen's Chambers, along with a tape-recorder carried by the stenographer, who remained in the room.

"So, no doubt you've heard about the threat?"

"Kate just told me, Judge," said Simon.

"OK. What do you both propose to do?"

They looked at each other.

"I don't want the trial to have to go off, not after three days," said Kate.

"Yeah, we all know why that is. If there's a retrial I'll make you serve Whelan's photos well in advance," said Simon, when perhaps he shouldn't have.

"Actually, it's nothing to do with that, Simon. Because, unless you haven't noticed, you're still running a set-up defence. So it would make no difference at all would it?"

Maybe not. Who knows?

"Alright, rather than bicker, let's think about what we're going to do," said the Judge.

"I don't mind a Jury of eleven," said Simon.

"That's what I was wondering, Simon. I can just discharge the Jury member who received the threat and continue with the trial."

"Judge, while I don't mind, I should still take instructions."

"Oh, of course you should, Simon. What time is it now?" asked the Judge, looking at her watch, "11 o'clock or thereabouts. Tell you what, let's all meet back here at 11.30 and you can tell me how far you've got – how about that?"

"Will do," said Simon.

The first port of call in these circumstances should be the cells, where Danny would be sitting. Instructions could be taken from him and the Judge could be appraised. But so much had changed lately that Simon didn't do that. Not straight away at least. First of all, he went down to the canteen and spoke to the boys.

"Oi Oi!" shouted Houdini.

They were all smiling.

"Good morning Mr Silver," said Billy, standing up to shake his hand.

"That's very formal," said Simon, half-smiling and half-scared.

"Well, it's not every day you meet a love God!" laughed Billy. They all joined in.

"So? Tell us what happened then," said Stobbsy, "we're all dying to know!"

"What do you mean? Melissa?"

"Yeah yeah, don't pretend you don't know. Come on, tell us," said Davey.

"I was a perfect gentleman, as you would expect!"

"That's not what we heard!" laughed Billy.

"What did she say?"

"Nowt, I'm only messing with you, she'll still be in bed anyway, it's not lunchtime yet."

There was silence for a noticeable time.

"You're not going to tell us are you?" asked Davey.

"I've got something more important to tell you, and I mean you, Davey."

"Oh aye?"

"One of the Jury has turned up this morning, saying that he got threatened last night."

"Threatened?"

"Yeah, I don't know exactly what was said, but apparently someone phoned him up and, you know, advised him to find Danny Not Guilty."

"Fucking hell, who would do a thing like that?" asked Davey.

"Someone who wrote the Jury's names down, Davey. Someone like that."

Davey knew that Simon must have seen him taking notes on Monday. And his face changed.

"What are you going to do?"

"What can I do?"

Davey was starting to worry now.

"Well…"

"I don't know anything about it do I? I couldn't prove a

thing, even if I wanted to, which I don't particularly," said Simon with a smile.

Davey smiled too now.

"You're getting the hang of this game aren't you?"

"I'm doing you a favour, you've all been very honest with me, and I'm going to be honest in return. There's not a thing that you can accomplish by making threats. And by the way, I don't mean that you should carry the threats out, I mean that you shouldn't make them in the first place."

"It's a bit different with Courts though, Simon, we don't usually make threats, I told you as much last night. But if something happened to the Jury then there would just be a retrial with anonymous Jurors."

"Look, Danny is going to get convicted, there's no doubt about it. He knows it, I know it and I think that in all fairness, you know it too."

"Well, aye, that's why whoever rang the Juror thought things needed a little push."

Simon was desperately trying to justify this conversation. Davey was as good as admitting that he had made the threat. That was a crime and Simon had a duty as a Barrister to report it. But so far, Davey had not said that it was him who had made the call. It may well not have been. Clearly, if he didn't make the call, then he got someone else to do so. This still made Davey a criminal, if only in a conspiratorial sense. Really can't have this conversation.

"Anyway, Simon. Who's to say that the coppers didn't do it?"

"Why would the coppers do it?"

"To make it look like one of us did it."

It was a fair point. And the conversation became justified by it.

"Right, I'm going down to see Danny."

"Say hello for us," said Billy.

"Will do."

"Here, before you go – what's going to happen with this threat?"

"I don't think it will make a big difference. There'll probably just be eleven Jurors instead of twelve who see the case through. Nobody wants a retrial cos they've got him well and truly convicted. And even if there was a retrial, Danny's not going to change his defence."

"Is there anything we can do?" asked Billy.

"Yeah, stay in here, and don't use telephones!" laughed Simon.

He really felt like one of the gang now. They felt it too.

★   ★   ★

"Right then, Danny," said Simon, as both men sat down, "there's a bit of a problem."

Walsh sighed.

"There always is, mate."

"Well this one is a bit of a puzzler. One of the Jury was threatened over the phone last night."

"Oh aye? Who by?"

He genuinely seemed not to know.

"Well, I don't know. Well, I think I do, but it doesn't really matter."

"Like hell it doesn't – who was it?"

"I think it was one of your boys."

"Aye – that's pretty obvious. But who?"

"I honestly don't know. I know that Davey made a note of the names of everyone on the Jury as they were read out."

"So what's going to happen?"

"The trial is probably going to go on with eleven Jurors instead of twelve."

"Will that make much difference?"

"It's impossible to say. But to be honest, I think the

evidence so far is so damaging that it won't make a scrap of difference how many Jurors there are."

"Aye, it's not going all too well is it?"

"Whelan saw to that."

"Aye, Whelan."

"So – what do you want me to say to the Judge? We've got a few minutes before I need to go back upstairs."

"I want it kicked, Simon. There's no way I'm having this."

Walsh was clearly getting irate now.

"OK – you know I don't think it will make a difference…"

"I know. But it's too much of a liberty you know? I didn't threaten anyone – why should I suffer just cos one of the lads did?"

"You shouldn't. But then, how much are you really suffering anyway with one less Juror?"

"That Juror could have been the one who was going to find me Not Guilty."

"Or he could have been one of the ones to find you Guilty. You can't play this on a guess, Danny."

Walsh stood up.

"Simon, I'm going back to my cell. Just go and tell the Judge I want it kicked. And I want bail until the re-trial."

* * *

Simon went to see the Judge as promised, at just after 11.30. She was not impressed.

"Bail? You must be kidding!"

It was one of those moments.

"Judge, those are my instructions," said Simon, without passion.

"OK Simon. Well that's just not going to happen I'm afraid."

Simon stayed silent.

"Don't be like that, Simon – I am not going to throw this

180

trial away when a retrial would make no difference. The defence will be the same won't it?"

"It will, yes."

"Why is he running this defence anyway? He's got no chance."

"The evidence is fairly damning, I agree."

She sighed.

"Well, it's his case I suppose. Now then, where's Kate?"

Kate walked into the Judge's Chambers a second or two after that.

"Sorry, Judge."

"Quite alright, Kate. Now, I wanted to wait until you were both here before I said anything. Have a seat, both of you."

They sat down.

"Now it gets worse I'm afraid! I have been informed that a relative of another of the Jurors has telephoned the Court. Apparently she was taken to hospital last night and she was kept in overnight. Nothing to worry about, though. She hasn't been threatened or anything."

That was below the belt.

"The hospital intend to discharge her today and she will be perfectly fit to attend Court tomorrow. I didn't enquire as to what the problem was, not really any of my business. But I'm afraid that I'm going to have to adjourn until tomorrow morning to continue the trial."

Simon suddenly thought what he could do for the rest of the day. And then he thought about Melissa.

"So, what I propose to do is to go into Court and formally discharge the Jury for the day. Any observations?"

"No," said Simon.

"None," said Kate.

"Very well. I'll do that then. I daresay you can wait for me in Court?"

They both stood up to leave.

Danny Walsh was brought up from the cells and a public address call was put out for all parties to attend Court. The lads sat in Court too and Simon wondered whether that was such a good idea. The Police would be sitting with them in the public gallery. Hopefully, nothing would happen. Simon had only a few seconds to go and speak to Walsh in the dock to tell him what was going to happen, before there was a knock on the door.

The Court stood as the Judge came back in and sat down after she had done so.

"This morning two matters have come to light," she began.

"The first is this. Last night, around twenty past nine, a member of the Jury was contacted by an unknown caller on the telephone. Threats were made to this man to find the Defendant Not Guilty."

Hang on. I was with these lads at that time last night.

Simon looked to the public gallery – he could just about see five faces looking back at him, wondering what the hell was going on.

"In consultation with Counsel for both sides, I have decided that this particular member of the Jury should take no further part in the trial and I hereby formally discharge him from further involvement in the case."

This was strange. It made no sense. But, thinking about it, Davey hadn't actually admitted to having made the call. Who else had done it?

"Secondly, I have been informed that one of the members of the Jury is unwell and will not be able to attend Court today. I therefore adjourn this case until tomorrow morning."

The Judge stood up, as did the Clerk, together with the rest of the people in Court.

"All persons having anything to do before Her Majesty's Crown Court may now depart and give their attendance tomorrow morning at 10.30. God save the Queen."

Simon's thoughts while bowing his head were not

focussed on God saving the Queen, rather on just who in God's name had made the call.

★   ★   ★

"Hey – we were all with you at that time last night!" said Davey, as Simon joined them outside of the Courtroom.

"I know. I can't work it out. When we were downstairs, I thought you were hinting that you had made the call."

"No, I just assumed that one of the lads did. But it turns out that none of us could have made it!"

"I'm stumped. Unless the Police did it, to make it look like it was one of you."

"Maybe that's why nobody's been arrested?"

"Not yet, anyway. I would go home, lads. Keep out of the way for a bit. I'll see you all tomorrow."

"Not coming out tonight?"

"No, it's probably best I don't in the circumstances."

"You're probably right, mate."

There was another reason why Simon wasn't going out tonight. He was about to call her.

Thinking about it, who's to say that Melissa didn't make the call? She hadn't come to the club until after half past nine. Maybe she made the threats and then came into the club as though nothing had happened. And then took me home. Shit. Suddenly, Melissa started to feature heavily in Simon's mind, and not for the usual reasons. What if she had more to do with the case than ringing a Juror?

★   ★   ★

Simon was swapping over his collars when Shelley came running into the Robing Room.

"Mr Silver, have I missed anything?!"

183

"Hi Shelley. Actually you did miss a couple of things."

Shelley's face showed how worried she was.

"But it's ok. We're adjourned for the day."

"Why?"

Was it her fault?

"Two ticks, I'll get us a coffee and tell you all about it," Simon suggested, with his tie in between his teeth.

"No I'll get them," she replied, "meet you in there."

He joined her in the Advocates' Lounge.

"Shelley – you look far too worried," he said.

"I just hate being late, especially when it's not my fault," she replied.

"Has something happened?"

"No, nothing serious. Just that my car died on me and I had to push it off the road and find somewhere to get a bus from!"

"No..." Simon laughed. "I shouldn't laugh, Shelley, I'm sorry."

"It's ok."

"Actually, I remember once when I was doing your job, my car died at a roundabout on the A1. It was snowing and I had to be in Durham for 10 right? It was about 9.15. Anyway, I got out into the snow, pushed my car off the main road and got the bus into town, ran down to the train station – got on a train, which was of course delayed and ran all the way from Durham station up to the Court."

"God – how late were you?"

"Actually I wasn't all that late believe it or not."

"How? Are you a fast runner or something?!"

"No, nothing like that! Most people were late that day with the snow and all. So, yeah, technically I was late, but I was among the first to arrive."

"That was lucky!"

"Yeah. Anyway, so I know what you're going through with a car that dies so don't worry."

"Thanks."

"It's nice that someone actually believes me," she said.

"How do you mean?"

"Well, if it was anyone else they would have just thought I was some dizzy tart who slept in!"

"Well, some people are a bit full of themselves in this place. Silly really, cos most of them have very little about them, I find. You know, socially I mean. Not that I tend to socialise much with the Bar."

No, I have new friends now. Which reminds me.

"Anyway, the Jury is now a Jury of eleven instead of twelve as of this morning."

"Why?"

"Well, one of the Jurors was threatened last night by someone over the phone."

"Really? Do you think it was one of Danny's friends?"

"Well I thought so originally. But they all have, you know, an alibi for last night."

"Yeah right!"

"No, really."

Don't tell her. For God's sake don't be that stupid.

"Honestly. I was with them at the time the call is supposed to have been made."

"Oh right. Oh well fair enough. So who else might have threatened the Jury?"

"Well it was just one Juror, but anyway, yeah, I don't know who it could have been. Maybe the Police, trying to play dirty!"

"Or someone else that Danny knows. Someone who wasn't there last night with you?"

That narrowed it down to pretty much anyone in Newcastle with more than a couple of convictions.

* * *

Davey and the others were back in Vapour, as per usual. Not much else to do these days except sit there and drink, what with Danny on remand and unable to give orders. As long as the club was still being run properly, they were doing enough. As much as they could in the circumstances.

"I thought it must have been one of you that made that call to the Jury," he said.

"Well, I thought it was you, mate – you were the one who wrote the names down," said Stobbsy.

"So did I," said Billy.

"This fucking stinks, this does," said Terry, "I don't like it one bit. Someone's playing us for twats."

"Terry, don't be so paranoid. It was probably just the coppers having a laugh," said Billy.

"Yeah well I still think we should watch out for anything, you know, unusual."

"I think he's right, like," said Davey, "I mean, I was just messing around when we were talking to Simon. I thought it was one of you then, but now I know it wasn't I can't think who it could have been."

"I think I know," said Terry.

★   ★   ★

"Sarge? What do you want to do about this threatening call?"

David Whelan looked at this young PC.

"Well, investigating it would be a good idea – don't you think?"

"Yes Sarge. Do I take it that you want me to go and speak to the Juror?"

"Yes, but don't go on your own."

"Well, it's just that I don't know the details of where the Juror lives."

"Oh, good point. I'll sort that out for you. Stay here and make me a cup of coffee. I'll be back in five minutes."

Sergeant Whelan wasn't supposed to know the details of the Jury's names and addresses. He should know no more than anyone else in Court. Jury selection is a matter for the Court. And he didn't know. He gave the impression to the officers under his command that he was omniscient. To them, perhaps he was, in comparison. But in truth he had no idea about how to get the details of this Juror's address. The listing office was probably a good place to start.

"Hello, I need to speak to the Chief Clerk. Fairly urgent if you don't mind," he said to a young girl in the listing office, who feared his uniform as much as most non-criminals do.

He met with the Chief Clerk, who had to go to speak to someone else before returning with the address. It didn't, strictly speaking, matter any more since this person was no longer a member of the Jury. But procedures are there to be followed. Whelan still got a little bit annoyed at this, even though he was the King of the by-the-book approach. And it annoyed him further that his five-minute time estimate was off by almost a quarter of an hour. His coffee would be cold.

"Here you go, there's the address," he said, walking back into the Police room.

"Thanks Sarge. We'll go round straight away. Although, actually, you probably need another cup of coffee now. I'll go and make one for you."

PC Cheung walked into the kitchen area, while Whelan sat down. He boiled the kettle again and made a point of spitting into the second cup just as he had done in the first.

★   ★   ★

"So what's happened to your car anyway?" asked Simon.
"No idea – all I know is that it died!" replied Shelley.

"No no, I mean, are you getting it towed?"

"Oh right. No, I didn't bother, I just came straight in."

"Well, I'll give you a lift back and we can sort out a tow."

"Thanks. Actually, I should probably get back to the office."

Damn.

"Bollocks to that! Let's go and get some lunch!"

"OK," she smiled.

"I'll just make a call. Meet you back here in a minute."

Simon walked up a quiet corridor and took out his mobile phone.

"Simon!"

"Alright Billy – here, do you know anyone in the motor trade?"

"Aye – why? Do you need an MOT doing?"

"No, I need to get a car towed."

"Oh right. Aye, no bother."

"How much?"

"Fuck off man."

Simon laughed.

"Cheers mate, I'll ring you back in a bit 'cos I don't know exactly where the car is, I'll have to find out."

"No bother."

Simon and Shelley left the Court building and decided on one of the Italian restaurants on the Quayside. They walked inside and sat down.

"Anything to drink?" asked the waiter as soon as they had done so.

"I'll just have an orange juice thanks. Shelley?"

"Er, actually I might have a red wine since I'm not driving!"

"Why not?" smiled Simon.

The waiter left them to look over the menu.

"Actually, Shelley, give me your car keys and I'll get it towed for you."

"Oh right – thanks. How?"

"Well, you know how it is. I know a fella who knows a fella!"

No, Simon. You are *involved* with a fella who knows a fella.

"How much will it cost to tow?"

"Don't worry about that, Shelley."

"Thanks! That's really nice of you. I was going to get my boyfriend to ring the RAC and see if they would pick it up for me. But now I don't have to!"

Boyfriend? Oh, for God's sake.

* * *

Lunch was eaten fairly swiftly. And Simon had to make a call to get Shelley's car picked up for her. What a waste of time that was! Not to worry though, there were other women. One of which was Melissa and Simon remembered that he needed to speak to her. Well, he didn't really need to. He wanted to see her. But in the event that she thought he was being clingy, even on day three of their liaison, he had the excuse of the Jury threat to hide behind. If calling her ended up freaking her out, at least he could say he was only ringing about the threat. Perfect.

"Hello?" asked a voice that sounded like this was the first word it had said all day.

"Hi Melissa, it's Simon."

"Oh hi babe," she said, still with a tired voice. It sounded so sexy. "What are you up to?"

"Well, we're adjourned for the day. I need to speak to you actually."

"Oh well just come round. Where are you?"

"In town."

"Are you coming straight round?"

Say that you've got something else to do first. Don't go straight round. It makes you look desperate. Say no.

"Yeah, can do."

"OK babe see you in a few minutes then."

Well, no harm done.

Simon was at Melissa's flat within twenty minutes. Far too early really. But then, it didn't look like she would mind too much. He parked up and walked to the door, ringing the one buzzer that didn't have a surname beside it. It seemed that everyone just knew her as Melissa. It occurred to Simon that he didn't know her full name. Not that it mattered.

"Hello?"

"Hi, it's Simon."

"Come up babe."

Melissa was still in bed when Simon walked into the flat. Remnants of Melissa's cocaine habit were still visible on one of the bedside tables and ought really to have served as a reminder of the fact that Simon shouldn't be standing where he was, but he chose to overlook the issue. It's only powder. Not like she's a murderer or something. Anyway, everyone does it these days. Not Simon, though. Why? It doesn't look too clever if a lawyer gets caught taking drugs. But these days, would anyone really care? Stressful job and all that... *More* justification. A habit itself, perhaps.

"Simon, you'll have to help yourself to a drink," she said, snuggling herself under the covers, "it's not time for me to get up yet."

"OK – do you want anything?"

"Coffee, of course!"

"Milk? Sugar?"

"Yes, honey!"

The old ones are the best. Anyway, she could say whatever the hell she wanted. She had a get-out-of-jail-free card as far as clichés were concerned, such was her beauty, even before she had got out of bed.

The question Simon battled with now was whether or not to make Melissa some breakfast. Would that look too needy? Constantly being subservient? Probably. But who cares?

"Would you put me some toast on?" she shouted through to the kitchen.

Oh well, that answers that question.

"OK," he shouted back.

Simon had no idea how to bring the subject up. He was dying to start off with some small talk. Melissa hadn't been living in this particular flat for very long, as she had told him the night before. Maybe he could start with something about that. The fact that the place looked different in the day time. Absolute rubbish, really. Anyway, most things *do* have a habit of looking different in the light! As it turned out, Melissa started with her own forgivable vacant small-talk.

"So," she said as Simon brought in a tray of coffee and toast, "good day?"

He took the liberty of sitting down on the bed beside her.

"Well, there's something I need to talk to you about to be honest."

"You sound serious. What's up?"

He was clearly nervous. It showed by the fact that he couldn't look her in the eye. Maybe because he didn't know how to ask the question he was going to have to ask.

The answer to it would be an important one.

"Right, Melissa, the thing is, yeah, last night one of the Jury got a threatening phone call."

"Really?"

"Yeah, and my first thought was that one of the lads had made the call."

"Well, that's not impossible."

"No, it's not is it? But, look, the thing is, it wasn't them who made the call."

He paused.

"I really need to know it wasn't you."

"Me?!"

He looked her in the eye now. She seemed genuinely offended.

"I hate to ask you Melissa. But I really need to know."

"Would you believe me anyway?"

"Of course I would."

"Well of course I didn't."

Now there was another pause. And it was an uncomfortable one.

"Melissa – I'm really sorry I had to ask."

"Well, you've got your career to think about haven't you? It's no good being seen with a tramp like me."

"Hey, don't say that."

"Why not? It's what you think isn't it?! Why are you even here, Simon? Why don't you just go back to your nice little life?!"

She was close to tears. This was not an argument for the sake of having one.

"Melissa…"

"Just go," she said, lying back.

"I don't want to go. I want to spend the day with you."

"Yeah? What else are you going to accuse me of?"

"Look, I had to ask. I'm sorry."

"Why? Why did you *have* to ask?"

"Because if it was you that made the call, I would have to go right now and not see you again. And I don't like the thought of that."

"Yeah?"

"Of course 'yeah'!"

The crying started to subside. And he could see the beginnings of a smile.

"Well I suppose I can forgive you."

"Look, I know we've only known each other for a few days, three days in fact. But, you know, I'd hate for something to happen that would make it, like, you know, *only* be three days. God I'm rambling. I'm useless at this."

There was another pause.

"Simon?"

"Yeah?"

"Kiss me."

He did. And it didn't stop there.

★   ★   ★

It was after four o'clock now. Simon lay beside Melissa in her bed with his arm around her, her head nestled into his shoulder. They had been lying like that for almost an hour now. She sighed. A sigh that suggested calm and contentment.

"Do you think I should get up at all today?" she asked.

"No, just stay here."

"It's nice isn't it?"

"Yeah."

"I'd love a coffee though – will you make me one?" she smiled up at him.

"Yeah, ok." Simon got up. "Stay there and look sexy for when I get back!" he laughed.

"Ooh, what are you going to do?" she smiled.

"Lots of things – in fact, your coffee might go cold!"

"Then maybe you should forget about the coffee and just come back to bed."

"Yeah go on then," he laughed, crawling speedily back beneath the covers to be greeted by Melissa's warm body and an initial giggling that turned into quiet enjoyment.

Simon didn't make any coffee until over an hour later. And when he did, he sat with Melissa under the covers of her bed, neither of them saying a word. Nothing needed to be said. This was not the kind of silence that made Simon nervous, or search for something to say. He could pretty much say whatever he felt like saying and it probably wouldn't matter.

"Hey, Melissa," he said, putting his cup on the bedside table, "did you know the lad that used to work for Danny? The lad they used to call Fivers?"

"Oh yes, I knew Fivers. God – Danny was shitty to him, he really was."

"Yeah, I've heard a few stories about that. The lads told me about the time Danny beat him up."

"Which time was that then? It wasn't just the once you know."

"Yeah?"

"God yeah, and it wasn't just Fivers either. Danny even beat up the poor kid's mother."

"Really?"

It was gut-wrenching to hear that. Especially since Simon was of the opinion that beating up a woman was against the code. Maybe he had the code all wrong.

"Yeah. I remember him coming round here after it happened. He saw me as, kind of, you know, someone to look out for him. He was in bits, Simon, honestly. He didn't know what the hell to do about it."

"Oh right, I didn't know you were friends."

"Yeah, he was a bit shy to begin with, but he started to talk to me after about, well, a few weeks or so!"

"Well, maybe that's because he thought you were as beautiful as I think you are!"

Simon got a kiss for that. And that was no bad thing, because it was one of the cheesiest things he could remember having said for a good few years.

"That was around the time when Danny and me, you know, fell out."

"Oh right – because of that?"

"Yeah. Why?"

"To be honest I got the impression that he, sorry to say this babe, but…like, dumped you."

"He would say that. I really hate that about him. He has to look like he's the man, you know, all the time."

"I suppose his reputation can't tolerate him being dumped."

"Yeah well, he knows what really happened. He even started on me the night that Fivers came round here. He was full of hell. And Fivers, bless him, he tried to stick up for me, but he was too scared of Danny to do anything physical about it."

"What happened?"

"Nothing serious, don't get me wrong. He just pushed me about a bit. Didn't hit me or anything. I think he would have if I hadn't just told him to grow up and stop being paranoid."

"Paranoid? What about?"

"Well, think about it, he turns up here and finds Fivers and me sitting at the end of this bed. He thought we were at it!"

"But you weren't?"

"Of course not! He was only a kid!"

"Well, you never know!"

"I suppose. Anyway, Danny's just like anyone else – if you stand up to them, they tend not to pick on you."

"What did you do?"

"I just shouted back at him. Told him that if he didn't go right there and then, that I would tell the whole of Newcastle that he liked to beat up women. So he left! In fairness, he did get his two pence worth on the way out. He always has to have the last word, so I let him say what he said and then he went."

"What did he say?"

"He said that he liked beating up men even more and he slapped Fivers across the face. Then he grabbed him by the shirt, looked him in the eye and told him he was going to cut him up, said something about finishing the job with his mother as well."

"That's quite a 'last word'."

"Yeah, well, Fivers thought he was a dead man anyway. Tell you what, though. It was weird. You know how he was, like, the kind of 'man with the plan'?"

"Yeah"

"Well, he'd come here, all teary-eyed and scared about what would happen to his mother. And after Danny left, he had such a look of fright on his face."

"Not surprising…"

"Mmm. Anyway, he sat for a while, said nothing. I didn't know what to say to him to be honest. So we just sat there for a while, in silence. And he looked deep in thought, like he was mulling something over in his head. He seemed to totally calm himself down after a while. And then he looked up at me, I'll never forget it. He looked me in the eye and said he was going to have to go. But not just home. It was like he was saying goodbye forever. It was quite chilling to be honest, the way his eyes looked sad but full of hatred at the same time."

"So when did you last see him?"

"Well, that's just it. I haven't seen him since that day. He stayed around for a while after that apparently, but the day before Danny got arrested, he disappeared."

If anyone really *had* set Danny up, Fivers was an obvious choice. Surely it was no coincidence that he disappeared the night before Danny's arrest. Of course, Danny could well have been guilty for all Simon knew. And Fivers might well have simply called the Police the night he left. Perhaps no-one planted the drugs after all.

But there was a more troubling image in Simon's mind. What better time would there have been for *Melissa* to set Danny up? Make it look like Fivers had done it.

There were now a million questions. If Melissa was behind all this, what the hell was he doing here in her flat?! In fact, what on earth possessed him to come here in the first place??!! It was surely the most dangerous thing he could possibly have done. His career was one thing. But, as Simon asked himself, was he in any danger? Did she have plans for Simon that involved anything other than spending time in bed?

Nervously, with a desire to find out more, coupled with a fear that the truth might be best left alone, Simon looked up at Melissa.

"So, anyway, why the hell did Danny beat up Fivers' mother?" he asked.

"Well," replied Melissa, "Fivers had started dealing again you see. Danny didn't take too kindly to that."

*   *   *

It was almost a year now since Danny Walsh had imposed himself on Fivers' life and livelihood. Perhaps it was because of this impending anniversary that Fivers had started to think more about his position. Here he was, a year older, considerably less well off, doing work for a man who did not treat him well, financially or physically. Nothing at all had changed in Fivers' life for the better. His mother was still stuck in the shithole where they lived together. He had not moved on financially. He was helping Walsh and the group by formulating water-tight plans that assured both wealth and freedom from prosecution. And what did he get for it? Hardly any money, for one thing. And he dared not step out of line, for fear of further beatings at the hands of a man that no-one except Kev Wardle would dare to step in and dissuade.

Fivers had an imagination. This made him something of a dreamer. But it also made him the most profitable employee that Walsh had ever had. Why, then, was he so far from being appreciated? He was taken for granted now, as much as he had been on the first day. Walsh would never see this of course. He would say Fivers was lucky not to be still lying in hospital for having dealt drugs in Walsh's town.

He seemed convinced that it was his town. Why did he feel it necessary to be *his* town? Why did he need to be so ambitious? He would never be the richest man in the area – his methods of accumulating wealth meant that he could never show it off anyway. But he had to be in charge. Fair enough, Fivers didn't mind that so much. But isn't a true leader someone who doesn't need to be seen to lead? Should they not enjoy a reputation that relieves them from the need to impose themselves?

In a year, Fivers could have made tens of thousands of pounds. He still had the money under the bed that Walsh had ignored. But the cost of getting involved with Walsh was that he had had to take a huge pay cut. And for what? To be constantly patronised? Never taken seriously? Yes, they followed his plans but only after a lot of persuasion. Why? They were perfect plans. They needed no explanation, at least not to those with Fivers' intelligence. But that was the problem in itself. He was so far above the rest of the group that while his mind wandered off in the direction of genius, the minds of the others remained firmly rooted in a lack of foresight that endangered both them and Fivers, through his association with them.

Where was his life going now? Was he headed for another year of the same? Thinking about it, Fivers could not see how he could expect anything else. Walsh's attitude was not going to change simply because a year had passed. He had his mind made up. Fivers was a nobody, useful for helping to line his own pocket and nothing more.

Fivers took his inspiration not from a need to prove himself to Walsh – it was a waste of time anyway – but from his mother. That's what lead him to deal in the first place. All he wanted was a way out. He didn't need to make millions. Just enough to buy a house in a quiet country village with enough left over to allow him and his mother some level of enjoyment. And not enjoyment in the usual sense. Enjoyment to her meant a new pair of shoes more than once every two years. A restaurant meal once in a while. The things that middle-class teenagers do without a thought. It is perhaps worryingly simple. They had it. Fivers and his mother didn't. That's why he tried any possible way that he could think of to make some money. Then he would be in the league where he belonged. Free to explore his own potential and see where it would go. Like normal people, really.

He had started to really hate Walsh lately. He never liked him much anyway; few people did. But recently, again perhaps due to his employment anniversary, everything that Danny did, or said, had wound Fivers up. Little comments about where he was taking Melissa that night. How much he had spent on various mindless floozies for a night in the sack with them. Money that would be better spent on treating his newest employee, and his infirm mother, for providing a level of covert brilliance that enabled Walsh to be able to have money to spend in the first place.

Within this year, nothing had changed for Fivers. But the whole world had changed for Danny Walsh. He was always at the top of the local criminal chain anyway, but he had established himself almost at a national level now. People came to him from as far down as Sheffield and Manchester. Not all the time, but enough to make his name a well-known one. He had moved away from mere drugs and racketeering and was now involved in large-scale robberies and jewellery trading. All because of Fivers and an imagination that scared those who benefited from it to the point where they felt the need to suppress it by what was an almost systematic patronising.

Keep the kid young. Then he won't get too clever for himself.

It occurred to Fivers one night that it might be interesting to calculate just how much business he had created. How much Walsh had made from him. He would even take off the costs of sorting out the Joe MacRae mess to give an accurate amount. And when he did, the figure he came up with was still in excess of two million pounds. In a year. And all because of ideas that Fivers had had.

The national average wage is supposed to be around fifteen thousand pounds a year. Fivers had barely earned ten this past year. And Walsh had taken seven figures. Fivers knew that he would never himself have been able to turn over that much on his own – he would need people to work for him and he didn't trust anyone on earth enough to allow that. But then, he didn't need that much money anyway. Half a million or so would do it. And then he and his mother would be set for life. He could get a job, like other people do. Maybe do some night classes and one day get to university. Like other people do.

*　*　*

The problem that Fivers faced was that there was no way on earth that even the most creative mind would be able to find a way to work for Walsh and deal for himself at the same time. It would be impossible not to get caught. But it was the only way. He only needed another hundred thousand pounds or so. That would take a year or two, keeping things on a fairly low level to minimise the risk of exposure. Then he could retire with his mother. But he knew he would get caught. Not by the Police – they were easy enough to fool. By Walsh. He was far from being a criminal mastermind in the true sense, but to be fair to him he did have the requisite experience to be able to smell a rat when there was a rat to smell.

Fivers would have to rebuild his old empire from scratch. That meant finding out where the old customers had gone. And he needed to buy some new clothes so he could dress himself in such a way as to pass for a university student. That's always the best place to start dealing. University campuses with hundreds of students, policed by those with no real savvy when it came to anything any more serious than people making a noise or leaving the kitchen untidy.

Fivers was the sole reason for the Firm's growth in the last year. He knew it. They knew it. But Walsh would never admit it. He cursed the fact that he had provided so much. He knew why he had. He wanted to impress, perhaps in the foolish hope that the cut that he received would grow with time. A year in, he was fed up with waiting for a larger cut with each job or deal. He had given Walsh too many chances. Too much respect. If Kev knew what he was thinking, he would have had a fit. But Kev did his own thing. So there should be no reason why Fivers shouldn't.

He cursed himself further. Helping to establish Walsh on a national level had meant that the only options open to Fivers now were rooted in the local drug market. It was clear that he could plan just about anything to perfection. But he had to work alone in order to not get caught. He did think about canvassing a few ideas with Billy and the others, but then he discounted the idea immediately, chastising himself for what was a rare moment of what he saw as foolishness. If they weren't up for it then they would be alerted to the fact that Fivers was planning on doing a bit of moonlighting and they would tell Walsh. No, that was not a good idea at all and Fivers felt like an amateur for having allowed such a runt of a thought to enter his head. He was far too strict with himself. But then, it was that internal self-discipline that allowed for external success.

The drugs market was the only realistic way that Fivers thought he could make money as a sole trader. Of course, there was always the option of chancing the odd blagging here and there, but then you tend to risk an awful lot for the contents of a till. They always hammer you on sentence when you hold up a wine shop or a newsagent. Sticking a gun in the face of a middle-aged woman never looks good to the Judge passing sentence. No amount of personal mitigation can negate the fear caused to someone who didn't deserve it. Besides, eight years is a long time for a couple of hundred quid.

The way to guarantee a decent score is to hold-up a post office van or a private security service van after a few ATM pickups. But doing that alone was almost impossible. There was always a way of course, and Fivers was the man to find it but even so, there was no way that he could risk jail. It was an inconvenience more than anything. Plus, Walsh would know that Fivers had been working for himself and in all likelihood, he would go round and collect the boxes of money from under his bed just to piss him off. That being the case, he would also find out that Fivers had lied to him about how much money he actually had. And on the day Fivers came out of prison, Walsh's temper would probably still be active enough that Fivers would, on release, end up being transferred from one government institution to another, namely one of the city's hospitals.

It had to be drugs. It was the only way. Keeping it small means you rarely get caught. Another foolish thought. Walsh had caught him last year. This time would be different though. Yes, Fivers had neglected to factor in the fact that the snow on the roof had not set due to the heat from his cannabis farm. That was a mistake. But a forgivable one. One from which he had learned to think beyond the usual considerations that a small-scale drug dealer thinks about – police interest and the discreet nature of customers. It had occurred to Fivers, and again he cursed himself for his stupidity, that he had never needed to hoard all of his cash in the first place. He had a fortune hidden under the bed. Was it not better spent on a quantity of drugs that could be sold on at a profit? That would relieve him of the need to set up another farm. After all, it was almost a year since Walsh had found him out. You never know, it might start snowing again.

The question was where to go to buy in bulk. Fivers had a thousand contacts now but couldn't use any of them. The thought depressed him. The only way to make some money was by dealing again. And the only way to do that was to buy in bulk from someone that Walsh didn't know. Did such a person even exist? He had thought it all through, as he usually did. But now he realised that he faced an impossible challenge. Half an hour spent thinking, ruined in a second's realisation.

Back to square one again. Another year of patronising. Oh well.

* * *

A few more depressing days spent in the company of Walsh and the Firm, being asked to formulate ways of covertly getting rid of diamonds was enough to make Fivers start thinking again. And while he sat alone in Vapour a few days later, waiting for a friend of Walsh's to turn up for a meeting, he realised, out of the blue, that there *was* a way of getting a bulk load of drugs to deal without having to risk buying from one of Walsh's many contacts. It was a bit extreme though. Stealing drugs from drug-dealers isn't particularly safe. But as Fivers' track-record showed – the more bizarre the idea, the more likely it was to work.

Walsh had, at one time, bought in bulk from a man named Marshall. No-one knew his first name. Maybe Marshall was his first name, in which case no-one knew his surname. Either way, he was the sort of person who liked to restrict his identity to a level no higher than it needed to be. 'Marshall' and a regularly changed contact number were all people needed, and all he would allow them to know.

Marshall was the representative of a large-scale importer of heroin and cocaine, based somewhere in the South East. He sold large quantities of the substances to anyone with the money to pay for them. There was no partisan element in the operation that Marshall represented – the buyers could easily be rival gangs, Marshall didn't care. And the operation was too well-established for anyone to dare to challenge it, and too covert for anyone to know where to start challenging it in the first place. Fivers set himself the task of overcoming this problem.

The first part of the problem was that Walsh was no longer dealing drugs. He had moved on. Fivers had helped him to do so. Compared to major rackets, drugs tend not to bring in the sort of money that justifies the risks posed by dealing them. Dealing drugs is a step on the criminal ladder, but there are a hundred steps above it. Unless of course you are Marshall, or whoever it was that he worked for. But that group had the advantage of foreign contacts, whereas Walsh did not. If he had, perhaps he would have continued to deal.

This really was a problem, because Fivers could not justifiably make contact with Marshall without Walsh finding out about it. Of course, Fivers could easily make contact with Marshall if he wanted to buy a bulk deal – Marshall didn't care who he sold to. But this was a long term plan – Walsh could never be allowed to find out about it. Besides that, Fivers preferred the idea of stealing the drugs. It meant keeping all of the money he had saved over the years. It was a curious situation – if he was an honest customer, Marshall would know who he was and Walsh might one day learn of his purchase. On the other hand, if he was dishonest, Marshall would have no idea. And Fivers would be spared the bother of having to part with money. That was, after all, the overriding goal.

*　*　*

"How do you know all that anyway?" asked Simon.

"Well, Fivers told me. Like I say, he saw me as someone he could talk to, probably because we both started to hate Danny at the same time!"

Hang on. In bed, with someone who used to be my client's girlfriend, who now hates my client. I must be insane. I need to go right now.

Come on, get up, put your clothes on, make your excuses and leave.

"Simon?"

"Yeah?"

She cuddled up to him.

"Will you go and make me another coffee?" she asked playfully.

No, come on. Time to go. Really shouldn't be here. Should never have started this.

"Please?" she asked, running a hand down his side and kissing him, "I'll do rude things if you do," she smiled.

"Yeah ok."

*　*　*

Fivers had never met Marshall personally. Only Walsh knew him to look at. It was almost like a privilege reserved for those with a background of regular custom. No-one else in the Firm, except Billy, knew Marshall by sight. And Billy only knew him because he had driven Walsh to meet him every so often. He wouldn't have known him otherwise.

Contacting him would be easy enough by phone. But the problem remained that in order for Fivers to be able to steal a load of drugs from him, he would have to find Marshall without his knowledge. Ringing him up wouldn't achieve a great deal. All it would serve to do would be to provide Marshall with another person to suspect when he found out he had been fleeced.

Fivers had no idea where Marshall was based. He could narrow it down to the South East of England, which was no kind of narrowing down at all in essence. There was no clue to be had from the telephone number that Walsh used to contact him either – it was a mobile phone and so allowed no way to pinpoint his whereabouts.

The only thing that Fivers could possibly do would be to try to bring Marshall's name up in conversation with members of the Firm. Maybe that way, he could piece together something. But he thought about it. How long would that take? By the time he found out, Walsh would probably have stopped patronising him. Hell would have frozen over by this point too.

Like most of Fivers' plans, there was a spine of simplicity that formed its basis. It started with a question. Now that Walsh is out of the local drug market, who has taken it over?

Why had Fivers not thought of that before? He cursed himself. All he needed to do was find out who the low-level dealers were. That would lead him to the level above them. And theoretically, he could follow the path right to Marshall.

Fivers smiled to himself. This plan was not a bad one. In fact, it was so simple that he felt slightly bad for daring to call it a plan. Anyone could do it. Kids' stuff. Even the Police would be able to pull this one off, were it not for the fact that make the low-level arrests too early. And then the papers find out. The larger dealers are then nowhere to be found, grateful for the forewarning from those who want to catch them.

The difference here was that once Fivers had taken his first step up the ladder, there would be no publicity. No-one up the ladder would be alerted. He would find Marshall covertly. And, with any luck, he would be able to sneak away just as silently.

★　★　★

"Danny, me mam's not well so I'm just going to go home tonight instead of staying out. Is that ok? You don't need me do you?"

"No, get yourself away – less drinks for me to pay for! Not that you can drink all that much anyway, being a lightweight, like."

It was stuff like that.

"Yeah well, I'm only little," laughed Fivers.

"Alright Fivers, see you tomorrow."

He didn't even tell Fivers to pass on his regards. No chance of a 'get well soon' from this sort of man. In truth, there was nothing wrong with Fivers' mother, but still…

Fivers didn't go home. Instead, he took a bus from the Quayside up to the Haymarket, from where he took another bus up through the East End. It's always darker round there. More chance of finding out what Fivers wanted to know, without being seen to do so.

It was eight o'clock. Fivers walked around for a while, his eyes wide open for the type of person he was looking for. It didn't take all that long. By the Metro station, a small group of lads were sitting, making a little bit of noise, enough to make an elderly person slightly nervous but not nearly loud enough to warrant being moved on by the Police. This shouldn't take too long.

He caught the eye of one of them as he approached them. Usually, it didn't do to stare at someone. But it didn't matter. He was going to talk to one of them anyway.

"Alright?"

"Who are you?"

"Oh, you don't know me, don't worry. I was just wondering if you knew anywhere I could score some tac?"

They looked at each other. They knew. Of course they did.

But they weren't about to give the information away without a little bit more conversation. For all they knew, Fivers could be a copper.

"I just want a tenner's worth," said Fivers, "if you don't know, it's ok I'll just ask somebody else."

They stayed silent.

"Thing is, I don't really want to go around asking loads of people 'cos, you know, I might end up asking some fucking off-duty copper or something daft like that."

One of them laughed. The older-looking one. The Danny Walsh of this particular little group.

"Tell you what, give us a tenner and I'll go and sort you out."

This was a bit of a surprise. And presented something of a problem. Fivers needed to know where the place was. Not only that, but this kid looked like he might well do off with the money.

"I know you'll probably lamp me for saying this, but how do I know you'll not just take my money?"

"Do I look like a thief? You calling me a thief?" said the kid, standing up.

Oh for God's sake. This was Fivers' old life, a life he had left behind a year ago. At least with Walsh, for all his negative points, people didn't start fights over nothing.

Fivers was supposed to be at home. He would be watching the telly with his mother. Either that, or he would be in the club with Walsh and the Firm. Instead, here he was having taken two buses to get to a Metro Station in the East End of Newcastle where he was talking to a few kids he had never met and was in all likelihood going to get jumped by them.

"Do *I* look like a thief?" asked Fivers.

"Eh?"

"Come on, do I?"

"Well maybe you do."

"But am I one?"

"I don't know."

"No, you don't. So I could be, couldn't I?"

"You taking the piss?"

"No, I'm saying that for all you know I might be a thief. You don't know me. And so I don't take offence. So neither should you."

The lad was beaten. Four sentences in one breath tends to have that effect on some people. But he wasn't going to leave it there.

"You might be a copper."

Fivers laughed.

"If I was a copper, do you not think I would have arrested you once you started getting all excited about me calling you a thief?!"

"What for?"

"Coppers always think of something. Do you not know that? Maybe you aren't the right people to ask where to score gear from. Maybe you're just a bunch of kids who hang around the Metro drinking cider. I bet none of you have even been in a Police car in your life! It's alright, I'll go and ask someone else."

"No, no – hang on. What do you mean?"

"Doesn't matter," said Fivers, beginning to walk away.

It is a curious way to offend someone, pointing out to them that they are not a criminal. It offended these lads. They weren't really criminals either. Yes, there was some noise, the odd fight and maybe a few petty thefts between them. But they weren't *criminals*.

"Oi! Come back!"

Fivers turned round.

"I'll take you for twenty quid," said the larger lad.

"OK," said Fivers, bowing his head to conceal a cheeky half-smile.

Fivers walked with the group of lads through a few streets. None of them spoke to him. They seemed satisfied that he was above-board. Fivers would never take someone at face value so readily, but then he was a victim of his own imagination at times. He was always looking out for a conspiracy, a way of getting trapped by people. And that meant *anybody* – the danger of being caught out by someone cannot be ascertained by mere appearance. Only a fool would assume that it can.

The house to which the group led Fivers was normal in every respect. Just one house in a row of many. The older lad knocked on the door and after a twitch or two of an upstairs curtain, it was answered by a ragged-looking kid about Fivers' age.

"Who's this?" he asked, pointing at Fivers but looking at the older kid.

"A mate. Can you do us out a tenner?"

"Aye, come in."

They all walked in.

"Mandy!" shouted the lad.

"What?!"

"Come down!"

"What?!"

"Come downstairs man!"

"Hang on!"

"Fucking women eh?" said the dealer, looking to Fivers with his eyes rolled.

Fivers laughed.

"Aye, nightmare," replied Fivers.

"What's your name anyway?"

"Danny," said Fivers, a testament perhaps to the way he saw himself compared to this bunch of half-arsed chancers.

"Right Danny, stay down here with the lads and talk to Mandy for a bit while I go and sort you out."

Mandy came downstairs, half-wearing a dressing gown which she proceeded to tie up once she got to the bottom of the stairs. You could see one of her breasts quite clearly, though she didn't seem to mind all that much.

As they all sat down in the cramped living room, one of the lads took out a pouch of tobacco and some papers.

"Hey, you're not fucking skinning up here!" said Mandy with a ferocity that perhaps even Mental Kev would have struggled to match.

"Here, I'm just rolling a tab!" said the lad.

"Well, you'll not be here long enough to smoke it. Gary doesn't like people to stay too long. Roll me one while you're at it though."

"Fuck's sake..."

'Gary'. Thanks.

Fivers and the other lads left Gary's house having paid for the ten-pound deal. Fivers kept to his word and passed the older lad a ten-pound note for his trouble.

"Cheers mate, see you later," he said as he and his crew walked on ahead.

Fivers took a mental note of the house number and the name of the street before walking in the opposite direction to find a bus stop, discarding the cannabis down a drain as he walked around the corner. A Newcastle rat would sleep well tonight.

★ ★ ★

It was another week before Fivers went round to see Gary again. He bought a tenner again. In the following weeks, he did the same again. On the eighth week, he asked Gary how much he could get for a thousand pounds.

"Fucking hell, Danny, I haven't got that much to sell you!"

Fivers sighed and Gary went on.

"I mean, I only keep a few hundred quid's worth here in the house. You know, in case I ever get rumbled!"

"Yeah, I suppose."

"Why do you want that much anyway? Looking to start dealing?!"

"No, don't be daft. It just saves me coming round all the time. Anyway, it's better for you isn't it?"

"How's that like?"

"Well, if people come round less, then you've got less chance of being seen by the coppers. They would think it was a bit weird you having loads of people coming round the house all the time."

"Hey, I never thought about it like that."

"You know what I mean? I know what you're saying, you don't want loads of gear left lying around the place, but to be fair, you're risking just as much by selling loads of little deals cos that means loads of visitors coming round and staying for five minutes at a time. If the coppers get wind of that they'll start watching the house."

"Mandy!"

"What?!"

"Come downstairs!"

"In a minute!"

"Mandy! Jesus…"

Fivers laughed. These were genuine people. Genuinely hilarious too.

"What do you want? Oh, hiya Danny," said Mandy, walking into the living room, tying her dressing gown as she did so. This time, she was exposing her other breast, the one with "Gary" tattooed on it.

"Danny was just saying he wants to buy a grand's worth of gear."

"What for?"

"Well, to smoke, you would think…"

"Why do you want that much?"

"Well, it's like I was saying to Gary, it saves me coming round all the time. And more than that, it means it doesn't look as suspicious for you two having loads of customers coming round for five minutes at a time."

"Suspicious to who, like?"

"To the coppers."

"Coppers? Don't be daft."

"Mandy, he's right you know. Remember Cairnsy who got done last year?"

"Oh aye, Cairnsy."

"Well, the coppers were watching him for weeks, that's how they got him."

Mandy twigged at the potential significance of what Gary was saying.

"How do we know you're not a copper?"

Fivers sighed.

"Here, I've been here loads of times Mandy – if I was a copper, d'you not think I would have arrested you by now?"

That seemed to stop her paranoia from growing.

"Aye, I suppose."

"So, Danny, you want a grand's worth?" asked Gary.

"Aye," Fivers confirmed.

"Well, I'll need the money up front, mind."

"Hey, don't think you're leaving a fucking grand's worth of gear in my house!" shouted Mandy.

"Your house?! How's it *your* house?!"

" 'Cos I fucking live here, that's how!"

"Well so do I!"

"Er…I didn't want to cause trouble," said Fivers, failing to hide a smile.

"Don't worry Danny, she shouts at me all the time anyway. *Your* house – fucking hell…"

"OK, look. I'll go – right?" said Fivers, "but here, before I do, I've got an idea."

Fivers always had the ideas. And working for Danny Walsh meant that he was used to having to explain fully to the unimaginative every single idea that he had. So talking to Gary and Mandy was no real trouble to him. Especially since they amused him. Mandy wore the trousers here, there was no doubt about that. And she seemed to disagree with Gary just for the sake of it. That could be helpful. Fivers just needed to come up with a way to make Gary want to do one thing, where Mandy would demand that he do the opposite. A bit of conversational engineering was required. The sort of thing that lawyers do in cross-examination.

"Go on then, what's your idea?"

"Well, the next time you go and see your, you know, supplier or whatever, let me know and I'll meet you somewhere afterwards and give you the money."

"I wasn't going to go 'til next week."

"That's ok. One more week won't make a difference. I'll take a tenner now and meet you next week for the rest."

"You're not fucking driving up there and getting the usual amount, plus another fucking grand's worth Gary! No way."

Thanks Mandy.

"Why not?"

"Cos if you get caught with that much then you'll get fucking hammered!"

"That's true, actually, Gary. Sorry Mandy, that was a daft idea."

"Don't you 'sorry Mandy' me!"

"Tell you what, why don't we both drive up? I'll follow you in the car and you can take me to the supplier. And to say thanks I'll courier your gear back down."

"Thanks for what?"

"Well, for taking me. And for the fact that I'm not buying it from you."

"Fuck off," said Mandy.

"Eh?" asked Fivers.

"What's in it for Gary if you're buying direct from our supplier?"

Fivers raised his palms towards Mandy. Nearly there.

"OK, I see what you mean. Sorry. Tell you what, how about I pay for my gear and give you a hundred quid towards yours?"

Gary looked to his boss to see what she made of the proposal.

"Aye, sounds canny," said Mandy.

Some people are just too easy.

Fivers then realised that he would have to buy a car. Well, it was about time. But nothing flash. An old banger would do. Anything else looks suspicious. He wondered for a second where he might be able to buy such a car. Had to be a cheap one, in case Danny found out. He couldn't be seen to buy anything expensive.

Fortunately, Danny Walsh knew a scrap dealer.

"Do it first. Do it yourself. And keep on doing it."
Tony Camonte in *Scarface,* 1932
(dir. Howard Hawks © The Caddo Co)

Fivers opened the box of fifty pound notes under his bed and removed enough money to keep Mandy from going berserk. He placed a hundred pounds in his pocket, the money he had promised to Gary. He put a thousand pounds in another pocket and went outside to start the car. He called Gary on the way.

"Alright mate? I'm just about to join the A1."

"From yours?"

"Yeah, I'm coming straight from home."

"No bother, I'm about three or four miles up from there."

"OK I'll flash you when I can see you."

The journey to the factory where Gary got his supplies was not a long one. Fivers knew the area but not the specific location of the supplier. So while he could well have eventually found the place on his own, it was no good going around knocking on doors asking for cannabis to the value of a thousand pounds. That might just arouse suspicion!

Gary pulled up outside a factory in an industrial estate in Blaydon. Fivers pulled alongside him and they both got out.

"Here you are mate, a hundred," said Fivers.

"Fifty pound notes eh?"

"Aye, is that ok?"

"Just means I'll have to pay it into the bank that's all. Shops tend to laugh in your face when you try to spend fifties!"

Should have thought of that. It makes no difference at all. But still, should have thought about it.

"Maybe you can get change from your supplier? He'll not mind going to the bank – he'll be paying money in all the time won't he?"

"Actually, mate, the supplier is a woman."

"Oh right."

Gary thought twice about letting Fivers meet the supplier. In fact, he already felt slightly bad for having revealed her gender. He owed her some anonymity. But it didn't matter. As it turned out she came out to meet him anyway.

"Hello Gary. Come in."

"This is a mate of mine – Danny."

"Hi," she said.

"Alright," said Fivers.

They walked inside together. It was a small factory, fronted obviously by this woman, that appeared on the outside to deal in fish products. Fivers wondered whether the workers here knew of the fact that their jobs were merely in existence to give the impression that this factory dealt only in fish, and nothing else. He concluded that they probably had no idea, especially since the woman opened a coded door and led both him and Gary down a flight of stairs into a room with a further coded door at the rear of it.

It was a funny mix of secrecy and welcoming. It made Fivers nervous. The woman had not seemed to be even slightly bothered that he was accompanying Gary on this visit. Maybe it was one of those situations where silent understanding was enough – she didn't need to ask anything at all. If Gary was happy then so was she. He would take the blame should something happen to compromise the operation and until such time arose, he would be taken on trust. Strange to think of such professional courtesy in the world of drugs.

Fivers was soon shown that this was not the case. As the woman turned on the light and ushered Gary and Fivers past her, she closed the door behind them and did not enter the room herself.

"What the fuck?!" Gary said with true fear on his face.

Fivers was a little worried too. It showed by the ferocity with which he banged on the door and shouted to be let out.

"What's going on?!" asked Fivers.

"I don't know. Shit, this is too fucking weird this is."

"I can cope with weird, mate. In fact, I live for weird. What I don't like so much is being locked in a room full of fucking cannabis plants by a woman who's supposed to be your pal."

"Hey I'm as panicked as you, man."

Fivers banged on the door again. For a good while. Fivers' imagination, strong and varied as it was, got the better of him at times, and this was one such time. He imagined being left here. Beaten. Killed, even. He thought about his mother and the look on her face as she was being given the news.

Human nature dictates that people give up after a while in such situations. Fivers and Gary did just that after an hour or so. And they began to wander around the room, looking at the plants and the stacks of cannabis products ready to be moved on. Evidently, there was another entrance to this room via a door at the far end and it was from there that the woman emerged, holding two Polaroids and in the company of a couple of sizeable 'gentlemen'.

"Sorry, Gary. But you should know better than to bring fucking strangers here with you."

This was slightly troubling. Especially since the two men didn't look all that pleased with the situation either. But, what were the Polaroid photographs for?

"Here you go, one each."

The woman passed Gary and Fivers a photograph of each of them standing in a well-lit room, seemingly inspecting a large cannabis crop. She then produced some similar photographs and held them up for all to see.

"Now, I dare say you can guess what these are for," she said.

Fivers knew. And he wondered whether a certain wheel-chair-bound internet businessman was behind this operation.

She looked at Fivers.

"I'm sure you're a lovely kid. Trustworthy, et cetera et cetera. But this is our insurance policy ok? You tell anyone about this place, the Police see these photos and you go down with it."

"Yeah, I understand," he said with a smile.

It seemed as though the MacRae technique was now in wide business use.

"Something funny?"

"No," he said, still smiling, "I'm just happy that you only wanted photos of us – my mind was taking me all sorts of places!"

The woman smiled. This kid seemed ok.

"Yeah well, just remember that feeling if you ever feel like talking to people about this place."

"I won't tell anyone. Not with the money I intend to spend here."

"Oh yeah?"

Fivers handed over the thousand pounds he had in his pocket. He let the woman hold it. Feel the weight of it in her hands.

"How much can I get for that?"

"Quite a bit," she smiled, "come with me."

He followed her over to what was perhaps best described as the loading area, where packages of cannabis products were piled, ready to be dispatched.

"Now what are you looking to buy?"

"Just tac, it's still more popular with fiver-deal-buying little shits than skunk is!"

"True enough!" she laughed, "and it's easier to hide in your car as well. Doesn't take up as much room. You taking it now?"

"Yeah."

"OK, tell you what. Bring your car round the back of the factory, Gary'll show you. We'll bring the stuff up."

"Alright," said Fivers, about to walk off.

"Usual amount Gary?"

"Yeah," he said, handing over two hundred pounds and feeling a little outdone.

★   ★   ★

"Are you pissed off?" asked Fivers, as they were about to get into their cars outside the factory.

"No, why?" asked Gary.

"Well, I kind of put you in the shit there."

"It's alright man, they're just being careful."

"What about the fact that I told them I would be spending a lot of money here?"

"That's your business, mate."

"Seriously? You don't mind? It means I'm not buying from you."

"I don't care, I don't like the hassle to be honest. I just like to take a hundred quid a week or so from this, for me and wor lass at the weekends. Take her somewhere posh for the odd night out you know?"

Fivers understood what that was like. It was a bit like his own situation. Of course, the difference was that he wanted a house and car rather than just the odd posh meal.

"Right, I best be off. Keep in touch, mate," said Gary.

He seemed to have forgotten that Fivers was supposed to be couriering all of the cannabis resin back to Gary's house. It looked like he just wanted to be out of the place.

Fivers had a look around the factory and its car park. He looked beyond it and up towards Blaydon bank. Several nice little spots to sit and watch the factory one night this week. Have a look and see who makes the deliveries. Then try and work out where they come from. Hopefully not be noticed.

★ ★ ★

"So who was the woman?" asked Simon.

"No idea," replied Melissa, "Fivers never mentioned her again after that. He was quite impressed by the way she took his photo though. It was the sort of thing he would do."

"Yeah that sounds like Fivers from what I've heard. Did he find out who was above her in the ladder?"

"Well, he almost didn't bother, cos there was enough in the factory for him to steal, but the trouble was that he was working alone and he wasn't sure whether he would be able to break in or not."

"So what did he do?"

"He went back a few nights later, had a snoop around. He saw a few trucks coming and going. He couldn't see what was being delivered, but at least he saw the logos on the trucks. They had the same name as the factory, but the logos were a bit, you know, fancier, more colourful. The main thing that he noticed, though, was – and this is typical of Fivers, no-one else would spot something like this! – that they all arrived from the North."

"Clever lad."

"Yeah…"

★ ★ ★

A week later, Fivers sat in his car in a layby on the A1 north-bound, with a flask of coffee and a few bars of chocolate, waiting for a truck to pass on the southbound carriageway heading towards the fish factory in Blaydon. This was turning into a long-term plan. For around two months he had gained

Gary's trust. Now it was a week since he had been at the fish factory buying a bulk load of cannabis. How much longer was this going to take? Fivers was a patient kid, but even he was getting restless now. Of course, the passage of time had its advantages – he had long since lost any kind of nervousness about this particular plan. It was bland now, and that would more than likely be of assistance to him when the big steal was ready to happen.

He sat for a couple of hours, watching the traffic and thinking. It was quite tiring. He began to reflect on the way the Newcastle drug market now looked. It was impressive. Unknown to most of the population, Danny Walsh had been the top dog for a number of years. And now he had given it up. But the market was still there to be ruled and for the past year or so, a new organisation had been growing. A group unknown to Fivers, and to Walsh in all probability, was now clearly responsible for a large proportion of the cannabis market. But that was cannabis. There was money to be made there. More customers. Infrequent customers. Not addicts, though. The real money lies in heroin and cocaine. It's quick money – they take your hand off for the stuff. And there's no need to market your product. Purveyors of the best and worst stuff can do equally well.

Who was controlling the market in those substances? Hopefully, tracking the source of the fish factory lorries would lead to the supplier of the cannabis. And that in itself should mean Fivers was led to the supplier of heroin and cocaine too. He couldn't quite imagine the mass importation of drugs in the area to be carried out by rival groups. There must surely be just the one supplier at that level. That said, of course, it didn't really matter – as long as there was enough to steal it didn't matter whose it was. Fivers was working alone and looking for two simple things – a lot of drugs and an easy way to steal them by himself.

Three chocolate bars and two cups of coffee into the afternoon, Fivers saw a fish truck pass him on the other side of the road. That proved his point, he hoped. They definitely arrived from the north. Now it was just a matter of simple time and patience. Sitting at the side of the road, further north up the A1 each time, and watching to see where the trucks came from. Beyond boring. Who else would waste time doing that?

But if the result was right – did the method really matter?

Once Fivers had done this a few times, it became easier because it meant that he was outside of the busy city area of the road. There were six or seven slip roads on and off the A1 north of Blaydon but once past those, it was a good few miles between each one.

Within a month, sitting once or twice a week, Fivers had reverse-tracked the trucks to twenty miles north of the city.

* * *

You come to rely on luck when you work in this industry. Crime is not easy and it is filled with ambitious people whose victims can include their own family and friends. Even the most beautifully laid plans can fall prey to the struggle between those on one level trying to be the person who gets to the next one. Fivers had never needed any convincing about the benefits of working alone, avoiding such a struggle.

Here was Fivers, on his own. He didn't need luck. He was happy enough putting in the hours, working for Walsh for a few months while he found a way of going back to his old drug-dealing ways. But, just because you don't *need* luck, it doesn't mean that you don't sometimes get lucky. Fivers didn't know it at the time, but he was about to get lucky the day that Walsh asked him to make a visit to an inmate of Acklington prison, about thirty miles north of Newcastle. Up the A1, mostly.

He made the visit. He drove up to Acklington in his car, looking out for trucks on the way up, disappointed not to see any before he got to the turn-off that leads to the prison. His task was to speak to one of Kirby's crew who had been caught selling on diamonds that the Firm had acquired from a robbery. All he had to do was go and see him. Sit with him, buy him a cup of coffee and a bag of crisps. Just remind him that his mouth was best kept shut. No need to actually say so. In fact, there was no need to do anything other than have a laugh and a joke with him. Just as long as the lad could associate the fact that he was in prison with the fact that members of the Firm were still there to look after him, as long as he behaved himself. The simple act of sitting with Fivers should remind him to be a good boy.

Fivers came out of the visit and decided to drive back via the scenic route along the coast. Nothing really would be lost to his own plan by driving in the same direction that the trucks drove – he already knew they used the A1. So he decided to drive back the long way. Maybe get some fish and chips somewhere.

He saw the signs for Amble Marina and thought nothing of it. He drove on. Parked up. Bought some chips. Got back in the car and set off to find himself somewhere nice to sit and eat them. A car-park by the beach maybe.

The lucky event wasn't so dramatic that he dropped his chips or anything like that, but Fivers' heart did jump when he pulled into an out-of-the-way car park, switched off the engine, started shovelling chips into his mouth and saw one of the fish trucks pull into the very same car park. This really *was* good fortune. Maybe he was due some in all fairness.

The driver got out of the truck and walked to a rather indistinct-looking car that was parked beside it. He got in, started the engine and made off. This looked interesting. A car-switch. What was that all about?

Fivers chose not to finish his chips as he started his own engine and followed the car back up the road and into Amble Marina.

★ ★ ★

The plan was around three months old now. Three months of gathering information, watching people, making new contacts and, of course, working for Danny Walsh at the same time. And now he found himself parked up in Amble Marina having followed a car there, driven by the driver of a fish factory truck. And it started to make sense to him now. The drugs must come into the Marina, get picked up by car, delivered to the truck, which was then driven to the factory. But in broad daylight? Apparently so. Perhaps the best place to hide really is right under everyone's nose. Let the world go on its merry way while you pick up consignments of drugs. After all, who would dare to do it in public? It just wouldn't occur to anyone – even the Police would probably think it unlikely.

Fivers could see the car he had followed, parked up on the other side of the Marina. Just waiting, or so it seemed. So Fivers decided to do just the same. He watched, for a good while although it seemed to pass quickly since his heart was racing for the first time since the night he met Gary.

After an hour or so, a small boat sailed into the Marina and moored up. The driver of the car got out and walked towards the boat to be met by one of the crew. Hands were shaken, money exchanged. The man climbed aboard and disappeared from view.

Fivers knew nothing about boats. All he knew was, rich people had them and he didn't. The boat in his eye at the moment was a small one, like a mini-yacht. Nothing particularly distinctive about it. Hard, therefore, to pick out from the others when Fivers returned, which he was going to have to do, in order to work out whether this boat tended to deliver just cannabis, or whether it brought in heroin or cocaine. A closer look was required. Maybe that would reveal something distinctive.

He had to look like he was doing something though. What was everyone else doing? Tending to boats. Walking dogs. Fivers had neither and so feared he might look out-of-place. The criminal reaction to something out-of-place is to assume that it relates to the Police and to react by lying low for a while. Fivers didn't want to alarm anyone into doing that. God knows it had taken far too long to get this far already. Maybe it would be better to come back later tonight. Then again, how would he know which boat to inspect more closely? Another stupid idea that Fivers cursed himself for allowing even a moment's consideration.

The answer was given to him. Sometimes you can over-prepare. Better to let things happen and deal with them as they present themselves. Fivers watched as the man disembarked, carrying a large parcel which he placed into his car. He left it there and returned to the boat. He emerged again, carrying another parcel. This was done three times in all. And then four men from the boat joined the man that Fivers had followed. There was a small restaurant on the edge of the marina, and they all went inside. Now he had the opportunity.

But something occurred to him. He didn't know what was in the boxes. Was it all cannabis? What if the three boxes were filled with different products? And he was disgusted with himself for not having thought about whether or not there was more than one fish factory that received the deliveries. The factory that Gary had taken him to had been stocked with cannabis. What if there were other factories that stored other drugs? Why hadn't he thought of that? No wonder Walsh took the piss – Fivers started to believe that maybe he was right after all. Maybe he just wasn't professional enough.

He walked over to the boat. In blue italic script was the

name *Angelina*, written on the side of the hull. Simple as that. He didn't even need to stop, inspect the boat and look suspicious. That was the distinctive feature of this particular boat. But it occurred to Fivers that perhaps stealing from the boat was unnecessary. If what was contained in the boxes was, as he began to suspect, a combination of drugs, then he needn't steal them from here. He had a better idea.

He walked back to his car. There was no way he could steal the unknown man's car. Not here, not in broad daylight. Even if he did manage it, he would have to leave his own car here. No good.

He got back into his own car, watching as the four men emerged from the pub. They weren't in there long. A few minutes. Probably just using the toilet. But then, wouldn't there be a toilet on the boat? Maybe they were just bribing the harbour-master. Maybe he was in on this too. Is there such a person? God knows, Fivers had no knowledge of things maritime.

It made no difference though – if Fivers was right, he would never need to come back to Amble Marina. Unless of course he was mooring his own yacht.

★   ★   ★

Fivers had been to Amble Marina on a Monday. So the plan was easy enough – go back to the car park the next week. The trucks had passed Fivers on the A1 on a daily basis, but then there was no guarantee that they were delivering anything more than fish products on days other than Monday. Maybe that was the delivery day. Best to keep it simple – stick to what you know. Fivers knew that a consignment was delivered on the day he had been to the Marina. It could have just been a load of fish, but then, why park the truck and take a car to the Marina? Plus, you can fit a lot less fish inside three boxes than

227

it would be worth going to collect. No, he was sure that the boxes contained illegal substances. The question was – exactly what? The answer was to have a look.

He had to take a day off from Walsh the next week. Walsh wasn't bothered. There was nothing that he needed Fivers to do that day. Lately, that seemed to be quite a regular thing. It meant a pay cut too. Fivers didn't care. He had his own little scheme to think about. That was going to pay far more.

He drove up to the car park, timing it to arrive around an hour before he had the previous week, just in case. Anyway, it would allow him to have a look around, make sure his idea would work.

He could see the same car parked up that he had seen a week earlier. He pulled up into a space far enough away from the car so as to look inconspicuous and got out to have a look around.

The truck would, if last week was anything to go by, reverse into a space beside where the car was parked. That meant that it was backed up against the small wooden fence that ran along the length of the car park. Behind the fence, the whole way along the car park's edge was effectively a row of long grass, the type that is typical of the sort found on sand dunes. Behind this was a makeshift path, worn away by a thousand dog walkers. Beyond that Fivers saw the land rise to a point behind which he assumed there would be a load of kids playing on the sand dunes.

His mind was on the long grass through which the path was cut. He imagined that, were he to lie there, behind the fence, no-one in the car park would be able to see him. Yes, that would work.

He walked back to the car and waited for the truck to arrive. Within a couple of hours, it did. And the driver got out, climbed into the car and drove away, much as he had done the week before. There was no-one around. Now would be a good time.

Fivers waited a moment, allowing himself a final check to make sure no-one could see him. By his calculation he had at least the time it would take for the man to drive to the Marina, pick up the goods and drive back. That meant around twenty minutes, going on simple travel time and assuming that the man didn't stop for any reason. So twenty minutes was his minimum time.

He got out of the car and walked to the back of the truck. Fivers was no master at picking locks. You don't have to be, really. He was inside within a minute, pulling the door shut and hearing it click locked.

He pulled a torch from his pocket and shone it around the interior of the truck. Boxes were piled up on both sides of the truck in such a way as to create a small path all the way to the driver's end. Fivers knew why that would be. Once the man came back he could stick the boxes of drugs at the driver's end and walk back to the entry-end of the container and use some of the boxes there to fill the gap, making the truck appear filled with fish products. Quite clever.

But for this plan, Fivers needed a decent place to hide inside the truck, but one that allowed him a quick escape from it. What he had in mind was a plan that required every single second between the driver locking the container door, walking back to the cab, starting the engine and driving away, to be used efficiently. Unlike the beautiful twenty minute cushion that he had in order to get *into* the truck, he was talking thirty seconds, tops, to get out.

He moved a few boxes around from one side of the container. He needed to free up enough space to be able to hide behind what would appear as undisturbed boxes. They were large enough that he only needed to get rid of two of them. He could crouch on top of a couple of boxes and pile two in front of him, while the man brought in the boxes from the Marina. It took him almost twenty minutes to create a decent hiding place.

That meant that the man could be returning at any time. Last chance to back out of this now, Fivers.

No way.

Fivers assumed his position in the hole he had created. He had the good sense to switch off his mobile phone too. He waited.

It seemed to take forever. It was just over an hour. He almost forgot why he was there after a while. But the sound of the door being opened alerted him as to the reason for his hiding painfully within the boxes of fish. Now it was time to start concentrating. He heard footsteps come towards him. They stopped as the man came to the cab-end of the container. Then he heard them again as the man left the container and closed the door. Fivers stood up and peered over the boxes behind which he was crouched. he hadn't stretched his legs in an hour and he struggled to stand at first. Just below him was a box similar to those he had seen from a distance the week before. What was in it? Cannabis? Pills? Heroin? No time to check right now though. The door was opened again and Fivers crouched down immediately.

Three boxes were placed at the cab-end. And Fivers began to worry. What if there was a fourth box – how would he know? The time it would take for the man to come back with a fourth box would be around the time it would take to get into the cab and start the truck's engine. By then, Fivers would be stuck inside the truck, alone with the hoard he wanted to steal, but unable to do so.

He had no choice. He had to peer over and look towards the door. The man didn't see him as he stood at the rear end of the container, musing over how best to construct the false frontage. Fivers couldn't think why. He had, after all, two extra boxes he could use – Fivers had given him them!

He began to pile up two sets of four boxes. And as he completed the task, Fivers jumped over the boxes he was hiding behind and picked up the three boxes of drugs. He could see why the man had made three trips from the car to *Angelina* – they were not particularly light boxes – probably filled with things heavy enough to make the boxes appear to be full of fish, on a cursory inspection at least.

He reached the false frontage. Ten seconds.

This was already taking too long. The man would be walking round the side of the truck by now. Shit.

Fivers, in a panic, began to dismantle the false frontage by moving the boxes and placing them behind him. Eight of them. Ten more seconds. He picked up the boxes of drugs and moved them to the door, which he opened as quickly as he could. The man would be inside the cab by now. He threw the three boxes out of the open door and over the fence, unknown to the driver, whose mirrors would not allow him a view of the back of the truck. Ten more seconds.

Fivers could feel his heart beating through his rib cage as he jumped out of the container. The engine was started just as he did so. Thank God. His timing was spot-on. He closed the door – the driver would not hear it – and dived over the fence himself, lying there and peering through the grass as he saw the truck drive out of the car park and up towards the Marina, probably heading to the A1 after that.

This was unbelievable. Military precision. Fivers was proud of himself. And he couldn't help but smile as he carried the three boxes to his own car. A pity he had had to park it so far away, given the weight of the boxes. Never mind. A small price to pay.

He put the boxes into the boot and proceeded to open them. A box of cannabis resin. A box of pills. And, last but not least, a box full of packets of heroin.

Fivers couldn't believe it. There must have been a quarter of a million pounds' worth of heroin in just one box.

Fivers had sold the cannabis that he bought from the fish factory, at a profit of about three hundred pounds. Not bad for just one thousand down. Thirty percent or so. Even better, however, to sell on the stuff he had stolen from the truck. God that was a buzz, that one. Fivers was still excited about it three days later. The trouble was that he was the only person who would ever know. He told Melissa, of course, but then she was the sort of girl you open your heart to. You drown in her eyes while you spout all sorts of things out of your mouth. Before you know it, you've told her everything. And just because she asked. You can fob most people off. But not her. She was one of those girls that make men behave. Ask and she gets. Some girls make requests, others can make demands – simple as that.

In fact, Melissa was one of Fivers' first customers as far as the pills were concerned. There were hundreds of them in the box. And Fivers found them pretty easy to shift. A pocketful every time he went to a club. They went like wildfire. Apparently they weren't bad either. Not that Fivers would know. To him, taking drugs was a mug's game. Decent profits though.

"I can't believe he pulled that one off!" laughed Simon.

"He was a genius, that kid. No doubt about it," said Melissa.

"So how much did he make from the drugs?"

"Thousands. But Danny stepped in, just like he had the year before."

"No way…"

"Yeah, I know. He only sold the cannabis and the pills though. I don't know what happened to the heroin. He's probably still got it, either that or he's sold it on. Either way, he's a rich kid!"

"No," said Simon, "I don't think he has it any more."

232

*"The way I saw it, everybody takes a beating
sometime."*
Henry Hill in *Goodfellas,* 1990
(dir. Martin Scorcese © Warner Bros Inc)

Simon sat with Danny on the fourth day of the trial, as usual, in the cells. Danny looked sick to death of the whole thing as they summed it up together.

"So, basically, what can we ask the rest of the witnesses?" asked Simon.

"Well, you're the Barrister, you tell me," said Danny, though he seemed indifferent as to whether Simon told him or not.

"We can call the rest of the officers if you want to, but we'll just be saying the same thing over and over – 'you set him up didn't you?' And you know what the answer will be."

"Well aye, they'll just say they didn't set me up."

"Right. Then add to that the fact that Whelan produced a photo, which – fair enough – he shouldn't have been allowed to do, but it shows that they didn't set you up."

"Well someone fucking did!"

"I know – but I think the Police have pretty much proved to the Jury that they didn't do it. As for who did, that's another story."

Simon sighed. He hated this bit.

"Danny, I'm going to have to agree their evidence."

"What does that mean?"

"It just means that their statements get read out. Their statements become evidence."

Walsh looked for something to get angry about. But there was nothing, and he knew as much."

"Aye, just have them read out."

"So, the other thing is, I need to know whether you want to give evidence."

"Too fucking right I do!"

That sorted that problem out. He wanted to give evidence. And so he would. If he messed it up, that was his problem.

"Fine, good. OK, now that means you'll probably give evidence this afternoon. Maybe even this morning. Happy enough with that?"

"No bother."

"Are any of the lads going to give evidence for you?"

"Nah. There's no point."

"Well, what about the girl you were with the night they found the car?"

"She's no good."

"Why not?"

"Just fucking leave it will you?!"

Simon backed away defensively.

"I'm sorry, mate, I'm just fucking wound up," sighed Danny.

"It's ok. I'm just trying to do what I can to win the case."

"Not much chance of that though, eh?"

"No."

The morning was taken up with trivial matters. Evidence from scientists who had tested the purity of the heroin. Evidence from Police Officers who had estimated the street value of it. The Jury looked bored. And convinced.

Kate Holloway closed her case just after half past twelve and Simon stood up to suggest that now would be an appropriate time to adjourn for lunch. He wouldn't be getting much lunch though – there was an examination-in-chief to think about. And Danny would probably want a word. As would the lads, no doubt.

"So – what's next?" asked Billy.

"Danny is going to give evidence this afternoon. Then, that's pretty much it. Speeches tomorrow I reckon. Get the Jury out late morning, early afternoon. Might even get a verdict tomorrow."

"What are the chances of that?" asked Stobbsy.

"Pretty good to be honest. I think their minds are fairly well made up."

Six men sighed almost in unison.

"I'm going to go and see Danny for a minute ok? They might let you go and see him. I doubt it, mind, but it's worth a go. Wish him luck and all that."

"Aye, cheers Simon," said Davey.

"Right, Danny," said Simon, as Danny sat down, "not much help this morning. No real damage, though. Just not much help."

"Well, what can you do? The heroin's in my car, it's worth however much it's worth."

"Yeah," Simon sighed, "so, you're giving evidence after lunch. Now I can't really take you through the evidence. You know what I'm going to ask you though. The question is, well, think about what you're going to be asked. They're going to put their case to you, which as you know is that you are at the head of a major drugs operation. Their questions are going to centre around that."

"Aye, I know. They'll try and trip me up."

"Well, yeah, they might. But I'm not too sure. There's not much to trip you up on. I think Kate will go fairly easy on you to be honest. She doesn't want to look too harsh. She doesn't really need to though – she's got enough evidence to convince a Jury. You know that as well as I do."

"Go and get your lunch, mate, don't worry about me."

"OK, I will, as long as you're happy enough. Cos the next time we speak I will be asking you questions in Court."

"No bother."

Simon's mobile was ringing in his pocket, though he didn't know it as he had switched it to 'silent' before going into the cells. You're not supposed to take phones into the cells in case defendants get their hands on them. Not that you can get a signal anyway. He took it out of his pocket quite by chance, just to see if he had had any messages and saw that someone was calling.

"Hi Melissa," he said.

"I just woke up," she sighed.

"You lazy girl!"

"Yeah well I blame you for wearing me out!"

Simon laughed.

"Yesterday was fun wasn't it?"

"Oh yeah. What's happening at Court?"

"Not a lot. Danny's giving evidence this afternoon. You coming down?"

"No, I'm going shopping!"

"Fair enough. Leave me here to work while you go and have fun!"

"Come round after work. I'm going to buy something naughty to wear."

"Er...ok."

"See you later, babe."

What was left to do? Nothing much. Go and finalise examination-in-chief. That meant looking over the trial notes. And Simon hadn't made very many. That was Shelley's job. Where was she?

"Oh, you're here," said Simon, walking into the public canteen, "how come you're not eating through there?"

"I don't really like the advocates' room. Everyone's really boring!"

"OK, can I eat in here with you then?"

"Yeah, pull up a chair."

"Thanks, I'll go and order some food first. Want anything?"

"No, I'm OK thanks."

Simon joined Shelley in the public canteen. They were joined soon after by Billy and Stobbsy.

"Sorry to interrupt, mate," said Billy.

"That's ok – you know Shelley don't you?"

"Aye, seen you in Court."

"We're just about to go over the trial notes, make sure I've got everything for when Danny gives evidence."

"Yeah right – we believe you! Sitting there chatting up young girls! We'll leave you to it, come on Stobbsy."

"Who are they?" asked Shelley.

"They are Danny's friends. And they represent the danger of eating in the public canteen. It might be boring next door, but it's dangerous in here."

"Dangerous?"

"Yeah, you don't want to end up making friends with people like that. They do you a favour and then they remind you about it a few months later. Not good."

"Has that happened to you?"

"Not yet."

"So they think you're chatting me up?" said Shelley after a pause.

"They're just lads, having a laugh."

"So you're not?"

This was interesting. And out-of-the-blue.

"Well, no, I mean, if I was I would probably talk about something better than where is the best place to eat in Court!"

"Oh."

Shelley bowed her head.

"Are you ok?" asked Simon.

"Yeah I'm fine," she replied, with her head still bowed.

"No you're not, what's the matter?"

"Nothing."

More silence.

"OK, well, my boyfriend finished with me."

"Shit. Why?"

"He's been seeing someone else."

"Eh? That doesn't make sense. He finished with *you*?"

"Yeah, he just said he had been seeing someone else and it was over between us."

"Sorry, Shelley, but, you know, is he blind?"

She smiled.

"I know this is the wrong time to be talking about it. We should look over my notes."

"Don't be so professional! OK, you're right. But we can talk later if you want."

"Yeah, we can get some coffee or something."

"OK, let's have a look through these notes."

⋆   ⋆   ⋆

It was a quarter to two. Everyone was due back in Court at two o'clock to continue with the trial. And there had been nothing from Shelley's notes that Simon hadn't remembered anyway. That was not due to Shelley, that was due to the fact that Simon had nothing of any use to put to the Jury – the evidence had not afforded him that luxury. So he robed and walked upstairs with Shelley, ready for the crucial part of the trial. How good a witness Danny Walsh would be was uncertain. He was a professional – no doubt about it. But he could be a live wire at times. If he lost his cool in the witness box then the trial was over. In truth, it was over the minute that David Whelan had produced the photograph two days ago.

"Your Honour, I call Daniel Walsh," said Simon.

Walsh was escorted to the witness box by a member of the security staff. He took the bible in his right hand and read from a card. It was strange to think that someone like Walsh believed in God. Maybe he didn't, it was perhaps just for show.

"Could you state your full name for the Court?" asked Simon.

Walsh paused.

"Daniel Francis Warren Walsh."

What an awful name, thought Simon.

"Mr Walsh, what do you do for a living?"

"I'm a company director."

That's one way of putting it.

"And what does your company do?"

"I own a nightclub."

"Do your business interests involve the trafficking of drugs such as heroin?"

"No, not at all."

"Are you involved in the drugs trade in any way?"

"Some people would call alcohol a drug. I sell that. But that's as far as it goes."

Good answer, Danny.

"Do you own a Jaguar XK8?"

"For now, yes."

OK, don't get clever, Danny.

"And was it your car in which the heroin was found by Officers who gave evidence earlier this week?"

"It was."

"It will no doubt be suggested to you that you owned that heroin."

"Not true. It was definitely not mine."

"Do you know who it belonged to?"

"I have my suspicions. I can't prove anything though."

"In the course of your trade, is everyone that you meet a friend of yours?"

"Mostly. You can make enemies though."

"Enemies?"

"Yes."

"Do you have any enemies Mr Walsh?"

"Several."

"Are you prepared to name them?"

"No."

"Why not? It would help your case wouldn't it?"

"Yes, but I would be in more danger from them than I would from the Court."

"How do you feel about that?"

"Well, to be honest, Mr Silver, it's a very irritating position to be in."

"So, you're not prepared to name names, but are you prepared to describe these enemies? How they came to be enemies?"

"Well, no names. But yeah, I have made enemies of people who I have had removed from the club."

"Why were they removed from the club?"

"For selling drugs."

"On your patch?"

Might as well ask it. Kate will.

"In my club. Not on my patch. I don't have a patch."

"Have you made other enemies?"

"Yes."

"In what circumstances?"

"Being a successful businessman makes you a target for protection rackets."

"Just so we're clear, what do you mean by a protection racket?"

He should be able to explain that phrase quite easily.

"It's a bit like bully-money. People have threatened to burn down my club if I don't pay them a certain amount each week."

"Really? How much?"

"Five hundred pounds."

"Five hundred pounds per week? How much do you make in a week?"

"Well, it depends. I pay myself through the company, which is quite normal, about a thousand pounds per week."

"So really you're only left with five hundred pounds out of that?"

"If I paid up I would be, yes."

"And do you?"

"No way."

"Why not?"

"Why should I? If I get a grand a week, about half of that goes on tax anyway. So I would be giving away just about all of my net income."

Look at the Jury.

"Mr Walsh, you have told the Court that the heroin was not yours. Are you suggesting it was put there by someone else?"

"Well, it would have to have been put there. Like I say, it's not mine."

"Where were you when the Police found your car?"

"I was in bed."

"What had you been doing the night before?"

"Working at the club. Then I went to the house where the Police found my car."

"Was that your house?"

"No."

"Whose was it?"

"I'm not prepared to say. Just a friend of mine."

"A friend who deals in heroin?"

"No."

"Mr Walsh, let's go back, if we can, to the issue of your enemies. Just to sum up what you've said in evidence so far:

you have, over time, made enemies of drug-dealers that you have had ejected from your club?"

"Yes."

"And further, you have made enemies of those to whom you have refused to pay protection money?"

"Yes."

Nicely summed up. Pause.

"Now, you can't say whether or not these people have set you up; like you say, you can't prove it anyway. However, there is one thing arising out of that which you can give evidence about. Have you ever been threatened by any of these enemies of yours?"

Danny laughed to himself.

"Just a bit, yeah."

"Elaborate please."

"Well, when I've had lads chucked out of the club for dealing, they've said they would get me."

"Get you?"

"Yeah, you know, do me in or whatever."

"And has that ever happened?"

"No."

"Have they made other threats?"

"Well, not the dealers. I have only ever been threatened, like I just said, by words like 'I'll get you'."

"People other than the dealers then?"

"Well, I have obviously been threatened by people working the racket."

"What sort of things have you been threatened with?"

"Having the club burned down...being attacked...that sort of thing."

"Have either of those things ever happened?"

"No."

"So, let's recap. You have received threats from those you call your enemies. Those threats have centred around attacks on you, or on your club."

"Yes."

"But none of the threats were ever carried out?"

"Correct."

"Is it conceivable, then, that instead of carrying out the threats that these people made, that someone has exacted their revenge on you by setting you up?"

Kate stood up.

"Your Honour, I don't see how the Defendant can answer this question."

"I'm only asking whether it is conceivable, Your Honour, not whether it happened," Simon replied.

"Well, that's not really evidence is it? There are many things in this world that are conceivable," said Her Honour.

He knew. He had done it on purpose. It's naughty, but why not?! The seed was planted at least. No need to labour the point. Go for some "no" answers.

"Your Honour, I shall move on," said Simon, "Mr Walsh, are you guilty of the offence of possession of heroin with intent to supply?"

"No I am not."

"Was the heroin yours?"

"No."

"Was it in your possession?"

"No."

"Did you know it was in your car?"

"No."

"Could you wait there please – my Learned Friend will have some questions."

Kate stood up. She looked like she was about to enjoy herself.

"Mr Walsh, the heroin in your car was in fact yours wasn't it?"

"No, I've already said."

"Indeed you have. How did it get into your car then?"

"I have no idea."

"If you didn't put it there, then who did?"

"I don't know for sure."

"You mean, you can't invent a name?"

"Someone set me up ok?!"

Don't lose it Danny. That's just what she wants.

"Someone set you up. But you refuse to name them?"

"I don't know exactly who it was. If I said a name then you would just say I can't prove it."

"No I wouldn't. I have to prove the case. Give me a name."

Danny looked at Simon.

"I think it was a lad who used to work for me."

"What is his name?"

"Fivers."

"Fivers? That must be a nickname is it?"

"Well, yeah."

"And what is Fivers' real name?"

Shit.

"Adam."

"Adam? Adam what?"

Oh God.

"I don't know his surname."

"And yet he worked for you?"

Danny, stop digging.

"Yes, he used to do work for me."

"What sort of work?"

Shit.

"He worked, you know, in the club."

"You employed him?"

"Yes."

"Yet you can't remember his surname?"

"No, I can't."

"But surely you must have interviewed him for the job?"

"Yeah, but you interview a lot of people."

"But you don't employ them all do you? Otherwise there would be no need to interview anybody."

"No."

"As an employer, you must have paid part of your employees' national insurance contributions. You don't evade your tax duties do you?"

"No, I run a tight ship. It's all completely above board."

"Mr Walsh, did you pay Adam, or Fivers as you call him, weekly or monthly?"

"Er, weekly I think."

"You think?"

"Weekly. Definitely."

Careful, Danny.

"How much did you pay him?"

A bit of mental arithmetic – multiply the national minimum wage by 40. Then add a bit on. Hurry up. They're waiting for an answer.

"About £180 a week."

"And do you use your own payslips?"

"Yes."

"Won't those payslips have the employee's name on?"

"Yes, they do."

"So how come you don't remember Adam's surname?"

"I don't get to see the payslips."

Oh shit. Now I have to say who does get to see them.

"So you have someone who is in charge of human resources?"

"Kind of."

"And what's their name?"

Silence.

"Mr Walsh? Their name please."

"I'm not prepared to say."

"Really? Why not?"

"Because this is just a fucking joke! What's this got to do with heroin? You're just trying to wind me up!"

And succeeding, Danny. That's why she gets lots of work. She's brilliant.

"Mr Walsh, I will warn you once, and only once. Do not use language like that in my Court, do you understand?"

"I do, Your Honour. Sorry."

"Very well, now answer the question please."

Danny sighed.

"OK, I don't know Fivers' real name. I paid him in cash, out of the till."

"Thank you Mr Walsh," said Kate, "an honest answer. From a man dishonest enough to evade tax liability by paying cash-in-hand."

Harsh. But Simon would have done the same.

"So, now that we've finished our little detour, why is it that you say that Fivers set you up?"

"Because we fell out."

"You fell out? How?"

"We just fell out, ok?"

"That must have been some falling out. Enough to make him spend a quarter of a million pounds on heroin, place it in your car and call the Police, thereby losing the heroin. Do you honestly expect anyone to believe that?"

Danny sighed again. It did sound ridiculous.

"All I know is, someone put it there. It might not have been Fivers. Maybe it was someone else."

"Someone wealthy enough to waste a quarter of a million pounds on heroin to set you up with?"

"Well, I think the Police had something to do with it."

"Yes, Mr Silver mentioned that a few times when cross-examining the Officers. This brings me to my final point you see, Mr Walsh. You will no doubt remember seeing a photograph produced by Sergeant Whelan on Tuesday?"

"Yes."

"And that photograph showed your car with heroin inside it?"

"Yes."

"But the door was closed and the windows were all intact weren't they?"

"Yes."

"Mr Walsh, how do you explain the fact that a quarter of a million pounds' worth of heroin was found in your fully intact car?"

"I can't explain it."

"There's no way to explain it is there?"

"Someone could have used my key."

"Could they?"

"Possibly."

"When? In the middle of the night?"

"Yes."

"Where were you that night again? Oh that's right, you refused to say."

"I don't want to say where I was. I was just with a friend of mine."

"So, you were with a friend, and while you were there, someone stole your key, opened your car door, placed the heroin inside, locked the door, returned the key to you and then called the Police. That's your evidence is it?"

"Well, it would make sense."

"Mr Walsh, that's the very thing that it doesn't do. It makes no sense at all."

Silence.

"The key to your car must have been in the house with you then?"

"Yes."

"So, someone must have broken in and stolen the key while you were asleep?"

"Yes."

"And then returned it to you."

"Yes, they must have."

"Mr Walsh, the only person who could have done that would surely be this friend of yours."

"No way, she would never do that."

"So your friend was a woman then?"

"Yeah ok, Sherlock fucking Holmes, I was at a woman's house."

"Mr Walsh, you are in contempt of Court," pronounced the Judge.

"Am I? Oh well, not to worry."

Now he is being childish. That won't help at all.

"So, Mr Walsh, who was this woman?"

Oh God don't say it. Please don't say it.

"She's called Melissa. She was my girlfriend at the time."

Shit.

"So, don't you think Melissa could have set you up?"

"Maybe."

"Is she wealthy?"

"I don't think so."

"Is she a drug-dealer?"

Remember the code.

"No, she's not."

"So, how would she get access to that much heroin?"

"I don't know."

"Let's recap Mr Walsh. Someone set you up. But you don't know who. What we do know is that it must be someone with enough money and knowledge of the drug market to gain access to a quarter of a million pounds' worth of heroin. Your car was not tampered with in any way, we can see that from the photograph. And so the only way you could have been set up was by someone breaking into Melissa's house while you both slept, planting the drugs and then returning the key to you."

"Yes."

"Mr Walsh, there is only one sensible explanation for the presence of heroin in your car isn't there?"

Silence.

"The heroin was yours, Mr Walsh. You are a major player in the drugs market and you were going to sell the heroin that you were carrying in your car, weren't you?"

"No."

Simon had no re-examination. The Judge had no questions. What would be the point anyway?

* * *

Walsh was going to be convicted of the charge against him. There was no doubt about that. He had made a complete idiot of himself when he gave evidence. No-one in their right mind would believe his ridiculous theory. It just made him look stupid. Like he was floundering, clutching at straws. Trying anything he possibly could to explain away the inexplicable. And Simon was left trying to defend the indefensible. No-one could win this one. No-one at all, not even the best lawyer that ever existed. Making a threatening phone call to the Jury was probably not a bad idea in the circumstances. There was no other way out. With hindsight, Simon could almost see the sense in it. But he still didn't know who had made the call. Not that it mattered any more.

Simon's mind was not on the case now. It was elsewhere. It was with Billy. With the lads. With Melissa.

* * *

Four days ago, Simon's life had changed. He had been tempted. And he had succumbed. It is an attractive life. Most people would cave in the circumstances. But he knew it was time to stop. When Danny had spoken Melissa's name in the witness box, it had given a final sense of reality to that which he had justified. He was not a man who socialised with other men in a club. He was not a man who had just met a woman and was exploring his feelings for her. He was a lawyer who had socialised with his gangland client's friends. And spent the night with his ex-girlfriend. It had to stop.

Simon walked into Vapour around 7 o'clock that evening.

"Oi Oi Simon!" shouted Houdini.

"Alright lads?" said Simon, sounding as glum as he felt.

"What's wrong with your face?" asked Terry.

"Well," he said, sitting down, "I had a bit of a reality check this afternoon."

"Oh aye? What – when Danny said that stuff about Melissa?"

"Yeah."

"Are you going to call it off with her then?" asked Billy.

"Why?" asked Davey, "do you fancy your chances, like?!"

"Fuck off Davey," said Billy, giving Davey the finger.

"Lads, look, this is serious," said Simon.

"Oh, go on then," said Davey.

"I'm a bit freaked out to be honest."

"Because of what Danny said?"

"Not what he said, more that he said her name, you know?"

"Not really, mate."

"Well, it made it all a bit more real, like. It felt wrong."

"There's nowt wrong with meeting a bird, Simon. If you weren't representing Danny then it wouldn't matter would it? So why should it matter now?"

"For that very reason. Because Danny is my client."

"But he's not bothered."

"I know. But…"

This was going to cause offence.

"…it's just, like, a bit dirty. Me hanging about with my client's mates. Seeing his ex."

"Dirty?"

"I know I know, dirty is the wrong word. You're all really nice people. But I don't want to get myself into trouble. And I don't want you to get into trouble."

"How would we get into trouble?"

"It might look like you've got me on a retainer or something. You know what the coppers are like, they'll make something out of nothing."

"You worry too much."

Terry cut in.

"He's right, lads."

"Oh, I might have known you would have something to say!" said Stobbsy.

"No, think about it. We don't want to draw attention to ourselves. Especially if Danny goes down."

"What do you mean?" asked Houdini.

"I mean, if people see us knocking about with Simon they'll wonder what the fuck's going on. And if they start investigating us all then we might find ourselves in a bit of a pickle."

"But we're doing nowt wrong!" said Davey.

"Not with Simon, we're not. But what I mean is, they might start looking at other, like, aspects of our business."

There was no arguing against that. Thankfully.

"I should probably go, lads," said Simon.

"Aye, whatever," said Billy.

Simon stood up.

"I'm not going anywhere until you shake my hand, Billy. I want no hard feelings."

"Simon, just get yourself away eh? You wouldn't want to be seen shaking my hand would you?"

"Billy, don't be like that. It's for the best."

"Aye right. See you tomorrow for the verdict."

Simon had never seen Billy like this. He seemed genuinely upset.

"Thanks for everything, lads. I've had a good laugh this week."

Silence.

"OK then. See you all tomorrow. Fingers crossed eh?"

Silence.

Terry stood up.

"Simon, it was nice to meet you. We'll see you tomorrow mate."

Hands were shaken. And Simon left. Seconds later, Billy Cameron's mobile phone rang.

★   ★   ★

"Hi, it's Simon," he said, into the intercom.

"Come up!"

Simon walked into Melissa's flat. For the last time. She didn't know that yet. She welcomed him at the door with a kiss, which he reciprocated for a second or two, before breaking off and walking into the lounge area.

"I heard something about you today," he said, without looking at her.

"Oh?"

"Yeah. 'Oh'. It turns out that you were with Danny on the night he got set up."

She looked down. There was no explaining it.

"Sorry. I didn't think you would understand if I had told you."

Simon sighed.

"I wouldn't have understood. You're right. And you were probably right not to tell me. I might never have found out."

"Have I messed things up?"

"No, *you* haven't. But, Melissa, things are fucking messed up."

She covered her eyes with her hand and rubbed her eyebrows. Simon approached her.

"Hey, don't cry."

He put a hand on her arm and she wasn't dramatic enough to brush him off.

"I'm not going to see you again am I?"

He sighed. And tears formed in his own eyes as he realised what he was about to do.

"This is really killing me. I really don't want this to end."

"But it *is* ending isn't it?"

"Yeah," he sighed, tears starting to build up.

They embraced for the last time. And, as had happened before, it didn't stop there.

It was an hour before Simon left, got back into his car and was about to start the engine.

His mobile rang.

"Simon? It's Billy."

"Billy. Look, no offence mate, but we said…"

"I know, I know. But I had to tell you. You'll never believe who's just rang me."

"Who?" asked Simon.

"Fivers," replied Billy.

"No…really?"

"Seriously. He rang just after you left. Been on the phone about an hour."

"What – just catching up?"

"Not exactly, mate. He rang to tell me he's been keeping an eye on the trial. Now that Danny has finished giving evidence, he thought he'd give me a bell."

"Why now?"

" 'Cos now there's absolutely nothing you can do about the fact that he is the one who set Danny up."

So there it was. Confirmation of something that Simon had long suspected. In part at least. But there were still questions. And he asked them.

"How? Why? Was Melissa involved?"

* * *

Fivers was by no means an empire builder. He had little ambition to speak of. A house for his mother and him to live in. A car that didn't need to much persuasion to start when you turned the key. To be able to eat in a restaurant without searching through newspapers for a money-off coupon. Walsh didn't have to worry about things like that. He had several houses. A villa in Portugal. Lovely car. And he ate out all the time. Fivers didn't need any of that. Just enough to be comfortable.

He was, despite his active, questioning mind and startling imagination, still a human being. He was as fallible as anyone. And he was as tempted by the promise of money as any other person would be. And when he sold the cannabis he had stolen, making almost ten thousand pounds from it, he was eager to get rid of the MDMA that came with the haul. Really eager. And even he got sloppy. Stupid really. Because Danny Walsh found him out easily.

He had, as he had planned, sold most of the cannabis at the university halls of residence. Easy money, lots of customers, little chance of being sprung. It might even have been worth buying some more in bulk. Make another few thousand, less the cost of purchase this time (since stealing from the same person twice is never a good idea).

But there were still tablets to be sold off. And they were far more likely to make Fivers even more money than the cannabis resin was. These days, people prefer to be stimulated rather than sent to sleep. And rather than keep it simple, Fivers entered into the 'right here, right now' mentality that swallows up most dealers and goes against Fivers' own better judgement. Quick money is the most dangerous kind of money. It has a habit of disappearing shortly after it is made. But that's what he wanted. And that's what he got.

He faced a small problem. People don't buy ecstasy tablets for a quiet night in. And so Fivers' ecstasy customers were going to have to be different people to those who bought tac from him. It was a tough situation for Fivers. His boss owned the very sort of place where he could shift the tablets easily. But right under Walsh's nose? That was madness, surely. Or was it? Marshall shipped in bulk loads of drugs in broad daylight. That seemed to work. Provided Fivers wasn't watching, of course. So why not deal in Vapour? Where else could Fivers justifiably go in town?

The answer should have been to sell them to Gary and Mandy. They would have bought them. It would have meant getting rid of the tablets for less money, but at least they would have been shifted. And it wasn't as though Fivers had had to pay for them.

But, faced with the happy prospect of lots of money, very quickly, Fivers came up with the idea to sell the tablets in Vapour. That way, he would get five pounds for each of them – which made him smile given his nickname – rather than two or three quid each if he sold them in bulk. Because the box he had stolen contained thousands of tablets. He stood to make at least thirty grand from them. Not bad for a nil-down investment.

It was going to take a while to shift that many tablets though . Patience being the now-departed virtue that it was, Fivers got restless. Once he got going, he was selling up to a hundred tablets every night. People tend to buy up to five at a time for themselves, mugs that they are, and with a capacity of twelve hundred people, Vapour was a good place to find twenty customers in an evening. It was, for a while at least, also a good place not to be seen dealing.

It was a real buzz, selling in the club. Fivers would wander off to the toilet, leaving the Firm sat at a table, and sell to a couple of people at a time. The place opened at nine and closed at two. Five hours. Lots of trips to the toilet. Easily shifting fifty tablets a night. His record was one hundred and twelve.

But still, it was taking time. He didn't like to sell every night, he still had sense enough to realise that to do so would be too risky. But thinking about it, it was going to take months to shift the tablets. That was too long. It had taken months to get the boxes. And if it was going to take months to sell it, there was just no point. Thirty grand was all well and good, but not if it took almost a year to earn.

The answer, of course, was to start selling the heroin. That was the obvious choice. But the crazy thing was, Fivers was dying to get rid of the tablets first. As though he would somehow fail if he didn't sell everything that he had stolen. Would it not insult his genius to fail now? Would he forever chastise himself for it? Probably. But he should have known that given the choice between making money and being caught, there really is only one option. He was just too blinded by pound signs to recognise that the choice existed.

Pills first. Not long now. Just step up the frequency. Increase the quantity. Then it's time to dig the heroin up from the side of the road where you hid it the night you stole it from Marshall.

*   *   *

You can't exactly advertise in the local press when you sell drugs for a living. You rely on quality, availability and word of mouth. That's what keeps existing customers coming back. And it's what attracts new customers. Unfortunately, word of mouth can backfire.

"Fivers, mate," said Walsh, on one perfectly normal night.
"Yeah?"
"A word."

The Firm knew what that meant. And they all felt that Fivers deserved what was coming. But *only* Fivers deserved it. Anything else was just plain evil.

Walsh beckoned to Fivers to follow him into the office behind the main bar in Vapour. He could sense why he was being asked to speak to Walsh in private. The Firm tended to have no secrets.

"I need your advice, mate," said Walsh. He was over-using the word 'mate' and it was fairly transparent as to why.

"What about?"

"Well, the thing is, right, I've heard a rumour. You know how it is, things get said, bandied about. Most of the time it's just bollocks, but it's worth checking just to be sure."

"OK."

"Now, I overheard something last night when I was walking back through here to use the phone. It was pretty noisy, so I suppose you could say that I can't be sure what I heard, and maybe I would agree, but basically I heard this lad ask another lad whether he knew if he could score a couple of e's."

Shit.

"Yeah? In here?"

"Yeah. That's what I thought, mate. There are no drugs in here. We don't deal in drugs anymore, us lot. Anyway, I thought to myself, come on Danny, this lad's probably just here for the first time and he wants to know if he can buy a couple of pills. He wouldn't know that I want to keep this place completely fucking drug-free in case the coppers do a raid. You know, what with them dying to find something to do me for."

"Well, yeah. He probably was."

"Aye. But then, you see, I heard what the other lad said. He told the first lad that he would definitely be able to buy that sort of thing in here. In fact, it turns out that the first lad bought pills in here all the time."

"Fucking hell eh?"

"Precisely. I was a little bit annoyed about that, Fivers. So what I did was, I introduced myself to the lad who was being asked about pills and I told him I needed to speak to him. He looked a bit startled, like, but he followed me through into here. Absolutely no fuss, like."

"Did he? What did he say?"

Oh God. What did he say?

"Well, he didn't say much to start with. Then, Fivers, I got a bit excited about the whole affair, you know? Started to ask him the same question again and again, louder each time. 'Who is selling pills in my fucking club?' I asked. He didn't know the lad's name. But he did give me quite a good description. I was a bit surprised, like, when I realised who it was."

"Who was it?"

"Turn out your fucking pockets, Fivers."

Shit.

Fivers grudgingly opened out his trouser pockets, and those of his jacket. There were three small plastic bags full of pills. Danny's face was getting redder by the second.

"How long's this been going on?" he asked.

"Not long, Danny, honestly."

"Honestly? That's a funny word to use, Fivers. You made me a promise last year, you've broken it, and now you want me to believe that it's fucking *honestly* not been going on for long?"

"I'm telling you the truth."

"And I want to believe you, Fivers. But how can I? When you've betrayed me like this?"

Why was he being so calm? For once, Fivers was not being patronised. He was being talked to on Walsh's level.

"Betrayed you? That's *you* using a funny word, Danny."

"Oh aye? And how's that?"

"Because for the last year, all you've done is fucking put me down, all the time. Everything I do, everything I say, you all just take the piss! And how much money have you made because of me? Eh? Half a million? A million? And what have I got for that? Eh? Fuck all. Ten grand and the piss taken out of me all the fucking time!"

"Whoa, hey, calm down!"

"No I fucking won't! It's time this got said. I'm sick of it! Sick of all of you!"

Danny seemed to be taking it in. That didn't feel right at all.

"I didn't know you felt like that."

Walsh's calmness began to rub off on Fivers now.

"Well I do," he said, "and it's long overdue being said. Danny, I'm sorry, but I just don't feel like part of the group these days you know? I didn't even feel all that bad for dealing in here. I know that's a shitty thing to say, but you know…"

"I know *now*. I didn't realise you felt patronised."

"Yeah, well."

"Where did that little outburst come from eh?" he laughed.

"Pent-up frustration, Danny. I'm sorry."

"Hey, if it needed saying, it needed saying."

Walsh handed Fivers the bags of pills.

"Now, look. Go and flush these down the toilet. And don't deal in here any more. You can keep whatever you've made, cos in fairness there's no harm done. But you have to realise, mate, I can't have drugs being sold in here. You know how it is, the coppers would love that. Any excuse to shut me down. Do you know why?"

" 'Cos they hate you."

"Well, yeah, they hate me, but there's another reason."

"What?"

"If I lose the club, how am I supposed to make a living?

Dealing? Blaggings? They know that's what I would have to do. And they would be ready and waiting."

"Oh. I hadn't thought of that."

"It's ok. You'll learn. Now go and get rid of these pills."

"OK. Thanks, Danny."

"That's alright. Now, I'm taking Billy and Stobbsy on a job in a few minutes so just stay with Houdini and them and we'll see you when we get back."

"OK."

Walsh walked back through into the club and over to the table where the Firm sat.

"Billy, Stobbsy, we're going out."

"Where?"

"Never mind where, just come with me. Now, lads – come on," he said, walking towards the door.

Fivers emerged from the toilet, where he had duly got rid of the pills. The lads were surprised to see him in such good health.

"Fucking hell, Fivers, dealing under his nose, you must be mental," said Terry.

"Aye, I thought you were supposed to be clever," said Houdini.

"Yeah, well. I need the money."

"We could all do with money, Fivers. But shitting in your own nest isn't the way to do it," said Davey.

"Yeah, I know," said Fivers, with a sigh. It was a false sigh. He didn't really mind anyway. There was always the heroin. And he wasn't going to be selling *that* in the club.

★   ★   ★

When they returned to the club, Billy and Stobbsy looked almost shaken. They said nothing. Walsh looked his normal self though. In fact, he seemed to be in quite a good mood.

260

Fivers was surprised to be told that he could go home for the night, especially since he had, as Davey had suggested, soiled his own doorstep by selling pills in Walsh's club. He had expected much more trouble. He should have known better than to assume he would get away unharmed. And when he got home and walked through the front door, he found his mother lying face down on the living room floor.

"Mam!" he shouted, running over to her.

There was blood all over the carpet and as he turned her lifeless body over to face him, he almost didn't recognise her. Her eyes were already dark purple and puffed out. Her cheeks were bruised, her lips cut. Her whole face was covered in blood and her throat was bruised to the extent that he could make out finger marks around her neck where she had been grabbed and held.

"Mam no! Mam!" he kept on screaming.

This was his first taste of death. His first taste of the harshness of his employer's true way of life. He had seen it before of course. Helped to arrange it in fact. But it didn't matter when it was someone else taking a beating. He hadn't even thought about Joe MacRae since the night that Kev had cut off his legs. It didn't matter. That was just a way for Fivers to gain recognition. The lad who pissed himself in the Court toilets that time. That didn't matter either. They weren't *people*. They weren't Fivers' own mother.

It was something upon which Fivers prided himself, the fact that real villains don't make threats. They take action. Walsh had warned Fivers last year. And he had taken no notice of the warning. But he was not warned again. Action was taken. He cradled the result of that action in his arms as his tears dropped onto her face, diluting the almost-dried blood. He wished for one last warning now. Just one more. He wouldn't do it again. A really powerful wish. Like it was the only thing that would ever matter.

It was time to make a phone call now. But he had no idea what to say.

"Which service please?"

"Ambulance."

It arrived within ten minutes. And they took her away to accident and emergency. Apparently she was still alive. Only just.

★   ★   ★

It was a big step for Fivers to walk into Vapour a week later. He had not been in contact with the Firm for days. And they had not contacted him. Instead, he had stayed at his mother's side in the hospital. Talking to her and hating himself.

Fivers' mother spoke to him on the third day. He cried his eyes out. He was beyond sorry. He knew that he had effectively done this to his mother. He was responsible for her injuries. He was the reason she was here.

She remembered what had happened. Two men had held her down. She had seen one of them before. There was a third man, one who had shouted at her a year ago. He was the one who had beaten her while she was held down. She remembered his face. The look in his eyes. The passion for the job he was doing.

Fivers walked into the club. He wanted to convey the impression that he felt that nothing had happened. That he didn't care. That would be the hard-man thing to do. But Fivers was not like that. There was a reason why he never felt as though he fitted in. He *didn't* fit in. These were not his sort of people. There was no emotion. They were robotic. That's what made them successful in the industry. The minute you start to care in the criminal underworld is the minute you should look for other employment. The only emotion permitted is the passion to make more and more money. If mutilating someone is the way to safeguard your earning potential, then that's what you do. That's all it is. Business.

He could not convey the impression that he wanted to. They could all see it in his face. Everyone in the Firm knew what had happened. They all felt terrible about it. All, that is, except Walsh who couldn't have given a shit. Fivers was getting clever. A liability. He had to be taught a more firm lesson than merely taking some of his money and stopping him from dealing. Hopefully, this was a lesson he would have learned.

As he pulled up a chair, sat down at the table and looked at the members of the group, trying his best not to appear as though he cared, his eyes started to glaze. He looked Walsh in the eye. And he reacted to his employer's arrogance. He imagined him there with Billy and Stobbsy. Straddled over his helpless mother's body, smacking her over and over until the blood covered her eyes, preventing her from seeing any more of the numerous blows that continued to be delivered to her. He could no longer hide his emotions.

"What's wrong with your face?" asked Walsh, smiling.

"Nothing."

"Look at you, man, you fucking big girl's blouse! It's not like she's fucking dead!"

He was beyond credibility. He really didn't care at all.

"Howay Danny, man, there's no need for that," said Terry.

Walsh looked at Terry.

"The little fucker needs to learn. And you should know not to question me."

Terry got up.

"I'm going to get a drink," he said, walking over to the bar.

"She nearly died, Danny," said Fivers.

It was an odd sensation, talking like this to the man who had almost killed his mother.

"Aye, that's right, she *nearly* died. But she didn't die did she? So cheer the fuck up."

Fivers looked at Walsh. He was thinking as he did so. He wanted to punish him for what he had done, but he knew that to do so, in the way that he wanted to do it, would be to put an end to his job, the club, the lads. If Danny was dead, there was no Vapour, there was no reputation, there was no money. He had kept himself so far above everyone else that he was able to maintain his position as the backbone of the operation. It could not exist without him. He knew too many people. And those people would never consider the others to be anywhere near as capable as he was. The Firm would die with Danny. But, with images of his mother's bloodied face flashing in his head, Fivers simply didn't care one little bit. It was as good as over for him now anyway.

As he sat staring at Walsh, a million ideas floated around in his head, all fuelled by the hatred he felt for him. There are a million ways to avenge a grievance. The trick is to find the one that hurts the most. And for the longest time.

Fivers had become very profitable to the Firm. Not because he was a hard man. Not because he had contacts. But because he had imagination. His plans allowed an element of surprise and unpredictability. And they never got caught. He was a genius. A true villain needs to be strong, feared, creative and cunning. It was as though his lack of strength and his inability to engender fear had been compensated by his powerful mind. Newcastle had never seen anything like it.

He looked at Walsh for a few more seconds. Studying him, almost. His face, his ears, his hair even. As though he was mentally feeling around to know every facet of the man who he was about to destroy. He got up, made his excuses and headed for the door. There was work to be done. There was a spade somewhere in the house. He had left it there on the night he buried the box of heroin that he had stolen from the truck.

★ ★ ★

The plan was an easy one. Danny's car had remote central locking which, when activated, turned off the alarm. All Fivers needed to do was find out the frequency of it. Then he could match it, open the car undetected and gain access to it. It would be immobilised. But that didn't matter – he wasn't going to move it.

Fivers needed two things. First of all, he needed a device to work out the frequency. Second, he needed to be in Danny's presence when he got in or out of his car. Danny didn't need to know he was there. In fact, that would make it more enjoyable.

Fivers had such a scanner anyway. Perhaps that's where the idea came from in the first place. They are easy enough to get hold of. All he needed to do was wait until later that evening, until Danny went round to Melissa's flat. He would drive there, lock the car, and go upstairs for the night. That was what he did most of the time. Pretty much any time he wasn't out with someone else.

Fivers spent the afternoon at the hospital. His mother had been there for a week at this stage and she was almost ready to be discharged. There was very little that the doctors needed to keep her in for anyway. Prescribe her some painkillers and let her go home. That's just what they did later that afternoon. It took a while to leave the hospital. Fiver's mother was fairly unsteady on her feet to begin with, and he could sense that she was enjoying the pampering she was receiving. But he needed her home. Right now.

Fivers drove home with his mother, made her something to eat and then told her to rest while he packed her things for her. She didn't understand why. It took some explaining. She was surprised to find out how much money Fivers had secreted upstairs and it was perhaps this wealth that made her take him seriously enough to do what he asked.

He left the house just after midnight. The city centre has a habit of crawling with Police at that time of night and that was the one thing that worried him. But no-one noticed when he pulled over in a layby on the A1 and carried the spade up to the place where he had buried the heroin. Well, it was dark. And for now at least, he was not in the city centre.

He unearthed the packages and walked to the boot of his car, removing the spare tyre from its housing and throwing it into the bushes at the side of the road. In its place he packed the heroin and covered it over with the wooden flooring of the boot. With any luck, the plan would not fail due to him getting a puncture on the way to Melissa's flat. That would be the ultimate insult.

He drove without a hitch to Melissa's flat and waited for a while outside. Danny never stuck to a particular arrival time. Perhaps he liked to keep her waiting, so she would appreciate his arrival all the more when he did show up. Fivers hated the way in which she displayed this appreciation. She was far too good for the likes of him. But this was not about her. If she was stupid enough to be with Danny Walsh, that was her business. This was about revenge. It was about Fivers' mother.

He didn't even need to get out of the car to activate the scanner. He parked around the corner and simply left the scanner switched on, secreted in the hedge outside the flat. No-one would know that it was there.

Walsh arrived and went inside. Fivers got out of his car and walked towards the flat. He picked up the scanner, walked over to Danny's car and activated it again.

Almost there.

He tried the door. Still locked. Shit. He checked the scanner to make sure that it had registered the car's frequency. It had. But it looked unusual. Not like a frequency he had seen before. The simple reason for that, as Fivers realised when he noticed that the alarm light was no longer flashing, was that the scanner had turned off the alarm, but not opened the doors. It was dark. Late. And Fivers only knew how to use the scanner, not how to alter the way it worked to fit circumstances such as these.

He also knew when it was time to give up.

He activated the Danny's alarm again and walked back to his car. He didn't start the engine. Instead, he thought of his mother, hunched over the steering wheel and cried.

He started to sum up the last year or so in his head. Low-level drug dealer, selling cannabis to whoever wanted it. Making an unknown fortune. Caught by Walsh. Taken on by the Firm. Welcomed, in a way. Used for his mind. Sorting out Millsy. Sneaking a gun into Court to help Kirby out. Solving a racketeering problem. Patronised for it. Unappreciated.

And now what was there for this unknown mastermind? A mother released from hospital following a beating administered by Walsh in order to teach Fivers a lesson. For making some money. Perhaps he shouldn't have done it. Had he known what was coming he wouldn't have done it, there was no doubt about that. But enough was enough. He needed money. For his mother and him. For a new life. And they would have had it long before now, had he not been caught by Walsh. Maybe he should have left the area the day after he got caught. Instead, he had chosen to explore the Firm. Why? With hindsight, it had brought misery and very little besides.

Now Fivers was sitting in his battered old car, outside the flat of Walsh's beautiful girlfriend, who he cheated on with irritating regularity, crying his eyes out at the fact that he had failed to achieve the simplest of things – it was not a big deal to match a remote access frequency. People do it every day. People with no imagination. But in truth, Fivers' tears were not based on his failure. Failure is easy to deal with. You just try again until you get it right. His tears flowed because he knew that, without revenge for what Walsh had done, he would never get out of this city. His mother would grow old in that fucking house, with scars on her face to remind Fivers why they were still living there.

His mother had not blamed him. She had just taken it. He thought about what she must have gone through. What was she doing just before they came in and attacked her? Watching the television probably. Sitting quietly, waiting for him to come home so she could put the dinner on. What had she thought as they held her down and beat her? She was probably more worried about whether something had happened to him rather than what was happening to her. That was her way. The way mothers tend to be.

The fucking bastard in bed upstairs was the cause of every tear that fell from Fivers' eyes. He needed to punish him. To stop him. Permanently. Fivers could leave the area, he was no worse off financially than he was a year ago. In fact, the sale of the stolen cannabis and pills meant that he had another forty thousand or so to add to what he had under the bed. But he couldn't leave it like it was. He couldn't leave Walsh in Newcastle, unpunished for what he had done to Fivers' mother.

There was to be no more working for Walsh. Fivers was going to ruin him. To break him. And Walsh would have to know that Fivers was behind it. That would hurt even more. Inspiration can come from the strangest of places. And while he sat in the car, crying as passionately as he was, his imagination took hold of him. It was a quick one this time and it seemed to come from nowhere.

Fortunately, Danny Walsh knew a scrap dealer.

Fivers had a plan ready in under a minute and even *he* had to laugh at it.

* * *

This was perhaps Fivers' most ridiculous plan of all time. But it was so ridiculous that no-one would ever believe it. That's always handy.

They say there is a link between emotion and justice. He had never felt like this in his life. Sitting there in the car, he had felt as though he was going to explode. Emotions firing up into the sky, as though tangible. And he really had been crying – the sort of crying which tires you out. Almost athletic. Maybe the more extreme the emotion the more the universe tries to lend a hand. Or maybe he truly was a master of his craft. Either way, his plan was as extreme as his tears had been. And perhaps this gave him more of a chance of success.

It was after midnight now. Perhaps this plan was *too* unrealistic though. It had, to his knowledge, never been tried before. So maybe this was not the time to judge the prospects of success. That could be done after the event. It might work. It was, in truth, no more insane than the other option – that of waiting around for the rest of his life, working for Danny fucking Walsh.

Fivers needed several things. A hammer, a handheld vacuum cleaner and a screwdriver. They were easy. What wasn't easy was the fact that Fivers was going to have to break into the scrapyard and work out how to remove a Jaguar XK8 driver's door. In the dark.

He drove home first, in order to collect the tools that he had in the house. That was the easy part. His mother was asleep and he didn't wake her. Best to let her rest. Once he got back from doing what he was about to do, they were going to be going on quite a long drive. Which reminded Fivers to fill up the car with petrol once the job was done.

This job was a classic one-man endeavour. Too many people would mess it up.

⋆   ⋆   ⋆

It was three o'clock by the time he reached the yard. So far, so good. It was unfortunate that the yard was not nearer than it was. It meant risking more exposure. The longer he was driving around at this time of night, the more he risked being pulled over by the Police. Random checks seem to take place only at night. And there was hardly anyone on the road for the Police to choose from, in order to pull them over and ask that most irritating of questions – "this your car, is it?".

But he had been lucky. Perhaps fate was also intrigued as to whether this ridiculous idea might work. Perhaps fate was the very root of his good fortune all along.

Removing a car door is not difficult. Especially in a scrap yard where the doors tend to be left open for people to fish around for interior parts. The problem was first of all getting into the yard and second of all getting back out again. There was another problem. It was dark and cold. And utterly ridiculous.

Then again, plans like these are only ridiculous if they fail. No-one criticises success. They envy it. But they can't deny it.

It didn't take Fivers too long to unscrew the door. And because no-one tends to steal scrap metal from this particular yard, as a general rule, the area was not covered by cameras. Fivers felt quite cheeky as he walked through the yard and climbed over the front gate. It took a while, carrying a car door, but he was back in the car within half an hour of having spotted the car in the yard in the first place.

Fivers was the sort of person who was painfully self-aware at the best of times. Now, in the early hours of the morning, having broken into a scrap yard, unscrewed a door from a Jaguar XK8 which was now lying in the boot of his car, on top of packages of heroin to the value of quarter of a million pounds, he began to question his own sanity. There were several trucks on the road – Fivers kept half an eye on the road and half on the lookout for trucks from the fish factory, just for interest's sake – but there was no-one else. So far. And he had to get back into town without getting stopped.

He considered making a hoax call, to divert the Police somewhere but he discounted it. For one thing, he didn't want more Police cars on the road. They seem to be in endless supply these days and it would only make matters worse if a load more were dispatched to attend a fictitious scene somewhere. They still need patrol cars to drive around. It would make no difference. So it was just a case of winging it, hoping to God that something ludicrous like a defective brake light wouldn't attract the attention of some Police jobsworth.

By four o'clock, Fivers was outside Melissa's flat again. Walsh's car was still in the side street where he had left it, alongside the hedge where Fivers had hidden the scanner. He tried it again, just in case. Once more, the alarm light went off, but the doors would not open. He was pleased in a way, though, it meant that he really did have to try out this idea. Crazy, but potentially his best yet.

First things first. Now that the alarm was off, he needed to get into the car. He fetched the hammer from his own car, wrapped it in a piece of cloth and made a slight tap on the bottom left side of the driver's window. That way, the glass would land on the seat and be easy to clean up. It didn't smash. He tried again, a little harder. This time the window shattered but no glass fell through. This was a tricky bit. Ideally, there would be as little glass in the car, or outside on the road, as possible and it took time to push enough glass through to allow Fivers' to reach in and open the door, but not overdo it at the same time. Leaving even one tiny piece of glass lying in the car or outside of it might make a discerning lawyer ask for it to be tested. That would be no good.

He opened the door carefully from inside and allowed himself to exhale having done so. Even though he knew the alarm was deactivated, he still worried. It's always best to worry – you make less mistakes that way. He removed the door and carried it carefully to his own car, leaning it against the side panels while he made room for it by removing the door from the scrap yard. He took out the packets of heroin and placed Walsh's door inside the now empty boot, knocking the glass into the well where the spare tyre should have been. He could sort that out later. It wasn't necessary to do it there and then.

The next step was to swap the locks over. He gave himself a mental slap on the wrists for not having already practiced this on the scrap yard door. Now he faced the task of doing something new for the first time, while on-site. Taking up time he could not afford to waste.

Twenty minutes was wasted and Fivers was sweating. He removed the lock from the scrap yard door and replaced it with Walsh's lock. This part didn't need to be perfect. As long as the door could be closed, that was all that mattered and he attached it quickly. Almost there.

He had to make two journeys with the heroin. There was a lot of it. He placed most of the packets in the footwell on the passenger side. The remaining few he left on the passenger seat. Now for the noisy part.

Fivers had left this until last for a very good reason. All there remained to do was to get rid of the glass that he had knocked onto the driver's seat when he smashed the window. And then he was pretty much home and dry, needing only to close the door and reactivate the alarm. He was beginning to feel like a champion. Like he was running the final mile of a marathon.

He had knocked only a small amount of glass onto the seat. There was none, as far as he could see, and therefore as far as anyone would bother looking, anywhere else. Not on the floor, nor anywhere in the lavish interior. He piled up the larger pieces, the visible ones, with his hands and carried them back to his own car, throwing them into the spare tyre well. A quick, though a little more noisy than he had hoped, once over with the handheld vacuum cleaner would remove any invisible pieces. It was no good having some copper sit in the seat and cut himself. That might have the effect of arousing suspicion.

A few seconds was too long and Fivers started to feel nervous. To be caught at this late stage would be unjust, considering that a plan that was laughable a couple of hours ago had pretty much now been carried out.

He closed the door quietly and re-activated the alarm. Job done.

He was buzzing now. He piled everything he needed to take with him back in his car and drove home. Now it was a matter of getting rid of the door. The Tyne was good enough for Kev Wardle and it was good enough for Fivers. It wouldn't matter where he threw it – unlike MacRae's legs, this would sink fairly quickly and not be seen. He smiled at the thought. A terrible thought, really. But, that's the business. You don't do it to make friends. You do it to make money. As quickly as possible. Then you can get out. It's the idiots who stay in the job because they like the fame that end up in trouble. Like Walsh would be once Fivers made a phone call.

He placed an anonymous call to the Police on the way back home. He walked inside, picked up some belongings and woke his mother up. It was almost six o'clock in the morning. Wherever they went, which was undecided, they would miss the traffic at least.

* * *

"Fuck off Billy, he's having you on!" said Simon.

"I believe him."

"There's no way that could be done. No way in the world. He's just taking the piss."

"Well, don't be so sure. That kid was a rare find, believe me."

"So was it true, what you did to his mother?"

"Simon, I still feel shit about that. I really do. I've never done anything like that before in my life. But, you know, when Danny wants you to do something, you don't argue."

Simon sighed. He couldn't agree. But defence work is a business too, and you have to keep your clients, and potential clients, happy. So sometimes you appear to agree with them.

"Yeah, I imagine it would have been hard to say no to Danny. I've never known him other than in the cells. I suppose he's different on the street."

"He is. A lot different. So anyway, is there definitely nothing you can do with that information in the trial?"

Simon had to laugh.

"Even if there was, mate, no Jury on Earth would swallow that story. I spin some yarns at times, but I don't think even I could make that one believable!"

"You really don't believe it?"

"I'll be honest, mate, it's a good story. But I still think he's having you on."

"Well, I reckon different. But fair enough."

A pause.

"I'll see you tomorrow," said Simon.

"Aye, see you."

Simon drove home, smiling to himself. He felt a bit like a gangster. Just left his moll in the flat upstairs, having spent a pleasant hour or so in bed with her, having just broken up. And then on the phone to a hoodlum to hear a ridiculous story about some kid switching car doors.

Was it ridiculous? Simon wondered, as he drove home. There were two things that troubled him. One, that someone would be capable of doing that sort of stitch-up job. God, no-one would be safe would they? If that was possible, anyone could be set-up at any time. What if Simon upset someone? They might take their revenge out on him by setting him up.

The second troubling thing was something of a wake-up call for Simon. The only thing, incredible though it was, that fitted the facts was the story that Billy had just told Simon over the phone. That Fivers had done this. It made sense. He was quite the creative young mind. He had organised all sorts of things for the Firm, some of which they had described to Simon this week.

He really *could* have set Walsh up in the way Billy had said. He had the imagination, the motivation. The more Simon thought about it, the more he realised that it was the only explanation that made sense. And as a final insult, Fivers had left it until the defence case closed before revealing the truth. So that no-one could actually do anything about it. Walsh was going to be convicted. And, officially now, he was entirely innocent of the charge against him.

"Now listen up, boys - I'm makin' a speech. And here it is."

Johnny Lovo in *Scarface*, 1932

(dir. Howard Hawks © The Caddo Co)

The next morning was full of delays. The prison bus was late, as was one of the Jurors. Kate's closing speech wasn't long – it didn't have to be really. But it was almost time for lunch so the Court gave itself a break before hearing Simon's speech which, as a desperate attempt to answer every question to Walsh's benefit, was expected to last a little longer than Kate's.

At least he had the so-called "short adjournment" in which to look over his speech. He never knew why Judges didn't call it lunch-time, because that's all it was. It's no great shame to admit that just because you are a Judge you still have to eat lunch. But everyone seemed to refer to it as the short adjourn-ment. Not a big deal, but Simon Silver was an analytical person. Perhaps more neurotic than analytical. He thought about words and what they meant. He thought about why people chose to say certain phrases instead of others. Basically, he daydreamed. It was no great surprise that he was daydreaming since there was little to concentrate on with the speech he was going to have to make after lunch. It was completely pointless. There was nothing really to say. He would have to think of something because you can't exactly *not* make a closing speech. But usually you have more to waffle about than Simon did today. There was no real defence. No alibi. No believable pointing of the finger. Just a very bland "it wasn't me, someone must have set me up". And they never work.

But then again, why not? Simon wondered what would happen if he was accused of a crime that happened a few weeks ago. What if he couldn't remember where he was? What if he couldn't realistically point the finger at someone else? That is quite a thought. Someone could accuse you of something serious and if you had no idea about who actually did it, or where you were, then what could you say? All you could say would be "no – it wasn't me". But you would be in Court – there's no smoke without fire so they say, and without any particular defence, the Jury would be more likely to find you guilty. Oh, he was at work at the time, fair enough, not guilty. Oh, this person has a grudge against him, that's why it's at Court. A reasonable doubt perhaps. Not Guilty.

But there would be none of that if you didn't come up with a defence. Maybe it actually pays to be a criminal, since you are more likely to get away with something. Simon was daydreaming again, but this daydream was a helpful one. Make the Jury imagine themselves in the same situation as an innocent man. What would they do if all they could say was "it wasn't me" and they were totally innocent? And didn't know any criminals. And couldn't imagine if there was someone with a grudge who was setting them up. Would they expect to be punished for being entirely innocent of something, when they could instead raise a reasonable doubt by saying they were set up? Or somewhere else at the time? There you go, Simon, that's not a bad start for a speech. Say that.

He knew that he should really have had his speech ready by now. But the trial was still ongoing up until this morning and there was no point in typing something out only for some surprise evidence to manifest itself and make you have to start again. That was the theory anyway, as it happened there had been nothing this morning that had pointed to anything other than guilt. And besides, they always tell you not to write out your speech otherwise you end up reading it. Simon had been making speech notes all the way through and he was just going to go through the evidence of each of the witnesses in turn and hope to undermine each one as he went. But there was little to pick on in terms of witness inconsistency. There were no holes in the evidence to speak of. So he was just going to have to use this hour to see if he could think of anything else. He had found a quiet spot in the Court library and was sitting there thinking things through. At least it was quiet. At least he had found an excuse to get away from the defendant's mates who were probably sitting through in the canteen. They were hard to say no to. And he had had some fun this week. Christ, he had nearly got involved himself.

It had been a normal start to the week. A Monday morning depression based on the fact that it was Monday, which was reason enough to be miserable, but based also on the fact that Simon had slept for about four hours, having stayed up late to make sure that the case was fully prepared. What a waste of time that had been.

In truth he would probably not have slept much anyway. This was his first gangland case. He was ready for it, but he was still really nervous. The reason being that if you win your first gangland case you get inundated with decent work from then on. But if you lose, you find yourself stuck, still doing the dross that even pupils aren't all that scared of.

*   *   *

Simon stood up and breathed in as deeply as usual. He almost felt like smiling and in fact he almost did. As if he was telling the Jury that he knew he was wasting everyone's time by making a closing speech. Everyone knew it was a waste of time. Even the Defendant knew it. Well, it was worth a go, running the trial. Better to give it a shot since he was looking at lengthy custody even on a guilty plea. He wasn't guilty, of course, at least not of what was alleged, but Fivers had stitched him up with such professionalism that no-one believe him. It was science-fiction. It was just implausible. In fact it was laughable. Certainly entertaining. The whole trial had been an almost light-hearted affair. The Jury were so enchanted by the romance of the gangland lifestyle that they were almost sorry to be leaving it behind to get on with their lives again.

But they already had their minds made up. They came into the trial hearing the word 'gangster' and had heard nothing to convince them of anything other than guilt during the last week. The doubts were just unreasonable. But there was also an element of sadness for some reason. Established criminals who live big attract an almost perverse support from the public. They become famous. Being associated with them is attractive. It's for that reason that we feel almost sorry to see them caught. But there was no other sensible verdict. Go on, Mr Silver, entertain us. You know we're going to find him Guilty.

Simon was in there now too. Representative of the under-world. He had done well to avoid getting involved himself. It was plain to him now why people do get involved in organised crime. The fast money, the status, the women, the cars, the camaraderie. Everyone looking out for each other, friends willing do time for you. The whole concept of reacting against the establishment in a way. It's almost political. Empire-building has been the same since before the modern calendar. Whoever has the most allies, whoever gets rid of the most people in their way, whoever dares to challenge the system as it is can rise to the top of it. Or be ruined by it. But at least you're in there, mixing it up. Not working a 40-hour week taking home an average wage. Buying a house by the time you're retired and realising that your kids are older than you were when you last had some fun. That's why the life is attractive. The romance of it. It's organic. Vibrant. People remember you.

Epilogue

Danny Walsh was convicted of possession with intent to supply a controlled substance of Class "A". He was slightly taken aback, it is fair to say, when he received a sentence of 12 years' imprisonment. As was his Barrister. The sentence is currently being appealed.

On return to prison that evening to begin his sentence, Walsh got one item of mail. He opened the envelope and found a card inside. It was blank on the outside. He opened it up, looked inside and saw that the inside was also blank and empty. Except for a crisp new five-pound note which made Walsh's heart beat so hard and fast that he could feel it through his prison-issue shirt.

Billy Cameron felt it the right thing to do to step into Walsh's shoes and lead the Firm until he got out again. He doesn't have the same panache. He, along with four other men, is currently remanded in custody following an allegation of blackmail. Simon Silver has been promised the brief to represent Cameron.

Walsh's car was confiscated under the Proceeds of Crime Act and sold at a Police auction a few months later. It fetched just over £8000. The buyer was a young lad, who looked as though he couldn't afford to pay that sort of price. The car was found abandoned and burned out later that same day, its parts indistinguishable from those of other cars of the same make and model, should anyone even think to look.

Fivers and his mother moved out of the area with as much as they could carry. Including around three hundred thousand pounds from boxes hidden under Fivers' bed, which Walsh never knew about. His current identity and location remain unknown.